BAD DREAM

BAD DREAM

John Christopher

SF
CHR

This first world edition published in Great Britain 2003 by
SEVERN HOUSE PUBLISHERS LTD of
9–15 High Street, Sutton, Surrey SM1 1DF.
This first world edition published in the USA 2003 by
SEVERN HOUSE PUBLISHERS INC of
595 Madison Avenue, New York, N.Y. 10022.

British Library Cataloguing in Publication Data

Christopher, John, 1922-
  Bad Dream
  1.   Science fiction
  I.   Title
  823.9'14 [F]

  ISBN 0-7278-5960-9

Typeset by Palimpsest Book Production Ltd.,
Polmont, Stirlingshire, Scotland.
Printed and bound in Great Britain by
MPG Books Ltd., Bodmin, Cornwall.

Remembering Jessica, and for my children

One

Frohsteig was forty kilometres north-west of Nuremberg, a distance gulped down in just under half an hour by the big, black Mercedes. They switched from autobahn to trunk road, to secondary road, and finally to a lane that windingly pierced the village. Headlamps lit high banks of white, then a grotesque inn sign – part deer, part sway-tailed fish – proclaiming the *Gasthaus Rehfisch*. Snow scattered as the board swung in the wind. It was not snowing at the moment, but Michael Frodsham guessed it was freezing sharply beyond the gently humming warmth of the car.

He noticed ice brimming the swift-running river as they crossed the creaking bridge and the road turned uphill, the fat snow tyres slipping slightly under the heavier traction. They halted before snow-mounded iron gates, and there was a shock of cold as Heinrich, the chauffeur, got out to punch buttons on a glimmering screen. Then they were off again, wheels whispering beneath an avenue of oaks.

John Frodsham, Michael's father, was waiting outside the front door to meet the three passengers. He hugged his daughter Anna first; then Michael. Heinrich was solicitously guiding Michael's grandfather, David Dorigny, inside, to where the butler was waiting. Anna scolded her father. 'You shouldn't have come out. It's bitter.'

Security lights outlined them distinctly against stone and snow. His father looked well, Michael thought, but older than his years. Sixty-two, was it, or sixty-three?

'I would have met you at the station, but I thought you'd be better off less cramped. Come in, come in!'

DD had pulled himself free of the butler's attentions. John Frodsham offered a hand, and he took it, grumbling. 'I'm too old for this sort of thing.'

'You look fine. Fitter than ever. But I appreciate it – that you make the effort.'

In the early years of his father's second marriage, Michael had joked about him acquiring a German accent; and even with the joke gone stale and long abandoned, he found himself listening for a difference when they met after an interval. It wasn't so much accent as phrasing. 'I appreciate it that you make the effort.' At least he hadn't put the verb at the end.

They passed beneath the glassy, indifferent glares of long-dead stags to the pink room, where logs a metre and a half in length crackled in a fireplace almost twice that width, the huge cast-iron plate behind them embossed with eagles. The room was hot rather than warm. He'd forgotten how high they kept their thermostats.

Moritz the butler was ready with drinks – cognac for DD, the Bell's whisky they reserved specially for Michael. Hot chocolate for Anna would be on the way. John Frodsham inquired about their journey.

'Fine,' Michael said, 'after the Tunnel. Before that . . . well, you must remember Southeast Rail.'

His father did not make the obvious comment that it would have been easier by plane: he knew DD's stubbornness in that respect. He asked about Sheaf, seeming eager for news of the town. There had been a time when Michael had felt sorry for him – Sheafless amid the alien corn – but he'd rid himself of that. John Frodsham was happy in Frohsteig. Michael asked after his stepmother: 'How's Maria-Mercedes?'

'In great form. She sends love and regrets. Early bed tonight.' He laughed. 'She's just back from the latest re-chiselling. It takes it out of her.'

2

His wife's commitment to cosmetic surgery was a family joke, at which she herself smiled blandly. The results, it had to be admitted, were impressive: she would pass for under forty rather than over fifty.

'And Johann? Hildy?'

Johann and Hildy Frodsham – Frods-Ham as the local pronunciation had it – were the fruits of his father's marriage to Maria-Mercedes, and so his step-siblings.

'Hildy's at a party in Nuremberg, a working party. Johann had something to finish here. He'll be down soon.' His father hesitated, then said abruptly: 'Travelling since breakfast – you may not have heard the news?'

'About Johann?

The head-shake was decisive but also uneasy. 'The trouble in London.'

'Trouble? No.' On his own he might have listened to the radio, but DD's hearing had deteriorated recently and it would have irritated him to have someone buzzing just out of comprehension. 'What trouble is that?'

'They burned down the Europa Building.'

'Burned it down?'

Since it had been erected opposite Harrods, the European Federation's London headquarters had been an object of ridicule even among Europhiles. An Albert Hall lacking the cosy Victorian charm, rendered yet more absurd by the circlet of overblown, illuminated stars thrusting out at roof level, it had become derisively known to all as 'The Christmas Pudding'. Among die-hard anti-Europeans, the laughter had a rougher edge: it stood for everything they loathed. Demonstrations centred on it, and windows had been broken until those within stone's throw were replaced by metal panels; but its very ugliness had seemed to proclaim permanence, invulnerability.

'There's been no official statement, but it looks as though it may have been gutted.' John Frodsham hesitated. 'I taped a news report in English if you—'

3

Anna broke in: 'Yes, please, Daddy.'

She had managed not to ask the question Michael knew would be tormenting her: did you see your grandson's face in the mob? A negative answer would not have been sufficient, anyway; she would need to look for herself.

The invitation to Frohsteig had naturally included Adam, and Anna had tried to persuade him to come with them, desisting only when reluctance turned into exasperation. Michael had put in a separate word, to which Adam's response had been terse: no way was he going to join a Christmas jamboree in Hunland.

Mastering an urge to kick his nephew, Michael had said only: 'Couldn't you make the effort? It hasn't been a good year, with Granny T. dying. It would make your mother feel easier. You know how she worries about you.'

'She enjoys worrying.' Seeing Michael's face, he added: 'I mean, she's stuck with her temperament. You can't ask me to spend my life reassuring her. It's like filling a bottomless pit. And I've promised I'll go to Joe and Sally.'

Active resentment of the ruthlessness of the young was probably just another indication of being outside that age-group. But there was something in what Adam said: Michael could understand the need to be free of that overwhelming caring. Predictably, Anna's immediate reaction had been to cry off from Frohsteig herself.

Until this year the family Christmas had always been celebrated at Sheaf, with a varying number of the German side – his father, Johann and Hildy usually, the rest occasionally – as guests. They had uncomplainingly accepted conditions more cramped than they were accustomed to – including being farmed out to a hotel when necessary – and John Frodsham's bid to switch venue following Granny T.'s death had not seemed unreasonable. DD had initially objected, claiming that being in his late eighties earned him the right not to move out of his accustomed surroundings.

Michael had managed to talk him round, but if he'd been aware of Anna's jibbing he would have backed out too. Fortunately DD lived mainly in a private world these days, paying little attention to those about him. He prevailed on Anna eventually, with the aid of a sworn guarantee from Adam to call them in Germany.

As his father picked up the remote control from a French rosewood table, Michael asked: 'How did anyone get close enough to set fire to it? It usually has a heavier police presence than New Scotland Yard.'

John Frodsham pressed a button to release the screen, which whispered down from its ceiling slot, masking the Chinese wallpaper. 'The police were there, all right. That's the worrying bit.'

The news was read by EuroLondon's chief newscaster, Caroline Rawden, who combined magnetic blonde beauty with a cool, somewhat flat delivery. She autocued against a background of the Europa Building with flames sprouting from its windows: 'As yet there is no conclusive explanation for the disturbance which resulted in the burning of the Federation's London headquarters this morning. In some quarters it has been linked with recent disturbances in Birmingham and Newcastle, but those were minor incidents which involved little damage.'

A face that Michael recognized was inset on screen, top right. 'The editor of the *Daily Mail* has dismissed suggestions that there could be a connection with today's front-page editorial, criticizing the Commission's prohibition of the flambéing of foods in restaurants. This regulation, based on possible carcinogenic effects from the ingestion of partly burnt alcohol, is of course a public-food order, and does not apply to food served in the home.'

The editor's face, set in an unconvincing smile, went full-screen. 'Mr Jason Redditch says there is no possibility that what he describes as just a facetious comment could be regarded as incitement to civil disorder.'

A boxed clip was inset across the face: If they're stopping us setting fire to our own Christmas puddings, why not set fire to theirs?

Redditch's voice came up: 'It's bloody ludicrous.' He had a robust northern accent – Leeds, wasn't it? – and a blustering delivery. 'A joke's a joke, and that's all. We've said we're opposed to the regulation, but we support law and order. The people who made trouble today don't go to restaurants – certainly not the kind where they pour brandy on the sweets and put a match to it. Any road, the ban isn't just for the UK. The French are going to have to do without their Creeps Oozette as well.'

Caroline Rawden resumed: 'Some concern has been voiced about the degree of planning that seems to have been involved. What appeared originally to be a peaceful demonstration was used by an organized minority to gain entry to the building.'

On screen, the door of an undamaged Europa Building, a copy of one of Ghiberti's doors in Florence, left open at an inviting camera angle, was flanked by federal guards. On the white-starred blue carpet covering the steps, a Sub-Commissioner and two assistants faced a man and woman bearing a scroll of signatures. Between them and the watching crowd was a line of mounted police. Suddenly, from different parts of the crowd, figures emerged, running through gaps in the police line towards the entrance. Some grappled with the federal guards while others ran in through the door, carrying what looked like small boxes. The police line did not budge.

Caroline Rawden said: 'The intruders are reported to have placed fire bombs at vulnerable points on the ground floor, using guns to keep members of staff at bay. No shots were fired, but the fire rapidly took hold.'

Now figures were running away from the building. Anna stared at the screen, hands clenched. She asked Michael: 'You didn't see . . . ?'

'No. Positively not.'

The camera panned along the police line. None moved. A horse reared, and the rider brought it back into control. Most faces showed no emotion, but across one or two, smiles flickered. The camera zoomed to a head-and-shoulders close-up of a bearded man, wearing a Superintendent's insignia and an impassive expression.

The next clip was of fire engines, with men unrolling hoses. Flames were already blossoming from the building's lower windows. Jets of water were aimed at them, more or less accurately, with no perceptible effect. Instead, flames burst out higher up.

Caroline Rawden continued: 'Fortunately emergency evacuation procedures went according to plan, so there was no loss of life or serious injury. A protest over the failure of the police to take action against the arsonists has been lodged by the Federal High Commissioner in London with both the Prime Minister and the Chief Commissioner of Police. The Prime Minister has expressed his personal shock and regret at this act of barbarity, and announced the immediate setting up of an inquiry. The Chief Commissioner, Roger Hawtree, also expressed regret, but called attention to the fact that last October the Federal High Commission declared enclave status for all their buildings in Britain, as a result of which local police are not permitted to enter them without an official request. Neither the Prime Minister nor Commissioner Hawtree was available for interview.

'The latest figures for economic growth, issued by the Bundesbank—' John Frodsham switched off, and the screen withdrew into its sheath.

Johann had entered the room during the last few moments. 'They seem to be playing it down as far as possible,' he said. 'Reasonably restrained cover, and no comment from Brussels. Sensible. How are you all? A good journey? Sorry I was kept.'

He shook hands with DD, kissed Anna, and crossed to

Michael, gripping an arm. 'Great to see you again. Thanks for bringing them.'

Johann, Michael's stepbrother, was a centimetre shorter, with a thin, mobile face and direct brown eyes. A scar on his right cheek accentuated rather than impaired his looks; although hinting at Heidelberg and duelling, it had come from a kick by a horse. His English accent was perfect, as it should be after Eton and Balliol, but his tone was warmer than one associated with those backgrounds. He said lightly: 'It's down to that fool, Perdrai.' Perdrai was Federal High Commissioner in London. 'We reckon Prussians are stiff-necked, but they've nothing on the French. Bonn was wrong to go for non-local HCs in the first place, but that was one outstandingly lousy appointment. His party-killer is the story about his grandfather carrying de Gaulle's briefcase on the re-entry to Paris.'

By Bonn he meant the European parliament, which had sat there for some years now.

Michael shook his head. 'It's a nasty business.'

'No one killed. One of the guards may have got a black eye. And I can't imagine anyone going into mourning for the building. London probably wasn't the right location in any case. Oxford would be more suitable, except it's vandalized enough as it is. What about Milton Keynes? Decentralization might take some of the heat out.'

'It was the police inaction I was thinking about. They can't ignore that.'

'I suppose not. Though that enclave stuff was asking for trouble: just because someone overreacted to a false tip about drugs. It's the customary cock-up situation, but it's not serious. I imagine Hawtree will have to go, but if they've any sense they'll take the opportunity to move Perdrai at the same time. Retire him, maybe. He's always saying how he's dying to get back to his property at Colombey.'

Anna joined them. 'I'm worried about Adam.'

She spoke to Johann in simple appeal, without the nervous evasion she frequently showed to others, even Michael.

Michael recalled how she had mothered Johann as a toddler, herself a blooming teenager and Maria-Mercedes a tolerant onlooker, casually pleased at having her son doted on by her English stepdaughter but not beginning to understand the passion of Anna's commitments. Or could that have merely been easygoing indifference?

Johann responded unhesitatingly. Grasping her shoulders, he fixed her worried grey eyes with his confident brown ones. 'Of course you're worried, darling Orfant.' That too was from his childhood, and an American comic book she used to read to him. 'You worry about all of us, even me, and Adam's special. He's with friends in London, isn't he? Do you have a phone number?'

She shook her head. 'He wasn't sure where he would be – moving about, he said. He promised he'd call here on Christmas Day.'

'If he said so, he will. And until then, you can relax. There've been no injuries, and no arrests.'

'They didn't mention arrests, but you said they were playing things down.'

Johann smiled. 'No pulling the wool over my Sussex sister's eyes, for all the sheep around Sheaf. So let's check.'

He lifted his wrist and dialled with a ballpoint. On the tiny screen, Michael had a glimpse of a woman in her thirties against an office background. Frohsteig Wissenschaftliches Verkehrs maintained a duty staff even this late on Christmas Eve.

'Trudi. Can you update London – the Europa fire. Any arrests, actual or pending?'

The woman keyed up a screen and studied it. Her whispering voice said: '*Ganz nichts*, Herr Johann.'

'*Danke schön*, Trudi.' He added in English: 'Happy Christmas!' His finger checked on the off button. 'If anything develops on this, call me. Anything, any time, OK?'

He slipped the ballpoint back and grasped Anna's hand. 'If there's anything you should know, I'll tell you. Wake you in the middle of the night if necessary. Now, drink your chocolate and off to bed. It's been a long day, but what matters is that you're here.' His gaze ranged affectionately. 'You're all here. I know it's not Sheaf, and Granny T.'s no longer with us, but the family's together.'

Michael saw his father's approving eye on his stepbrother. He was happy that he no longer resented it.

The tree, five metres tall and reaching almost to the elaborate gesso ceiling, had been set up in a corner of the hall and left deliberately unlit. A pink and gold cherub presided over green slopes studded with bright baubles to where beeswax candles glimmered in their fireproof holders. The family presents, organized by Maria-Mercedes' social secretary, were stacked neatly in front.

They would be opened after the champagne (actually vintage Sekt from the Frohsteig vineyard): a continuation of Sheaf tradition, though in recent years the wine at Sheaf had been Frascati. Michael wondered if his father had interpreted this as an economy which could now be rectified. It had in fact stemmed from a whim of DD, when a notion that the bubbles upset his stomach coincided with a fit of nostalgia for his young manhood in wartime Italy.

As a rosy-cheeked maid, out of uniform and into dirndl for the occasion, advanced on him with a tray, he was aware of another upgrading: barquettes of caviar instead of smoked salmon sandwiches. Nearby DD, munching with enthusiasm, held his glass out for topping up; presumably he had forgotten his complaint. Michael noticed him stiffen his back, and saw Otto von Frohsteig on the far side of the room, tottering behind his zimmer frame with a nurse at his heels. A brief appearance for the occasion, by the other head of family. DD looked pleased; Otto was ten years his junior.

Michael had seen Hildegard but failed to catch her eye.

Now she caught his and headed towards him, abandoning a young man with receding hair who gawped mournfully after her. She embraced him despite his encumbrance with glass and canapé, lips warm on his cheek, smelling of an unfamiliar but undoubtedly expensive scent.

'Michael, you grow more handsome. More and more!'

Freeing himself, he looked at her. She had been beautiful as a child, but now her beauty had flowered wonderfully, and was matched by adult poise. Her looks – high cheekbones and forehead, blonde hair, dark eyes and flawless mouth – resembled her mother's, but had none of that self-indulgent remoteness. Movements and gestures conveyed vitality, restlessness; and her skin wore the effortless perfection of youth rather than expert renovation.

'Hildy – my pretty lying sister.'

'Half, Michael, only half. *Mein Stiefbruder.* Still forbidden, alas. Have you brought Lucy? I want to meet her.'

He hadn't known she was aware of Lucy's existence, let alone her name. That information would have come from Johann, who had joined them for lunch in London the previous month.

He shook his head. 'She has family commitments.'

'Poor you. But it means I have you to myself.'

She had flirted with him since she was a schoolgirl, her yellow hair – cut now in a style he guessed had left no change from three hundred Euros – braided in pigtails. In recent years he had watched her perfecting her technique on other males. It was an entertaining spectator sport.

She took his arm, feeling biceps. 'And so healthy! Is that because you still play your strange game with the funny-shaped ball?'

'I do still play rugby. Don't knock it. There has to be something the Germans can't do.'

She laughed. 'We are less good at ballroom dancing, also.'

11

An English couple had won the European championship in Berlin a few days previously, with other British
couples coming second and fourth. Winners and runners-up
were both under Frohsteig advertising contracts. 'You must
teach me to dance, Michael, if you will not teach me to
play rugby.'

House servants filed in and took up positions before the
tree. Moritz seemed impressively unaware of how ridiculous
he looked in lederhosen. His concertina, after a preliminary
groan of protest, swung competently into 'Hark, the Herald
Angels sing', and the company gave tongue. It was a very
fair performance, clearly the fruit of strenuous practice.
John Frodsham, who had come to stand behind Michael
and Hildegard, linked arms with them.

They continued with 'The Holly and the Ivy', and inevitably wound up with 'Stille Nacht', Moritz's accompaniment
subdued and mournful. Maria-Mercedes initiated a round of
applause. As the singers trooped out, her brother Dieter
von Frohsteig appeared, broad and benevolent of face,
luxuriantly black-haired, and over two metres tall.

'Michael, I have not seen you yet!' Although strongly
accented, his English was competent: certainly better than
his sister's. 'It is so good that you come. How is work? You
still house the sick?'

Michael took the proffered hand, which closed strongly on
his. 'After a fashion. And you – still making the dreams?'

Dieter laughed, shaking his large head. 'A peddler of
corruption, as our American friends will say! What is
reported from your contacts – is the Amendment to be in
Aronheimer's program?'

The US President was up for re-election in November.
The amendment to the constitution, as provisionally outlined, would prohibit both use and provision of Virtual
Reality, except in limited and specific circumstances. 'Contacts' must refer to Lucy, who worked in the President's
office. She didn't talk much about her job, and as far as

Michael could remember it had not been mentioned during their lunch with Johann. But he was not too surprised at Dieter's knowing: he took pride in his information network.

He said: 'The Americans I've met seem to think it's too soon to say. It depends what happens in the early primaries.'

'I like Americans, except that they become so serious. And with such narrow focus. Dream-making is natural to the human animal. From the time that we live in caves, we seek help in fantasy. Homer, Shakespeare, Charlie Chaplin . . . always there is need for escape from the dullness, ugliness of the world. Not so?'

'It could be argued there's a difference between listening to a story or watching a clown, and living a substitute life.'

'When the storyteller stops talking, or the curtain descends in the theatre, life is there again to live. What difference?'

'It's a deeper involvement, surely. And Virtual is a stage on the road to Total, where it's a great deal more than glove-and-helmet. Being in a body cocoon, with drip feeding and automatic waste elimination, is a long way from real life.'

'For a period only, a limited period. Sleep, with pleasant dreams. Then they wake up, and walk away.'

'Provided they don't get addicted, and walk right back.'

Dieter shrugged. 'Those stories are exaggerations. But even if there are some, a few, who find Total more attractive than the life they have lived, is it right we blame them? No one knows how to understand another's problems, pressures, and make judgement. There are many worlds out there, and some are bleak. Shall we deny others comfort because we are lucky not to need it?'

It was a familiar argument, one of whose weaknesses, Michael felt, lay in the we-and-they aspect. Virtual, like mass holidays, was a lower-class indulgence, Total a vice of the defeated. No member of the executive class would admit to indulging in either.

Hildy said: 'There is another thing, Michael – will you ban Virtual and take the bread from your poor sister's mouth?'

She moved from him to hug her uncle in a close embrace. Michael had sometimes felt that Dieter was more a father to her than their own was: she certainly relaxed more easily with him. From Dieter's arms she laughed at him, displaying perfect teeth, though that particular perfection was not a gift of nature. She had lost two front teeth on a ski slope when she was twelve. He remembered her white face, and snow speckled with blood, and how brave she had been. Dieter had been there then also, comforting and reassuring her.

'I'm sure you could find another kind of bakery,' he said.

'Michael, Michael, you do not understand! It makes me happy to be part of the dreams of thousands – millions even. And what harm does that give? Does it hurt them if they imagine I am in their arms? Or maybe are you jealous?'

Plucking the glass from Michael's hand, she gave it to Dieter. She stretched to kiss him, this time on the lips. 'So – that is reality, not Virtual. And the difference is to you I am half a sister. Boring. So many memories, but all of familiar things. Dream is better, perhaps. Come. Mama is summoning us.'

She urged him in the direction of the tree. He wondered if she would like the brooch he had got for her, a little enamelled bird in flight. He wondered too when Lucy would be opening her present, and visualized the topaz cross, yellow sparkling against dark brown skin. More immediately he must brace himself to express proper thanks for the Frohsteig presents. They would, for a certainty, be expensive.

The Christmas feast was exactly as Michael had expected: long, heavily fuelled, and musically accompanied – a string ensemble played Schutz and Praetorius in the minstrels' gallery. It was after four when, gorged and fairly drunk, he got away to his room. He doubted if Lucy would call him here. He had tried to reach her from the train, finding privacy at the end of the swaying corridor while DD dozed and Anna was engrossed in a book. The time had been appropriate – seven a.m. in Washington DC – but the phone showed a lack of signal. He intended to try again but DD was restless about being on the wrong side of the Channel. By the time he relaxed it was nine o'clock Washington time, and Michael knew she would be on her way to her family in Middleburg.

It would now be late morning with her. He dialled the Middleburg number from the bedside console and got an engaged signal. He tried again, ten minutes later, with the same result and wondered if phone calls were being jammed before giving up. His room was stiflingly warm, but when he managed to open a window it admitted an arctic blast. Daylight had faded, but the snow was lit by a moon almost at full. He felt a need to clear his head, and found his fur jacket.

Paths had been cleared that morning, and though there had been some further snow it did not lie more than a few centimetres deep on them. He made his way between the swimming pool – dimly lit, with steam rising from the roof vents – and the shrouded tennis courts, towards the park. Deer at the salt lick lifted their heads but did not move away, safe in their ornamental role from the guns which might menace their wilder cousins. He saw a mound ahead, and recognized the Beinhaus.

It stood more than a metre below ground level, surrounded by a walkway to which, on all four sides, steps descended. There had been drifting here, and it wasn't easy to make out precisely where the steps were: he trod a cautious path down into the thicker snow. The door was locked, but a long, low window offered a view of the interior.

Michael unclipped a torch from his belt, and shone it inside. Nothing had changed, nor was likely to: the skulls were piled in the same elaborate cairn, with femurs and tibias in orderly lines beside them. Dieter's father, Otto, had shown him the Beinhaus on his first visit to Frohsteig, mentioning that the oldest skulls dated from the seventeenth century.

A voice from behind startled him: the snow had muffled approaching footsteps. Dieter's voice called: 'Michael! You consult the dead?'

He turned and saw him, looking even bigger outlined by moonlight. 'Not unless I can be sure of an answer. I was hoping to walk off the feast. You too?'

Dieter thumped down the steps in a flurry of snow. 'I looked out from my window, and saw you go into the park, and followed. Our dead are silent? That is wise. We modern Germans are garrulous. We can learn from our ancestors.'

He sounded drunk, and had certainly put away a lot of wine. He produced his own torch and flashed it into the Beinhaus.

'Quiet, yes. And most orderly. This was not always so. The Americans liberated them from order, in 1945. It took time and patience to bring them back to discipline. They played football with the skulls, I think.'

Otto had also told Michael that story. He'd mentioned it to DD, who'd commented that it sounded like standard military behaviour; his own regiment had similarly amused themselves while occupying a Schloss in Austria. He said: 'Soldiers often behave badly. Were you able to sort out who was who – *Grosstante* from *Grossonkel*?'

Dieter shrugged in the moonlight. 'No. The importance was that they should once more be orderly.' He laughed. 'We are German, after all! But let us be more serious, and speak of life, not death. Michael, I have wished to talk with you. The work you do, with hospitals – it contents you?'

'It's a job. And a reasonably useful one.'

'You are capable of better things.'

'Being in any gainful occupation is something, these days.'

'If you wish, there can be work for you here. Also useful, and better paid.'

'That's a kind thought, Dieter. I appreciate it. But it would make it more difficult to go on playing my game with the funny-shaped ball, as Hildy calls it.'

'And that is important to you? Anyway, I am not sure this is correct. Rugby is starting to be played in Germany, as you know.'

'I do. And I'm impressed.' He was also amused. 'But you have a way to go still.'

'Do not underestimate the possibilities. We may be late starters, but we work hard.'

His voice was sharp in the hush of night and isolation; as also, suddenly, was the buzz of Michael's phone. Lucy, he thought: she might have changed her mind about calling him here. It was a nuisance not being alone, but he could fix a time for getting back to her. He lifted his wrist, pressing the receive button. The faintly lit dial showed a face, but not hers. The miniature image was of Adam, in the frame of a callbox.

Adam asked uncertainly: 'Michael?'

Since Michael was not transmitting vision, Adam's screen would be blank. 'Yes, it's me,' he confirmed. 'Do you want your mother? I'm outside the house at present. Can I get her to call you?'

'No. That's not it.' There was nervous excitement in his voice. 'You've heard what's happening?'

'We heard about the Christmas Pudding. Your mother's been worried. Are you all right?'

'I'm all right, but there's a crackdown in progress. They're picking people up in a big way. I've a friend who needs help.'

'I don't see—'

'The thing is, he's in Germany. In Nuernberg in fact, near you. He needs to get back to England. His cards will have been cancelled. He needs money.'

'Well . . .'

'I'll pay you back,' Adam said impatiently. 'It's a question of immediate cash.'

His mother would pay, he meant, but that wasn't important. 'It's not that. I'll need to get to a cashpoint myself. And then there's the problem of contacting him. Can I call you back?'

'Mike, we're talking urgent plus. The German police will be looking for him. He has to get away fast.' Adam sounded manic; this was the kind of excitement he'd been looking for.

Michael said: 'I can't believe it's as bad as you think. From what I've heard—'

'You're not here! You don't know what it's like.'

He felt his wrist being firmly taken, and lifted. 'Adam, here is Dieter. Can your friend come to the Schloss?'

'Dieter!' There was relief in the thin distorted tones. Adam's anti-European fanaticism had never really extended to his German relations, and he seemed actually fond of Dieter, appearing to find relief from maternal fussing in his more impassive amiability. On holidays in Frohsteig they had spent hours together on the library floor, engrossed in war games.

'I am sure we can help,' Dieter said.

'I don't think it would be a good idea for him to try to get to you. It's a long way, and—'

'He is in Nuernberg, your friend? So he is accustomed to this city?'

'Yes.'

'Can you get word, so he is at the Bahnhof two hours from now?'

'Yes, I can do that.'

'The Bahnhof cafe stays open all night, even on this day.

18

We will be there, with money. Describe us to him. We will expect that he approaches us.'

'Dieter, that's great! I can't thank you . . .'

'No need. Call your mother now, but say nothing of this. She must not worry.'

They occupied a booth clearly visible from the door. There were three other customers – a middle-aged couple and a student dozing over a book and a cup of coffee – and a solitary girl serving. Dieter had ordered cafe cognac, and complained about Remy Martin not being available. Heinrich had the Mercedes parked outside the station.

Dieter spoke of the trouble in London, like Johann making light of it. But he criticized the federal authorities. For far too long they had been careless of British sensitivities.

'Europe is not Europe without Britain. Can I say England, since our Celtic friends are not listening? It is to England we look for stability, continuance, tradition. You kept your monarchy and nobility when others failed. There is talk of bringing back ennoblement in Germany, but that is impossible. There must be a fount of honour, not so?'

He said nothing of speaking as a von Frohsteig, though that was implicit. He didn't mention either what old Otto had once confided – that both name and title had been adopted when the family, formerly Mueller, acquired the property, together with the Beinhaus and its contents, in the thirties. They had been leather manufacturers, and there had been an increasing demand for the product as the Nazi movement gathered steam. They had also, Michael suspected, been well-placed party members, but Otto had not divulged that.

Dieter was still hymning the merits of the British class system when Michael touched his arm. 'Our man?'

The cafe was separated from the station proper by glass walls, decorated with etched and coloured glass featuring giant irises and bulrushes, and marsh life generally, in the fashionable neo-Nouveau style. An eye peered in, its owner concealed by a willow tree and heron. They watched as he made a careful survey. Then he moved quickly, almost beating the door's photo-electric trip, advancing to where they sat.

Thinning red hair was not a promising start. The face was raw-looking, freckled and sweating; he was of average height, more than average bulk, and generally out of condition. He ventured 'Dieter?' in a sub-cockney accent.

'Sit down,' Dieter said. 'Cafe cognac?'

'I don't know . . .'

Dieter clicked finger against thumb, and the girl jumped to it: Michael had always been impressed by the way he secured attention. He ordered for the newcomer with a repeat for himself, not disputing Michael's refusal. While the girl was away, he elicited information.

The redhead was a member of the European Parliament, Rivers by name: Anthony Rivers, he said, pronouncing the 'th'. He was additionally a member of Britain Awake! – the extreme anti-federalist group to which Adam belonged. He'd been told a warrant was out for his arrest in connection with investigations into the Christmas Pudding fire. He needed to get back to his friends in London. He was gabbling.

'Are you absolutely sure – about the warrant?' Michael pressed. 'We had the situation checked last night, on account of Adam. The report was positive that no arrests had been made or were contemplated.'

'Nothing official, no. This is Gestapo stuff.'

Gestapo was the name given by Britain Awake! to the Euro Geheimes Polizei, the special police unit which had been set up more than a year before, following bomb incidents in Palermo and Brighton. Doing his best to be reasonable, Michael said: 'The EGP doesn't have powers of arrest. That was made plain.'

'No,' Rivers said, with heavy scorn. 'All they have is power in an emergency to instruct the federal police to act. And they decide what constitutes an emergency.'

'They're answerable to the Council.'

'And who are the Council answerable to?' He was almost squeaking. 'Look, I'm not going to argue about this. Adam said one of you could lend me money. Can you, or not?'

Dieter raised a silencing hand as the girl approached with a tray. When she'd gone, he said quietly: 'It's all right, Anthony.' He even had a shot at the 'th'. 'We have brought money.'

'You'll be reimbursed.'

'Yes, I am sure. That is not important. What route do you take, to London?'

'They'll be checking the Tunnel route, but I know someone at Boulogne who can get me on a boat.'

'And to get to Boulogne?'

'They may be checking rail services generally. There's a long-distance motor coach.'

'Which will also be checked, probably.' He produced an envelope from an inside pocket. 'Money is here. Also a street map of Nuernberg, with an address marked. This is a car-hire company that can be trusted: we use them. I have telephoned, and they expect a client. You will not require money for this – it is charged to my account. The station taxi drivers have perhaps gone home for *Weihnacht*, but it is not far – no more than two kilometres.'

'Just over a mile,' Rivers said. 'I'll walk it anyway. Taxi drivers may be part of the net.' He looked to Dieter, ignoring Michael. 'Adam's told me about you. I won't forget this. We're not anti-German, you know – just British patriots. We want the right to govern ourselves. We had it for fifteen hundred years and we want it back.'

His voice wavered. Dieter said: 'If Adam speaks of me, I hope he tells of my admiration for the British. Best of luck.' He raised his brandy glass. 'Cheers! Better we wait here, and you go first.'

They watched him leave, some jauntiness recovered. The student was fully asleep, the couple deep in an urgent, low-pitched mutual harangue. Behind the bar the girl, earphoned, was engrossed in a DVD. The scene had the unnatural look of a public place abandoned to the emptiness of night.

'They do love whipping themselves into a frenzy,' Michael commented. 'At Adam's age it's understandable, but that one must be close on fifty. And that comic insistence on translating distances out of metric! As if it mattered.'

'I suppose it matters to them,' Dieter said. 'He means well, I think.' He pressed his quick-call button to alert Heinrich. 'And it costs us little. I think we can go home now.'

Two

They had been urged to stay on at Frohsteig for the New Year, but neither Anna nor DD was happy at the prospect. Anna was restless at the distance separating her from Adam, and DD just could not get used to being away from familiar surroundings – even more essential to him since Granny T.'s death. The Frodshams were regretful, but did not apply pressure.

Michael's father said: 'See you soon,' on parting, but it was a pious hope. He rarely visited England these days; they would be more likely to see Johann or Dieter.

Hildy, kissing her stepbrother goodbye, said: 'You may see me. There is a plan of filming in London.'

'Good. Why London, though?'

She shrugged, her shoulders lifting, white and fragile, out of a deep-necked, apricot-coloured angora sweater. 'Lower costs is what they say. Maybe to show to our local extras that there are cheaper places than Nuernberg. *Pour encourager.* But the real reason is that Leo is on the hunt. Will you believe that in his last virt-play I was cast as the older woman? Against a schoolboy . . . My victim was from London, and went back afterwards. Leo regards this as unfinished business.'

Leo, who had been to one of the Christmas parties at the Schloss, was her principal director, a pale anxious man who did not drink but chain-smoked. As always, the reference to her work embarrassed Michael, even though he had the

23

impression the porn was extremely soft. He said: 'So, some weekends in Sheaf, I hope.'

'*Ohne Zweifel.* But I also hope for fraternal lunches in London.'

'Dutch, if so. I know the sort of place you favour.'

'Darling Mikli, I'll pay. These days I am quite rich.'

They had a quiet New Year, with no one staying up to celebrate. DD went to bed as usual at ten, and Anna followed soon after: Adam had a party in London, but promised to come down in a day or so. Michael got through to Lucy prior to her setting out for a presidential shindig, and decided to have an early night himself. Subsequently he had a couple of days free in Sheaf before going back to work. The town lay in winter quiet, frozen snow crusted and discoloured in the gutters, but virgin white on some stretches of roof. Friars Hill was totally rather than moderately treacherous, cobbles snow-blanketed except for a narrow track beside the hand-rail. The immediate post-Christmas period was normally quite a popular time for tourists, but he saw none.

When he mentioned this in the Dragon, Andrew, the barman, pulling a half of Adnam's ale, said it was the Americans who were missing. Apparently there had been a White House announcement which Michael had failed to hear in Germany, advising against travel to England for the time being. He was surprised Lucy hadn't mentioned it, though it was true they had better things to talk about.

Andrew shook his shaggy head. 'That's what comes of burning down buildings. Bloody yobs.'

Adam had put in his belated appearance that morning, and Andrew's comment made Michael glad he had refused the suggestion of accompanying him to the pub: there had been antagonism between those two on previous occasions.

Michael had also been glad to get away from his nephew's political outrage. His present chief indignation centred on the fact that the federal troops drafted in following the fire were non-British. When Michael pointed out that this was established Euro policy, and that at least no German troops had been sent, it only made Adam angrier: it was the Germans who were doing the sending.

But it made Anna happy to have him home, if only for one night. She asked if he could stay longer, and he said no but with less display of irritation than usual. He also refused the money she tried to press on him. With an eye on Michael, he said she could repay Dieter what had been advanced to his friend, but he himself was all right.

They were in the upstairs sitting room. A remote sound of music indicated that DD was in his study; after giving up the harpsichord because of increasing hand tremor, he had taken refuge in his massive collection of discs and tapes and ancient LPs, largely featuring that instrument. Although remote, it was highly audible: since he put up the volume to compensate for deteriorating hearing, tinkle had turned to clang.

Michael asked: 'Did Rivers make it all right?'

'Yes. He's OK. For the moment.'

'You could bring him here,' Anna suggested, 'if there's a problem.'

'I'm afraid he needs a less conspicuous bolt-hole than Georgian House, Ma.'

Even if the paranoid innuendo was irritating, he was speaking gently to her. And the simple fact of his being there transformed her; just now she would pass for a woman at peace, fingers nimble over her gros-point. Adam sat in one of the bergere armchairs, and she had pulled her red velvet chair across to be close. They made a pleasing picture.

Relaxed, Adam was good-looking on a minor scale: he was less than one metre seven. His pale features were classically handsome apart from a chin verging on promi-nence; he had good cheekbones, a quick smile, and when not excited a warm, easy voice. He had been pretty as a child, and Anna's spoiling had not initially made him self-centred. That aspect had surfaced with his discovery of nationalist politics during his last year at Lancing, originally manifesting in contemptuous refusal of a place at Queens' College, Cambridge. He would, he announced, have no truck with universities that kow-towed to Euro rulings, which meant all universities.

The passions of nineteen, Michael reminded himself, were fleeting; in a few years they would all laugh about it. One needed to remember the happy, somewhat diffident boy who must still exist inside the frenetic super-patriot. In this interval, he could succeed in that. Recollection went back further and more personally: to abandonment and a shared loss. Not until a lot later had he understood the guilt Anna had felt over their mother's death, but she had seen and soothed his own. They had not exactly been babes in the wood – there was the familiar background of Sheaf, and Granny T. to provide food and fondness – but undeniably Anna had covered him with comforting leaves.

'There's one thing, Ma,' Adam said.

'What's that, darling?'

'I wondered if I could nick one of your paintings.'

She looked up, smiling. 'All of them, if you want.'

'Just that little one of the cat in the barrel.'

'Of course. You don't have to ask.'

During the twenty years in which artistic creativity had been supplanted by avid maternalism, Anna had shown a serene indifference to the products of those early years, hung all round the house by Granny T. It was maternalism which was gratified by Adam now wanting to take one. He had never previously shown interest in her work. At Frohsteig, Michael remembered, Dieter had spoken of his own collection of Anna Frodshams, expressing satisfaction at their recent rise on the international art market. One small oil had fetched five hundred thousand Euros at Sotheby's, Berlin, a few weeks earlier.

Michael suppressed an impulse to ask how much Adam expected the cat to contribute to the coffers of Britain Awake! The painting, one of his own favourites, was a worthwhile sacrifice to domestic harmony and Anna's peace of mind. All the same, he resented its conversion into funds for a crackpot organization.

He had suggested meeting Lucy at the airport, but she had vetoed that; they met at the Academy Club instead. Her kiss was cool, but she was not keen on public displays of affection. When he proposed a bottle of wine, she shook her head: she had an early evening meeting. Appreciatively, he watched her sipping Perrier. With those cheekbones, she could have been of south-east Asian rather than African origin. Her hair too was lustrously black, long and straight. He had always assumed cosmetic straightening, but now he wondered if he might have got that wrong.

It had been almost a month since their last meeting, and there were things to catch up on. She was deeply fond of her family, and of talking about them; though he had met none he knew quite a bit about them. They were high achievers: brothers an industrial architect and a paediatric surgeon, one sister an attorney with a leading Washington law firm, another majoring in Physics at Stanford. Lucy, for her part, was fascinated by his Anglo-German background; it had been her suggestion that Johann join them for lunch the last time she was in London.

She asked: 'How do the Frods-Hams feel about the Christmas Pudding?'

'Much the same as anyone with sense. Regrettable, but not too serious.'

'But that's not how Adam feels.'

'He's young, and going through a phase. What was that about presidential warnings to stay away from London?'

She shrugged. 'I'm here, OK? Straightforward ass-covering, I'd guess. This is election year.'

'Speaking of that, Dieter was wondering whether a ban on Virtual is likely to feature on Isak's priority list.'

Isak was President Aronheimer, elected three years earlier on a peace and harmony program during a temporary lull in transatlantic hostility. The last poll figures Michael had seen showed him fifteen points behind the front-running Republican.

'Johann's big-wheel uncle?' She smiled. 'I can understand why he'd like to know that. Their outfit has one of the few flourishing Euro export lines. They've a good eye for the market. Our home producers can't seem to match up to them.'

Michael sipped his white wine – from the very last case of New Zealand Chardonnay, the girl had said. How had that one started? He remembered: a stricter quota on southern-hemisphere lamb, European cheese banned in retaliation, wine in counter-retaliation. The trade war at least was thriving.

He wouldn't have pressed Lucy, but she volunteered information. 'I think the amendment will go in the program. There's a rising groundswell. We had a bad case of serial murder in Detroit a few weeks back. A kid of seventeen killed six girls and set up the bodies at freeway exits: very conspicuous, and with spectacular mutilations. He said he got it all from Virtual, and his attorney is pleading diminished responsibility on the grounds of Virtual addiction. It looks like it could run.'

He nodded. 'It has run here – took up most of the television news for a week.'

'On the good old knock-America principle, I guess. On our side, it works out as knock-the-Federation. That was an imported tape, and Europe's the probable source.'

'Not Frohsteig.'

'I'm sure you're right. But Europe's simply Europe to most Americans. And it ties in with stories about Total. We had one that started with a piece in *Twenty First Century*

Republic and got boosted in the media. This wasn't the old business of equating it with drugs, but the suggestion that it could be used as an economic weapon.'

Michael looked at her in query. 'That there might be plans for stowing whole sections of the workforce in Total cocoons, to take them off the labour market. Cheaper than Welfare, and you also save on riot control. Ethical considerations to one side, some economists figure it would give the Federation an unfair competitive edge.'

'That's ridiculous!'

'Maybe, but the story's out and about.'

'I spend a lot of my time visiting hospitals – in Europe as well as here. I'd know if anything of the sort was happening. Total Homes are on the increase, but not for unemployed workers. Basically, they're for the socially maladjusted. The system is voluntary, and medically supervised. You can quote me on that.'

She sipped her water. 'I might, if I thought it would do any good. No one wants to listen to anyone but Cassandra. America First is the flavour of the year, with Sock-the-Federation as the cherry on top. And it looks like it will get worse, not better.'

'Nothing serious though, surely? Just the usual tub-thumping.'

'Hope you're right.' She grinned, showing very white teeth; one, upper left, pleasingly out of line. 'I wouldn't want a war to come between us.'

'No.' Their gazes locked. 'I suppose you can't get out of this meeting?'

'No chance.' She was smiling.

'After it finishes?'

'Possible, I guess. But . . .'

'What?'

She looked at her watch. 'Half after one. I don't need to be on show till six.'

'Well, good!' Her elbow rested on the polished elm table;

he reached a hand to her upper arm and felt a muscle flex.
'Something to eat first?'

'You bet. I'm a gal who needs fuelling. But make it fast
food, OK?'

Thursday was a light day: he was scheduled to visit only
the Norman Hospital, less than twenty miles from Sheaf.
Anna insisted on cooking him breakfast, and joined him
and DD in the conservatory, looking happy and relaxed.
Family breakfasts had been important to Granny T., and
Anna obviously felt good presiding in her place. She had
also had a reasonably long and non-anxiety-provoking call
from Adam the previous evening.

It was a raw, late-January morning, but the garden was
full of birds. Anna kept the bird tables well stocked – both
the antique stone table and the wooden one she'd bought
at auction because the starlings were crowding the other
birds out – and news had travelled fast and wide on the
avian grapevine. It was an additional encouragement that
the garden had high brick walls and no predators. DD had
talked of getting another Burmese when Granny T.'s cat
died, deaf and near-blind and over twenty, within a month
of her; but Anna had resisted this with surprising vigour.
She had been attached to Tiffany, and taken a bigger part
than Granny T. in nursing her through the ailments of her
declining years, but birds came first now.

When away from Sheaf Michael didn't bother with
breakfast, but he quite enjoyed letting Anna indulge him.
Buttering toasted soda bread – a Granny T. speciality, well
copied – he remarked, gesturing with his knife: 'You now
have both tables swarming with starlings.'

'Pushy bastards,' DD observed. He anchored a shaking
right hand with his left. 'Huns of the bird world.'

'I like them.' Anna approached Michael with the coffee-
pot, and refilled his cup. 'They don't give up.' She stared out
at the kaleidoscope of squabbling wings. 'And they sparkle.'

Bad Dream

She had sparkled in her time: he recalled his early teens and watching, part resentful, part admiring, the flock of older males hovering about his pretty, gifted sister. It had been a shock when Marcus Reddaby, at forty not so much adult as ancient, moved in on them, and in the course of a hot summer punctuated by thunderstorms, routed the opposition with a laugh. His laugh, Michael reflected, had been the one distinctive thing about him. Physically he'd been below average height and narrow-chested; intellectually unenterprising and undistinguished – of value, one would have thought, only as a foil to her brilliant beauty.

Her devotion to him, though, had been complete, during the swift courtship, through the embarrassingly prompt pregnancy, and over the subsequent three years of their being together. They had not married, but Reddaby had come to live in Georgian House, at that time a fount of bustle and creativity, its five bedrooms, three sitting rooms and two studios almost continuously crammed with friends and family. There had also been DD, masterminding a renaissance of Sheaf ceramics in the pottery at the end of the garden. Michael watched his grandfather lift his coffee cup with care; the shake was cruelly in evidence today.

He could remember initial uncomprehending resentment at his father's abandonment of Sheaf, turning, over the years, into a puzzled awareness of how difficult it might have been for a non-artist like him to live in that throbbing hive of imagination. Dorignys and their partners, his grandmother and mother included, had been potting and painting in Sheaf for a hundred years. He, like his father, had found himself mute among song-birds, a blind man surrounded by passionate seers.

Had Reddaby come to feel that, too? At any rate he had suddenly left them for a girl even younger than Anna, taking his laugh with him. Michael had been baffled by his sister's reaction. A storm of weeping had been succeeded by a trade-wind of devotion to the three-year-old boy who, till

31

then, had seemed more a general family pet than a personal concern.

Just as abruptly, there had come an end to her painting, and to any participation in the intellectual and artistic dialogue pervading the house. This had not seemed to trouble her; apart from anxiety over Adam, nothing did. It was he who had read significance into her comment on the starlings. She, he was sure, had no regrets.

He left the house to a Bach cantata, the clamour of Zion's heart leaping for joy as the watchmen sang, leaving the space before the house empty. That also marked a change from the old days. Georgian House was unusual among the close-jumbled dwellings of Sheaf in having a courtyard with parking for five or six cars. Twenty years ago there had been four cars in permanent occupation; now only his battered Rover was left.

The car radio search button first offered him 'The Burgundy Browns', a soap about simple English folk learning to live the Euro dream in France; it had been kept on despite steadily dwindling audience figures. Pressing it again, he was successively offered three stations broadcasting non-American pop music, two distinctly Bavarian in flavour.

He finally accepted Radio Three, where a panel of broadsheet journalists were discussing Julie and Nige Tennant, the English Euro ballroom champions. A voice sounding like a dissolute and prematurely aged choirboy was going into ecstasies over their art – the flawless arc of Julie's body in the tango, Nige's exquisitely epicene salute in the Military Two-Step – and making comparisons with Fonteyn and Nureyev. He switched off on that.

He had taken the coastal rather than the inland road, if coastal was appropriate with the sea two or three miles distant. In a lay-by off the Loskenland bypass a couple of cars were parked, each singly occupied. A glance at the nearer one showed a helmeted head, and gloved hand on the steering wheel. He wondered what fantasy world was blotting out the bleak midwinter: it was a safe bet that sex came into it.

Traffic was very thin, and there was an empty straight of about five hundred metres ahead of him. Near the end on the left there was another lay-by, where in summer refreshments were sold from a catering van. The van had departed with the tourists, but there were vehicles in the lay-by now, the nearest a battered saloon car. As he was incuriously observing it, a figure appeared from the other side – a girl, waving.

Automatically he braked. Approaching the lay-by, he saw that the vehicle parked ahead of the saloon was a gypsy caravan. The shafts were empty, but a sorry-looking chestnut had been set to graze on the inner grass verge. There was room on this side of the saloon, and he pulled in. The girl who had waved stood irresolute, torn between looking to him and looking back. She was about fifteen, dark-haired and grubby, in a dirty green skirt and a man's brown leather jacket. She was thin and pale, and looked frightened.

'What's up?' he asked. 'Something wrong?'

Her accent was so thick he wasn't sure what she'd said; but in her quick, scared voice it sounded like: 'The little 'un's got a gun.'

A man appeared from behind her: late teens or early twenties, already beer-bellied, with fat, white, unshaven jowls and a small skull tattooed on his left cheek just above the line of straggly beard. He wore a green waterproof and flat cap, standard dress for his type of itinerant thug. He said to the girl with casual brutality: 'Get back.' His glance took in Michael. 'And bugger off, you.'

Aggressive stance, but poor physical shape: not a major problem, despite the belt with what looked like a sheath-knife attached. In fact he stood aside as Michael came forward. He could see the caravan clearly now, and take in the scene. A gypsy couple stood by the caravan steps, the woman with a baby in her arms. The man was a poorer specimen than the one who had told him to bugger off, and about half his size. He was coughing; it sounded tuberculous.

There were two other flat cap types, one standing close to the gypsies and the other just inside the caravan door. He was holding a battered ghetto blaster, which he threw out; it crashed beside the gypsies, the aerial breaking off. His mate was short and wiry – the little 'un? Both of these had belts and sheath-knives too.

The short wiry one said: 'You a bit deaf, mate? You was told to fuck off.'

'What are you up to?'

It was a weak remark, and he felt it came out sounding even weaker. The one he had addressed grinned. 'Bit of fun. You want to join in? These buggers aren't supposed to be here, and they know it.'

For several years, six or seven at least, European law had forbidden travellers to camp except in specified and properly regulated locations; there were half a dozen of these in England and Wales, another couple in Scotland. They were permitted to move between them, but not to squat en route. It was highly unlikely that this small family was attempting to do that – more likely they had accidentally become detached from one of the gypsy convoys which moved from site to authorized site, indulging what was left to them of an ancient wanderlust.

Michael asked the man with the cough: 'Are you camping here?'

He had to cough again before speaking. 'No, mister, we're not—'

The little 'un broke in with: 'They're all bloody liars and thieves. They put the horse to graze.'

It was a technical point, of a sort. Michael said: 'Then you should report them to the police, if you think they're infringing.'

He laughed this time. 'Don't want to bother the boys in blue, do we? We can sort this out.' He stared at Michael in calculation. 'And I reckon we can manage without you, mate. So just fuck off, like you've been told.'

The woman had started to cry, choking sobs which she tried to suppress. She looked to be in her middle thirties, breasts pendulous in a grubby grey jersey. He remembered gypsies coming to Georgian House in his childhood. He had disliked and feared their wildness and their importunities, hating it when he answered the doorbell to find one of them – usually Lydia or Polly – facing him with that false, demanding smile. It was Granny T. who had encouraged them, giving half a Euro for a bunch of primroses gathered from the hedgerows above Sheaf Hill. They walked three or four miles into town, she said, in all weathers, and they always offered something for what they took.

'What are you going to do with them?' he asked.

'Get going,' the little 'un said. 'Just get going. You're starting to look like a gyppo yourself.'

'The little 'un's got a gun . . .' Had he heard right, and anyway could the girl be sure the others didn't have guns as well? He moved towards the little 'un, hunching his body, hands held open placatingly in front of him.

'I see your point,' he said, 'and I don't want to cause any trouble. It's just . . .'

The right-hand pocket of the waterproof looked bulkier than the left. Michael launched his tackle from more than a metre away, putting his entire body weight into it. The man crashed to the ground, yelling. Michael was aware of shouts from the others, but he already had the gun. He rolled over, away from them, and came up with it, flicking off the safety catch. The other two had their knives out, but they backed away. He had got lucky: there only was one gun.

He cut short the protestations of gratitude and told the gypsies to harness the horse and get on their way. The old distaste was still there: it was a relief to see them go.

35

He waited till the caravan had disappeared round the bend before firing into the two front tyres of the other car. He would have fixed all four except that it seemed sensible to keep a reserve in case the remaining three got braver than they had been so far. They didn't argue when he set them walking in the opposite direction, towards Sheaf. He watched them get well along the straight before he got into the Rover.

'What in the name of God have you been doin' with yourself,' Mary Dwyer asked. 'You're plastered in mud.'

'I slipped on a bit of black ice. It's all right.'

'Take off your coat, and I'll get one of the orderlies to clean it up. Now give it over. They've time enough on their hands.'

The manager of the Norman Hospital was a southern Irish woman in her fifties, a round-bodied, soft-voiced lady with the stamp of past attractiveness. She had remained unmarried but not, he felt from the look in her eye, through lesbian orientation. She coped as well as most with the problems of a run-down institution within a run-down system, and without the ill-temper that commonly sprang from frustration. Michael suspected she might have something in her desk which helped; her breath was sometimes pepperminty, her speech marginally slurred.

This was not the case today, as she outlined a position which was, as usual, serious but not desperate – desperation being an horizon which retreated under the pressure of making do. He knew from the area health authority that there was yet another staffing crisis: two more doctors, one a consultant, had taken the transatlantic way out within the past month. At least one, she was convinced, had gone because of the persistent rumour that emigration might soon be prohibited.

Michael shook his head. 'No, that's not on the cards, I assure you.'

'Ah, but it's what they think, not what's likely to happen.'

He said, with a touch of irritation: 'It always amazes me that medics can be so stupid: they're meant to have better brains than the average. That's a federal issue, which means it must go through Bonn. As far as the continent's concerned the drain's no more than a trickle, and they're not going to take up a dodgy one like that just to please the UK government. Even if they did, it would be over a year getting passed. There'd be plenty of time to get out.'

'And where did ye get the notion that intelligence has anything to do with rationality?'

He grinned. 'That's the sort of remark I'd expect from a Catholic.'

She smiled with him. 'Would ye, now? Then it's not just doctors can jump to wrong conclusions. Five generations Church of Ireland in my family, that I know of. To business, though. When do we get that extension started?'

Michael shook his head. 'Alas.'

'It's been promised since ever I've been here. When he came down last August, the Minister swore it was certain for the new year.'

'I'm sure he meant it. But that was before the budget.'

'He said it would come as a federal grant.'

'Mary, do you have the faintest idea of the length of the line waiting for federal handouts in the NHS? There are plenty of hospitals worse off than the Norman. This place has only been built twenty years, and there's some have been falling apart for forty.'

She sighed, shaking her own head. 'Then God help anyone who has the managing of them. Those K wards would have been condemned as unfit for housing pigs in my young days. The only hope I have is for a reduction in cross-infections if they get any worse – the bugs will go lookin' for better quarters.'

'K wards – they're Virtuals, right?'

'Three Virtual, one Total.'

'I'll come and have a look.'

K1, K2 and K3 were straightforward medical wards, as usual cramped, as usual with a smell of Dettol masking God knew what. Addiction to Virtual Reality produced a variety of ills of inanition, not uncommonly as by-products of obesity. Apart from a natural tendency to snack between and even during sessions, addicts had long been targeted by junk-food producers. Food ingestion was a major feature of the average virt-play, adjunctive to the sex and carefully controlled violence. One might be vicariously sail-boarding in pursuit of a nubile blonde nymphet (or, gender-adjusted, being pursued by a hairy young sail-boarder) towards a tropic shore where consummation waited in the shade of murmuring palms, but in the script there would frequently be a handy bowl of Chockups or Candoodles or Mint-U-Toffs to nibble after orgasm. Dream and reality could profitably merge.

Addicts also suffered from the consequences of a life of near-immobility in having pronounced tendencies to digestive ailments, skin infections and haemorrhoids, but the main problem was depression. This could be crippling, rendering not just work but any purposeful activity well nigh impossible. Hospitalization in theory was dual-targeted: to cure physical illness while simultaneously weaning patients from their dependence on glove-and-helmet. As far as the latter aspect was concerned, statistics were ambiguous, and recidivism was common.

The first ward had something like twenty beds on each side, roughly double the official maximum. All had glove-and-helmet accessories as standard fittings, and all but two or three were currently in use. There was a sense of immobility and silence, punctuated by the occasional cough or munching sound. At the end desk, a dark-skinned male nurse was fiddling with a computer.

'Full occupation,' Michael commented.

'As usual. And with the usual waiting list.'

K2 and K3 were practically identical, except that in K3 a bed had been screened. In K4 the stillness was overwhelming, as was the overcrowding. An attendant could just about squeeze in between the tightly packed beds, each bearing its plastic cocoon connected to drips, waste tubes and monitors. Above the cocoons faintly glowing screens registered statistics: pulse, blood-pressure, calorific balance and programme identification. Michael stopped by the first.

'I suppose you wouldn't know off-hand what ELM/307 was?'

'I would,' Mary Dwyer said, 'but don't be impressed by that. It's an old favourite. Elizabethan, court and country, a knight with royal connections, middle twenties.'

'Handsome, rich, swashbuckling – and lusty . . .'

'Indeed, indeed. Beddings in fern and straw and satin sheets. The boars dying with a squeal, and opposing knights with a handsome groan of acknowledgement. With banquets between the fighting and the fucking: suckling pig and strawberries and cream, and claret and mead, and never a hint of indigestion or hangover.'

'How many variations, within categories?'

'A dozen, I think, in Elizabethan Male. Some of the more obscure types have only the one. Like Siamese Female: a princess with lovers, and a score of cats. It's really for cat-lovers, that one, with a bit of fornication on the side.'

'I've never thought much about it, but what about repetition? If they know what to expect . . .'

'It's no problem. The first signal blanks out a recognition area in the cortex. They know what to expect, but they know too it'll come fresh as a daisy.'

He remembered Granny T. using that phrase when he was five or six, and DD had been urging her to take a rest from potting. The smell of paint came back, together with the low roar of the furnace and the shadowy ranks of ceramics high up on the shelves. He'd asked why a daisy should be fresher than anything else, and she'd told him its real name was Day's Eye, because it slept at night and didn't open up again until the sun awoke it. He asked: 'Do they have daisies, in ELM/307?'

She looked surprised. 'Daisies? For what?'

'To stud those Elizabethan lawns.' He shook his head. 'It doesn't matter.'

She nodded, comprehending. 'I'd think so. Backgrounds are well researched, as they should be, the price authenticators charge. There's one lives up the road from me who's just changed his boat to a twelve-metre. Have ye not tried Virtual yourself?'

'No.'

It wasn't strictly true. He'd esp'd a couple of times, but only for a few minutes. Apart from the social stigma attaching to the practice, he hadn't relished the sense of being controlled – or, at least, not being in a position to exercise control.

He recalled what Lucy had said – the rumour that Total might be used to mothball redundant sections of the labour force. He asked Mary Dwyer if she'd heard of anything like that.

'Ah God, no! And where would we put them all, if so? We've a hundred and eighty beds here, and enough waiting to fill three times the number. And from what you tell me, we can forget about expansion – before my retirement, at any rate.'

'I was talking two or three years ahead, not twenty.'

She laughed, the sound loud in this ward where there was no other apart from the gentle hum of the machines: no coughs, no munching, no breathing one could hear.

'Away with ye! It's just eighteen months I have to do, providing I'm not on Total myself before then. Let's go back and have a cup of coffee.' She winked. 'It's terrible stuff, but I've a bottle of something will help it stand up.'

Three

The weather continued bitterly cold over Europe gener- ally, with press and television reiterating predictions, more pointed after two harsh winters and chilly summers, of a new ice age. In south and west England though, frost alternated with thaw. Rain during the night before the game against Bath turned the top layer of the pitch to chilly mud. The Wasps won 17–6 after a slogging contest, Michael scoring one of their tries and making the other. On Sunday morning he was called by Daniel Pugh, chairman of the selectors, and asked if he could play for England against France.

He did his best to rein back excitement, but it wasn't easy. He had been capped a couple of times previously, but that had been some years ago and he'd resigned himself to ending his rugby days as just an above-average club player. He mentioned it to DD while fixing pre-lunch Martinis, feeling he had to tell someone but assuming his grandfather would not make much of the news: DD's lack of interest in any game apart from croquet had always been notorious. On this occasion he made a vaguely approving comment, and immediately went on to labour a grievance about the poor quality of vermouth these days. When Anna came in from the kitchen, he made no reference to it.

It was therefore a surprise to Michael when he was called from Frohsteig that evening. 'Why didn't you tell us?' his father said accusingly.

'What?' He paused. 'Oh. Who did?'

41

'DD called.' Michael could hear him, presently drowning in Monteverdi in his study. 'A week on Saturday, isn't it? And at Twickenham?' Michael nodded to the camera. 'We'll be there.'

'I'm not sure about tickets. The allocation . . .'

'Don't worry. Dieter's organizing everything. Well done!'

'And I doubt it's worth the journey, anyway. I hear Ladbroke's are laying nine to two against.'

For the third time in a row France were the team of the year, having drawn with Scotland and walked all over Wales and Ireland. This was the final game of the season and they were assured of the championship if they didn't lose to England by more than ten points. Since England had lost all their matches, two of them heavily, the result of this one was taken for granted by everyone. Including, it was obvious, his father, who said gravely: 'It's being there that matters. On the hallowed turf.'

Would he have spoken of hallowed turf before the German marriage, Michael wondered? Perhaps so. He had a recollection of his mother laughing in response to some solemn observation by her husband and making even him aware – at what, seven? – of its absurdity. Something about the royal family? In the middle of laughing she had winced, inducing a different awareness: that her illness might be serious. His father's adaptation to the new life – *Lebensstil* said it better – had been so marked that perhaps there was a tendency to credit more to it than was warranted; though he had once heard Johann jokingly charge him with being more German than the Germans.

He said, awkwardly: 'As long as you don't expect too much . . .'

At breakfast next day, Michael found Anna in a flutter. Adam had called to say he might be coming down to Sheaf in the afternoon and bringing a friend. She needed Janice to prepare rooms, and wondered if she could be persuaded to come for a couple of hours in the morning in addition to her afternoon stint. She'd telephoned, but got no answer.

'They're probably still in bed.'

'Do you really think so?'

Anna looked at her watch, confirming with a glance at the long-case clock. Herself a passionate early riser, she found it hard to believe others might not be. Moreover she had inherited from Granny T. a conviction, founded in the latter's thirties childhood, of the superior stamina and steadfastness of the working class. Evidence of the more relaxed outlook which had long since replaced the work ethic hadn't really got through to her.

'It's nearly half past eight.'

Michael nodded. 'I'd give it till nine.'

She tried again as Michael was finishing his coffee. He was still on the local circuit and due to visit a hospital in Hythe that morning. She held the telephone against an anxious face.

'Do you think something could have happened to them?'

There had been a couple of mass murders recently, in which families had been massacred in the night, almost casually. Both had occurred in the West Country, nowhere near Sheaf, but Michael knew her capacity for imaginative alarm. Dropping his napkin, he said: 'I go past the top of their road. I'll give them a shout. You want her to come in as soon as possible?'

'Darling, would you? Whenever she can manage, really. But don't upset her.'

The look of relief had been only momentary. She was prepared to be worried about Janice now. And there was a good chance Adam wouldn't put in an appearance anyway: he had a record of consistent inconsistency.

'I'll rouse them very gently. I promise.'

He could remember Wilson Road from his childhood as a row of well kept council houses, with small lawned gardens in front and orderly allotment gardens behind. It was a slum now, the allotments, even in winter's bareness, a raggedly rioting wilderness. The council blamed lack of funds, and the residents, many of them redundant council workers, saw no reason to remedy the situation by personal effort. Number 78, with peeling paint, a broken kitchen window, and the hulk of a car rusting along with less identifiable chunks of metal on what had been the lawn, was no worse than average, but still depressing.

The upper windows had their curtains drawn and there was no sound as he stepped over cans and cartons, though a dog next door started a rhythmic barking. Reluctance to penetrate the squalor, enhanced by the suddenly over-whelming smell of last night's Indian take-away, made him momentarily irritated with Anna. He halted by a ground-floor window and looked in.

To his surprise, they were all there: the two fat girls on a sofa, Janice and husband Paul armchaired, the boy sprawling on a rug in front of the electric fire. None moved, and he wondered briefly if it might after all be the scene of a massacre. Then he saw that without exception they were wearing the mass-produced helmet and glove which was basic Virtual equipment (and included in the minimum standard of living index).

Obviously they had not heard the telephone: he had to rap the window sharply to attract attention. Janice slipped off the helmet but her right hand was still gloved when she came to the door. She was small and thin and blonde, like her son, and wore a tattered housecoat loose over her nightgown. At work she presented a neat enough appearance, but now her hair was a mess and he doubted if she had washed: she looked blotchy. She listened to his message with a vacant look and said yes, she'd go in. Despite the lack of response he believed it; she was fond of Anna.

His phone buzzed as he opened the car door. He waited till he was seat-belted before accepting the call, guessing it was from the office. Instead, Lucy's voice said: 'Hi. Where are you?'

'On my way to work. Where are *you*? At four thirty in the morning.'

She laughed. 'Wrong! It's half after midnight. We're in Anchorage. Aron had a sudden thought that the campaign in Alaska needing pepping up. It's been a heavy evening: they know how to put away liquor in the frozen north-east. I thought I'd call you before I sacked.'

'For a moment I hoped you might be in my time zone.'

'I will be, soon. Next week.'

'That cheers me.'

'No way I'd miss it – rooting for you on the big day.'

'How . . . ?'

'Johann got through to tell me. It couldn't have been easy, but he's persistent, that boy. But why didn't you?' She laughed. 'No, don't bother. I'm a sucker for that screwy British modesty. But would you have gotten round to telling me – before the game, I mean?'

'I was going to. But it's not much to boast about. We're in for a hiding.'

'And then again, other times – when I read it like defeatism – it makes me mad enough to want to kick you right off the edge of your off-shore island. Remember, I used to be a cheerleader at U. Virginia.'

'You're having me on. Short skirts and pom-poms?'

'No pom-poms, but very short skirts. Think I ought to wear them to Twicken-Ham, if I can find them in the attic? If I can still get into them.'

'It would make all the difference. Could promote the biggest upset since Agincourt.'

She laughed again. 'I'll be there. Remember you're in training. I'll see to relaxation, after the battle.'

Michael was in London the following Monday for a routine department meeting. His taxi took him past the shell of the

Christmas Pudding, surrounded by a barbed wire fence with Federal troops posted at twenty-metre intervals. The slim tartan belts and the badges on their picquet caps proclaimed them Scottish. He wondered if they were still aggrieved about the kilt having been ruled out as too subsidiarist a symbol, or whether, on a grey morning with waste paper in shivering flight along the pavement in front of Harrods, they were glad of the standard grey woollen trousers which had replaced it.

These meetings were chaired by Helen Rackham, the Deputy Minister. She was Australian by birth and British by marriage, but she had left her husband early in her career. He was a journalist, with four children from his new marriage: Helen was childless, and had formed no permanent second attachment. She was still attractive in her fifties, capable of using feminine charm, wiles even, and normally spoke in a gentle unaggressive voice. But the tone could change quickly; Michael had noticed that seemingly amiable telephone calls often concluded with a revealingly dismissive bark.

She was plainly ambitious, and he thought might be regretful at having chosen the path of national, rather than Federal, government. A couple of years ago the future of her boss, the Minister, had looked doubtful, but since then he'd reached an accommodation with the PM, and now seemed likely to stay the course. With attention mainly concentrated on Bonn, there had been limited opportunity to shine. On the other hand, he had to admit she was an efficient and decisive chairperson.

She listened closely to his report, thanked him, and was ready to move on. He felt he should put in a word for Mary Dwyer, and raised a query on funds for the Norman Hospital.

She looked at him with some impatience. 'They're bound by Treasury guidelines, like everyone else: the one and a half per cent maximum.'

'Which means three per cent undershoot, in real terms. They were promised a special allocation out of the rebuilding fund.'

Her smile seemed to acknowledge a feeble joke. 'Michael, there is no rebuilding fund. That was Federal, and all Federal funds are temporarily frozen. They'll have to make do, like everyone else.'

He persisted. 'Their waiting list is getting out of hand, on Virtual wards in particular.'

'Well, that's different. Virtual's a special case. I gather from Geoffrey we're due a new directive from Brussels. It's going to be taken out of general hospital administration and handled separately. Funded separately, as well. The plan is to transfer addicts to purpose-built clinics. Which means the Norman will win four wards, right?' Her memory for detail was always impressive. 'Meanwhile, they'll have to manage.'

Peter Graveny, from Northwest, said: 'Purpose-built clinics? I've not heard about that.'

'As I say, it's projected; not actually in the pipeline.'

'In which case, we can forget about it.'

'No. We're assured this one is high priority.'

'Fancy that,' Graveny said. He was tall, thin, disillusioned, a heavy drinker and near retirement. 'Anything to do with the story about putting redundant workers into hibernation to cut down on the social security budget?'

Helen Rackham stared bleakly at him. 'What story would that be?'

He pursed his lips. 'I've heard it around.'

'You should pick better places to do your listening.' Her look was icy. 'And frankly, I wouldn't expect an official of this Ministry to think anything so bloody silly worth repeating. Right, item seven.'

Graveny came out of the office with him. There was a pub, the Eagle & Lamb, a few doors along. 'One for the road?' he asked. When Michael hesitated he added: 'Not if you're worried about the Empress Helena spotting you, but she'll be tidying up for the next half hour at least.'

'It isn't that. I was heading that way, in fact. My nephew's meeting me there.'

'Well, that's all right. The road's long enough. No harm in making it two, or even three.'

They had whisky. Graveny ordered a double but did not attempt persuasion when Michael specified a single.

'Fair enough. Keep fit, and stuff the French. I'd have thought m'Lady might have offered a modest congratulation, incidentally.'

Michael shrugged. 'Mind on higher things. Where did you hear the story about redundant workers and Total?'

'Chap in the club. Not what one would call a reliable source – I only mentioned it to wind her up. His other one was about the Yanks landing a secret force in south-west Ireland.'

Adam came in a few minutes later, bringing with him a blast of winter. Michael was glad to note the oversized BA badge was missing from his jacket, but annoyed he wasn't wearing a coat; he rubbed his hands together, shivering. Graveny asked him what he would have, and he said a pint of Bass. The barman, a florid youth with a southern Irish accent, filled a glass and set it before him. Graveny said 'Cheers,' draining his own. Adam stared at the beer glass.

In a calm voice, he said: 'That's not what I asked for.'

The barman looked at the pump from which he had drawn the beer.

'It's Bass bitter, sure. I put it on the pump myself, an hour since.'

'I asked for a pint. Not a fucking half litre.'

His tone was still even, but contemptuous. The barman said: 'We've had neither pint nor half-pint glasses these past three weeks. There's a regulation on it. Not just here. I was in Dublin at the weekend, and it's the same there.'

Adam said: 'Yes, so I've heard. Maybe the Irish don't mind drinking according to Brussels rules.'

'In point of brutal fact,' Michael said, 'the pint measure was phased out by a directive from the UK Minister of the Environment, whose office is two streets from here.'

'Acting,' Adam said, 'on a Euro Order in Council.'

'Have a whisky,' Graveny said. 'I can remember when that was measured in gills, though I doubt if you can. Or something else?'

Adam smiled politely. 'No, thanks. Nothing. I prefer not to drink in a pub which won't serve an English pint, whatever the reason.'

'Don't you think this is being a bit silly?' Michael said.

'No, but I can see you do. Nothing like having a sense of humour. Hope you give the French a laugh on Saturday.'

'What staggers me,' Michael said, 'is the pettiness of it. You must have had this little ploy worked out when you said you'd meet me here.' He looked at Graveny. 'Sorry about this.' Graveny shrugged, amused, and he turned back to Adam. 'It's so bloody childish.'

'Is it? The brewers may not think so when their profits drop.'

'The profit on a half-litre? Do you really believe the rest of the country's likely to follow that sort of idiot gesture?'

'We'll see, won't we? Not if they share your indifference to losing basic liberties. But you could be wrong.'

Michael ordered another drink for Graveny. As it was being pressed from the optic, he said: 'Forget it. I wanted to see you about your mother. You let her down, not turning up last week.'

'I'm sorry about that.' He didn't sound sorry. 'But she understands the situation. Things crop up unexpectedly.'

'Do they? Anyway, as you know, she's coming up to London on Saturday – for that comic rugby match – but she and DD are staying overnight. Dieter's booked them in at the Adlon. She said she'd asked you to have dinner with them, but you'd been vague. Whatever crops up, I think you might manage to spare her a couple of hours.'

'I had to be vague. I don't enjoy disappointing her. But I'm not vague about it now.'

'So you'll be there?'

'No, I can't.'

Michael stared at him. 'What you always can manage is being a miserable little shit. I suppose you enjoy it.'

'Suppose what you like. It's bugger-all to do with you, but in point of fact I called her, and she understands. I've also told her I'll drop in and scrounge breakfast on Sunday morning. Not, as I say, that it's anything to do with you.' He turned to the barman, with a gesture that took in the whole of the bar. 'Bit empty for the time of day, wouldn't you say?' He nodded to Graveny and Michael. 'See you.'

As he left, producing another sharp drop in temperature, Graveny said: 'It may be silly, but in a way I envy the youthful enthusiasm. I can remember getting pissed when Maastricht went through. Out of frustration and anger. But you grow out of anger and get used to frustration.'

'It isn't a question of maybe. Can you imagine enough people boycotting pubs to make any impression at all?'

Graveny shook his head. 'In Lancashire they used to say they'd sup ale out of a sweaty clog. No, I can't see them working up a lather over half-litre glasses.'

There was a solid frost until Friday, when westerlies took over from the north-easters that had been dragging in Siberian iciness. The night stayed mild, and when Michael had a look at the pitch a couple of hours before kick-off, the grass was green and the sky reasonably blue. He was accompanying Bob Cheshire, the England fullback and captain who also captained Bath; an old buddy and antagonist. Their last previous rendezvous had been a tackle intended to slam Michael into touch two metres short of the corner flag: he'd handed Cheshire off and scored, but his left arm had ached for days, and there was still a fading bruise mark on Cheshire's neck.

The hallowed turf was rubbery underfoot. The adjective was not so ridiculous really. Michael looked up at the rows of empty seats, open except in the weather-proofed Guinness stand where they were shadowy behind tinted glass. There was a tingle in his spine. It always was there before a match, an almost sexual tension, but today the anticipation was more of a wedding night than a brief encounter.

Cheshire took a clasp knife from his pocket, and knelt to slide it into the turf. 'Permafrost at two inches, but above that it's cream cheese. Think it might throw them – just a little, maybe? They've had hard grounds all season, and they bank on moving fast.'

'If it slows them, it'll slow us. I can't say I'm ecstatic about having to play scrum-half.'

'You've been there before.'

'Not this season. Or last. And I'm not in the first flush of youth.'

'Needs must, with Andy flu-bugged. You underestimate yourself, Mike. You're a bit lofty for a scrum-half, but you can pull out a turn of speed on occasion. This may be it.' He looked up at the sky as they headed for the tunnel. 'Clouds gathering. A bit of rain could make things even more interesting.'

'Realistically, we're on a hiding to nothing. As a lot of people have been pointing out.'

Cheshire put a hand on his elbow, squeezing sharply. 'We've a heavy pack. Mud could help us. If we can get an early breakthrough, and then hold on . . .'

The massed array up in the stands, and the roar as they trotted on-field, were at once exhilarating and intimidating.

Cheshire lost the toss and the French kicked off, a good one which found touch behind the England 22 line. At the line-out, the French No. 8 performed a stag's leap to win the ball, twisting high in the air to flick it to his right wing. Their opposite winger had fallen back, and took a long pass beautifully clean. He set off up the field, side-stepping two men before passing to his inside centre. The whole line moved with scientific but graceful precision on to the England goal. Cheshire pulled him down, but the ball had already gone to the French winger, who went over comfortably at the corner.

The crowd's roar was different now: incredulous, even amused. Michael looked at the French half-back line as they hugged one another. They were less than a minute into the match, and he himself had not been within twenty metres of the ball. Madrite, the French hooker, took the kick. It was not an easy shot, with a cross-wind beginning to gust, but he made it look easy.

Ten minutes later, Madrite picked up from a maul and drop-kicked a second goal, putting the French nine points ahead. The sky had completely clouded over, and it started to rain. The pitch was already churning up.

It was a muddy slog after that, almost entirely in the England half. The weight of the English pack proved reasonably effective, but the French were always surer and quicker with the loose ball. Michael did manage to get a couple of moves started, but they fizzled against a fierce-tackling defence.

The rain came down steadily, in heavier bursts from time to time. They were moving leadenly through a world of wetness and greyness, principally a world of mud. He had lost all idea of time. The forwards were scrumming just above their 22 line: the French had put in, but were being forced back.

Michael had his eye on the French three-quarter line, watching for the ball going out in that direction, when the scrum unexpectedly collapsed. The referee ruled against the French, so it was Tony Barker who put in this time. It came through as a perfect Channel Three, slap into Michael's hands. As that happened, he saw that the French half-back line had drifted slightly, leaving a gap. Instead of passing, he lunged for it. He had a run of fifteen metres before he passed to his left centre, and was in position to take the ball back a moment or two later. The whole French defence had him as a target and in due course slammed him to the ground; but he was over the line as they piled on top. The half-time whistle blew as Barker's attempt at conversion dropped just short of the posts.

The Euro ruling of a compulsory ten-minute break in sporting contests lasting longer than an hour had put an end to standing around on the pitch at half-time. Michael couldn't believe what he saw as they stumbled into the dressing-room. Dieter, immaculate as always, stood with arms outstretched and thumbs up in a gesture of congratulation. Michael stared at him, wiping a muddy arm across his muddy face.

'How the hell did you get here?'

'Peter has brought me.' Another gesture indicated Peter Arnold, the England team manager, standing behind him. 'I am honoured above my deserving.'

Arnold looked embarrassed. 'We've been having a business talk, and since you and he are family . . .'

Dieter advanced to embrace Michael, allowing mud to smear his impeccable white shirt. 'Well done! The French are finding it not so easy as they guessed. It is the way I have always said: you must never underestimate the English. They may be beaten, but they are not defeated.'

Someone passed Michael a pitcher of lemonade, and he freed himself to drink thirstily.

Dieter said: 'You will come up after the game –' his gaze ranged comprehensively – 'everyone! So we celebrate.'

'I wouldn't say there's a lot to celebrate,' Cheshire said. '9–3 down at half-time.'

'Always there is something to celebrate,' Dieter said. 'Endurance – refusing to surrender. But not with champagne.

Let the French have that. We shall drink an honest wine,
Sekt from our Frohsteig vines, and toast the Anglo-Saxon
virtues.'

As they ran out again, Cheshire asked: 'Who was that,
for God's sake? Did Peter say family?'

Michael shook his head. 'Too long a story. I'll tell you
another time.'

The satisfaction he'd derived from the consolation try was
swallowed up by his annoyance with Dieter. It was typical
of him to bounce Arnold into letting him into the dressing-
room; even more typical to spout that condescending balls
about the English being beaten but not defeated.

The wind had dropped, but rain was drizzling thickly.
England kicked off and play settled into a midfield scramble
of surge and counter-surge. It was ten minutes before
Michael got a clean ball he could pass on. He thought
of Dieter up in the Guinness stand, looking down at
them through that ceiling-to-floor plate glass, and his anger
returned and sharpened. The other half-backs had a good run
upfield and the ball came to him again. He swerved clear of
two French defenders and stiff-armed a third, before scoring
between the posts.

The sensation he found himself experiencing was unmistakable, though it was fifteen years since he'd previously
known it. That had been in his final rugby season at school.
As now, it had come on him without warning: he'd been
counting himself lucky to get his team colours. It had
been a day totally unlike this, sunny and still and hot for
March, but the sensibility – the feeling of being not just at
some unaccountable peak of experience but both physically
and mentally master of a situation – was one he'd never
experienced before, or since. To the amazement of his team
mates, he'd played a blinder.

Today, with this weather, a sodden pitch, and the French
shocked into a fury of counter-attack, conditions were
altogether less favourable. But he could not put a foot

wrong, and whatever lifted him, as it had those years ago, seemed to communicate to the rest of the England side and lift them too. Their pack forced the French back relentlessly, and when the ball came out of scrums the half-backs moved with certainty and muddy grace. Again and again they broke through, giving Michael the ball as though deferring to a conquering and invincible commander. And with justification: he scored his fifth try just before the whistle blew for no-side. The final score was 27–9.

The seven-year-old Sekt came with heavy gold foil and a label bearing a dramatic version of the Imperial eagle. The food was an ingenious combination of English and German cuisines. Trays of very small Yorkshire and steak-and-kidney puddings, the former holding morsels of fillet steak streaked with horseradish sauce, were succeeded by others bearing equally miniature portions of Kessler-loin on sauerkraut, smoked oysters on halved quail eggs, and barquettes of smoked goose breast. Michael wondered how Dieter had got round the club's rule of allowing only their own caterers in; for that matter, how he'd wangled use of the Members' Room in the first place.

He felt woozy before the first sip of Sekt. The impact of the media immediately the match ended had been something for which he had no prior reference. He had been dimly aware of the rest of the team pummelling him and of being carried on their shoulders round the sodden pitch before a grinning Cheshire handed him over to the newsmen. Thereafter, a whirl of flashlights and hand-held cameras and booms probing for whatever idiotic words he managed to come up with. There had been a great deal of that before he was able to escape to the stinging benison of hot water, and then being hectored to hurry up and put clothes on because he was wanted upstairs.

The Germans surrounded him. He was kissed warmly by Hildy while Johann gripped one hand, his father the other, and Dieter smiled in the background. Johann said: 'That was the best, Mike, the absolute best. In their own word, *magnifique!* I'd no idea you had it in you. Something to tell the grandchildren. You in this will be *rememberéd*, as that great German poet put it.'

'I nearly wet myself,' Hildy said, giggling. Her scent was dizzying. *'Fantastisch.'*

'So proud of you,' his father said. He dabbed his eyes. 'Greatest day of my life. Greatest.'

Eventually they surrendered him to the Sheaf contingent. DD looked puzzled, either by the event itself or the tumultuous reaction to it. Anna smiled, biting her lip; he could remember an identical reaction when he'd won the hundred metres in his first year at prep school. That had been the day their father took them out for a meal, and introduced them to *Gewurtztraminer*, and over coffee, speaking rapidly and stumbling over the words, told them about Maria-Mercedes. He would be living in Germany, after they were married. It wouldn't affect their education – Michael would still be going to King's School in September – but they would have Frohsteig in the holidays. It was in a lovely part of Germany. Watching Anna, Michael had observed the tiny flicker of rejection, and spoken for both of them: they would rather spend their out-of-school time in Sheaf, if that was all right. He could remember also the look on his father's face, his first awareness of adult vulnerability, and thinking he perhaps ought to offer an excuse – maybe something about not upsetting Granny T. – but not doing so because his loyalty was to Anna, and her bitterness.

Adam appeared, behind her. Michael said: 'I thought you weren't going to be able to make it?'

'I'm glad I did. By God, that was good, Mikey!'

His usually pale face was flushed. He was wearing a white rollneck sweater, emblazoned with a shield bearing the red cross of St George. He looked happy; more relaxed than for a long time. Anna had noticed it too; she viewed

56

her son with familiar pride but rarer restfulness. His look was that of the boy of ten Michael had taught how to tackle and drop-kick on the Sheaf Flats. Michael stretched an arm round him, the other round his sister. This was his family; he felt himself swell with pride in an achievement which made them happy. And renewed confidence that Adam was going to be all right. The bad phase would pass, was maybe almost over.

His eye, which had intermittently been searching for Lucy, was attracted by movement near the door, heads swinging round. She appeared to sensational effect, wearing a loose cloak open down the front over a skimpy top and a skirt shorter than anything he had seen outside stage or television. The cloak was bright red, the outfit dark blue decorated with small birds, and her legs were sheerly sheathed in black. She came to him through the crowd with a challenging smile.

'Goodness,' Anna said. 'Isn't she gorgeous?'

As they kissed, Lucy whispered: 'You see, I managed to get into it. Four hours in a sauna – I hope it was worth it.'

'I love it. I'm not surprised the birds are blushing.'

'Shush, they're holy birds. Red Cardinals. The State of Virginia backing England.'

'You weren't on the touchline, though.'

'Cheering for England doesn't mean taking on English weather. And you won without it.'

'On second thoughts, that was just as well. The game would have had to be abandoned.'

None of the Sheaf party had previously met her. DD goggled openly as he was introduced, incongruous lust in his ancient eye, while Anna said: 'Michael never told us how beautiful you were. You almost make me want to pick up a brush again.'

'That's something you've never said to me, *geliebte Halbschwester*,' Hildy said, approaching with Johann. 'But you are right: she is beautiful.'

They offered a rewarding contrast: pink-cheeked blonde and tall elegant black. Michael had never thought of Hildy as particularly short, but she looked it beside the long-legged American. Her paleness seemed somehow lightweight.

Johann gave Lucy's hand a moment's admiring study before brushing it with his lips. 'My dear Lucy, I didn't see how you could improve with acquaintance, but I was wrong. I thought when we met you were out of my brother's class. You positively are, even now he's a conquering hero.'

Hildy took the hand Johann released. Michael wondered if she, for some quirky reason, was going to kiss it too. She didn't, but said: 'I think gold maybe should be prohibited to wear on any skins except black. Such an effect.'

Lucy's hand in fact was ringless but her wrist carried a close-fitting plain gold bangle. She smiled. 'That's OK by me.'

'I like the costume also. A new American style?'

She herself was wearing a black skirt with a bright yellow top, a kind of sweater in lamé. The skirt was below the knee but slit to thigh level. Lucy laughed.

'Not so's you'd notice. A very old one.'

Michael explained for her. Addressing Michael but looking at Lucy, Hildy said: '*Echt romantisch.* It is called cheerleading, not so? But now for England, not the High School.'

'University,' Lucy said. 'I didn't get picked at Junior High. We lived in an old-white area. Racial discrimination, or maybe I was a late developer.'

Hildy shrugged. 'High School, University . . . What you must not forget, Michael, is that Americans, in that great country of theirs, do not take little places like England seriously. Kinda cute, kinda quaint,' – she put on an exaggerated accent – 'but not important. OK for a vacation – all those neat ruins, some with residents – but not a place for real people to live.'

'There's an American in Sheaf,' Anna said. 'He's been there thirty years.'

'Self-deprecation may be the English art,' Johann said, 'but being half-English doesn't qualify us, Hildy. The opposite, I would say.'

'Oh, that view goes for Germany also. For Berlin, Germany, as well as London, England. And Paris, France, and Rome, Italy. All the little European countries.'

'Don't they constitute a great big Union now?' Lucy asked.

Dieter appeared, a black-tied galleon urbanely obliging lesser craft to give way. He gave Lucy an appreciative glance, but his attention was on Michael. Applying a large hand to his shoulder, he said: 'We need to talk.'

Hildy interrupted: 'I have a half-brother and an uncle, one either side, and I can read both their minds. He wishes to package you, Michael. Beware.'

'In part true, but only in part.'

'Michael Frodsham, a replacement for the Twinkling Tennants . . . but is it not a limited market? Only Britain and France. While the whole of Europe watches ballroom dancing.'

The husband-and-wife Tennant couple had been reigning Euro dance champions for the past three years, and under a Frohsteig contract for two. Dieter smiled expansively.

'That also is true, but maybe things change. It is something else to discuss. After dinner, perhaps. I thought we all have a family dinner at the Trefoil.'

The Trefoil took pride in being the most expensive restaurant in London. Michael shook his head. 'Not me, I'm afraid – not tonight.'

'Your beautiful girl from the golden west must also come. Family is not a limiting term.'

Lucy said: 'Don't think he was backing out on my account. Celebratory dinner with the boys.' She inclined her head, smiling. 'Right?'

'It's traditional, I'm afraid.'

'Good things are worth waiting for,' Lucy said. 'So I guess we both can wait.'

'You have right,' Dieter said. He looked at Michael. 'I will call you tomorrow.' Stretching out arms to the rest, he added, 'I hope I can rely on all others.'

'Not me,' Adam said. 'Sorry.'

Anna touched his arm. 'Darling, please.'

'I can't. But I really will nip in for breakfast, Ma. Promise.'

Michael said to Lucy: 'I'm sorry, too. But you know how it is, don't you?'

'Sure, I know about male bonding. I'm from the Golden West, remember? Don't worry.'

'No,' Johann said, 'don't worry one bit. I'll take care of her for you.'

It was after one in the morning when Michael paid off his taxi outside the small Bayswater hotel, fumbling with coins and eventually giving the driver a twenty-Euro piece, an act of bounty which was warmly received. The driver looked at him properly for the first time.

'Ain't you . . . ?'

'Yes. Night, then.'

A flow of congratulation followed as he made for the door and fished for his key; the hotel didn't run to a night porter. Lighting was low in the foyer, and the lift groaned reluctantly to the third floor. A distant noise suggested some insomniac was watching television: only when he opened his room door did he realize that was where it was coming from.

He was trying to remember if he could have left the set on earlier when Lucy's voice greeted him, from the bed.

'Not as bad as I expected. I thought you might come in with the milk.'

'How did you get here? I didn't give you a key.'

'Nor even an address. Johann told me this was where you

stay, and I kind of talked my way in. I'm not sure it's done your reputation any good.'

'Oh, but it has! Believe me.'

She was wearing a low-cut nightdress in white silk, wispy on her shoulders and clinging to her breasts. He put his hand between twin softnesses as he bent to kiss her.

'I was also wondering how drunk you were going to be.'

'Drunk indeed, but not too drunk.'

The television set was showing an old movie. He looked for the remote control but couldn't find it. Lucy detached herself and fished it out from under her pillow. As she was doing so, the screen went blank for a moment, returning to show the face of a newscaster. His expression was solemn, and NEWS FLASH ran in a continuous flashing band above his head.

'News is just coming in of an assassination attempt on the Federal High Commissioner in London, Henri-Jacques Perdrai. Monsieur Perdrai was shot outside his home in Hampstead when returning from a banquet hosted by the British Ministry for Energy and Research. He was taken by ambulance to the Wellington Hospital, where his condition is said to be critical.'

The newscaster's face was replaced by a still picture showing the entrance to a house in Bishop's Avenue. A figure lay huddled beside the gate.

'It is understood that two men formed the assassination team, of whom one escaped. The other was shot dead by one of Monsieur Perdrai's bodyguards.'

The camera moved into close-up on the figure by the gate. His face was hidden by a shielding arm, but the white rollneck sweater was plainly visible, with the outline of the cross of St George still discernible under the obscuring stain of a darker shade of red.

Four

The front of St Anselm's, hemmed close by shops and cottages and the rear of the Georgian town hall, did not offer a view of the churchyard, but Michael could hear the distant noise of the oaks and the two enormous copper beeches groaning under the onslaught of the gale. Gusts of rain swept the narrow north passage, drenching mourners as they came out of the comparative shelter of Eagle Street. Michael angled his umbrella to protect Anna, and found it tangling with his father's on her other side.

Inside, the great pendulum swung in its never-ending arc, beneath the gilt letters, almost invisible, spelling out the wisdom of Ecclesiastes. They proceeded to the empty front pews of an otherwise crowded church; he watched for signs of faltering but Anna's step was steady. He pulled forward a hassock, and knelt. Anna stayed upright beside him. He tried to pray for Adam, but found himself praying for her instead.

The organ gave tongue to the melody of the chorale from the St Matthew Passion. From further along he heard DD humming: he had chosen it for Granny T.'s funeral, and Michael had included it automatically in the present arrangements. He thought of how lost Adam had looked at that time, and his mind went further back: to showing him round the church as a boy of four or five. The thing that most fascinated him had been the stained-glass window, presented by a local dignitary to replace one lost to the Luftwaffe – mediaeval in style but featuring in the bottom left corner a

representation of the benefactor's Siamese cat. He'd asked
if the Germans had killed the cat as well as destroying
the window, and seemed reluctant to accept that it had no
significance beyond a personal whim.

Anna made no contribution to the service, not even
mouthing the Lord's Prayer; but she kept her composure.
On the way out, he placed her arm on his and his hand
over hers. She accepted the gesture without response. The
big black saloons took the funeral party down Eagle Street
and into the one-way system leading to Sheaf Hill. As they
made the slow crawl up to the cemetery, he noticed the rain
had stopped though the wind was still whipping the trees on
either side.

It was a couple of hundred metres' walk from the vehicle
turning-point to the spot where Granny T. was buried.
Yards, he heard Adam's voice protesting – *yards, not
fucking metres!* The sky was lighter, and there was a
specially bright patch to the south, where in good weather
one had a view of the English Channel. There was an
assembly here already, but he saw no one he knew. He
wondered about them vaguely: they were predominantly
young and male. They couldn't have been at the church
– those mourners were only now coming down the hill
behind them.

Nothing unusual happened until the very end. Michael's
attention was concentrated on Anna as the coffin was
lowered, and he was aware of Johann similarly alert as
she advanced towards the raw slash of mud among the
sodden green. She took the earth – how had it been kept
dry? – and dropped it, not flinching at the sound of its
impact on the coffin. He followed suit, and made way for
others; then, abruptly, there was the shock of music.

It lifted triumphantly over the rain-ravaged hillside and
the heads of the people gathered there. Over their heads? His
ear picked up a discrepancy – not over their heads but from
among them; and not from one direction but several. Out of

the orchestral groundswell a soprano voice rose, clear and commanding: 'Land of Hope and Glory . . .'

He realized, with a flush of anger, who the unfamiliar mourners must be. This was the anthem of Britain Awake!, the soloist, Mary Messiter, their emblematic angel. It had been she who, two years ago, had substituted that song for the Euro-anthem she was scheduled to sing on the Last Night of the Proms. She had not sung in public since; Adam had kept a collection of her recordings.

How had they managed it? The sound must be coming from a number of speakers: portable players, but what about the timing? Not portable players, of course – radios. BA must have set up a mobile transmitter close to the cemetery, with someone on the scene signalling the moment to broadcast: the others by the graveside would have had their sets switched on, waiting. Despite his resentment, he acknowledged their ingenuity.

The music stopped after just one verse. As that happened, balaclava-masked figures rushed towards the grave, from different parts of the crowd. They carried the Heckler-Koch light automatics which had replaced the Armalite. There was a murmur of alarm, and one or two cries of fear. As he grabbed Anna protectively, Michael was alarmed himself until he grasped the link. This was no more than the old IRA trick he recalled from childhood newscasts. Six of them took up position on either side of the grave, dropped to their knees and directed a ragged burst of fire into the sky.

Others blocked any possible pursuit as they ran back and were lost in the crowd. Not that it was necessary: there wasn't a single policeman present. Johann said quietly: 'My God . . . Impressive, though.'

'On the contrary,' Michael said, 'cheap and pointless.'

He walked to the grave to check something he had half-noticed just before the fusillade. A flag had been tossed in and lay across the coffin. It had been crumpled in someone's pocket and was only partially open, but the cross of St George was plain enough.

He went back to Anna. He had a feeling that, after such a long silence, she must be about to speak, and dreaded what she might say. But her expression was neither shocked nor particularly wretched, and her voice was steady.

'I think the sun's coming out,' she said. 'Yes, it is. Look.'

The bright spot in the south was bigger. The cloud was breaking, and there was even a patch of blue. She turned to him, smiling. 'I hope it's fine for the weekend. Just in case Adam can manage to get down.'

Lucy had had to go back to the States before the funeral, but was in England again a week later. They had dinner at Le Main Droit, supposedly the best of the zodiacal restaurants, and walked back to the Ronald Reagan Hotel, only ten minutes away. It was a cold, clear night, with stars visible even through the yellow fog of streetlights. Michael said: 'I can see why Pisces means you get nothing but fish, but why steamed – and why ginger with everything?'

'You didn't read your menu notes.'

'Well, tell me, since you obviously did.'

'It would take too long. And the interaction of stars and spices with the alimentary canal isn't a subject I'd choose for a romantic evening.'

'So why did you want to go there?'

'To see how it rates against the ones back home.'

'And how does it rate?'

'OK, I guess. But I don't think I've tried one out during Pisces before.'

They passed a road leading down to the Thames. It was much darker down there, but the limited illumination picked out the plastic pup-tents of the homeless, bunched on pavements and spilling into what was a street by day. Up here on the Strand, police with Heckler-Kochs maintained

65

the patrol that kept them from invading classified thorough-fares.

'What I find hard to understand is that you can start to take it seriously,' Michael said. 'With a mind as bright as yours.'

She stopped, making him do the same. She had been walking with arms folded, and as she dropped them the silver fox coat fell open.

'You do, don't you? You with that disciplined orderly mind, almost as bright as mine.' He thought she was annoyed, but her teeth gleamed in a smile. 'Did you know I check the stars before making an airplane booking?'

He asked, warily: 'Do you?'

She laughed. 'I maybe would, except I'd lose my job! When Aron wants something, his gofers take the very next plane. You ought to learn to relax and enjoy life's sweet disorders, Mike.'

'I find some hard to take. Fish with ginger, all right – but why nothing but rosés on the wine list? Incidentally, just what is the current mission? You didn't say.'

'Another great way of getting canned, or maybe winding up in Leavensworth, is to hand out government secrets to the first half-way good-looking foreigner who panders to my lust for zodiacal food.'

'Aron would be proud of your fidelity, not to speak of integrity and patriotism. We'll see what a nightcap of Scotch can do about that.'

'You're confident I'm asking you in?'

'Confident? Not really. Counting on it – yes. You owe me, for the steamed fish with ginger.'

She laughed again. 'Emotional blackmail! Next time we'll go to Simpson's, and I'll work on you.'

The Ronald Reagan, American-owned and run, was *de rigueur* for upper middle-class Americans and US govern-ment officials. Every room carried massively framed por-traits of both Lincoln and the destroyer of the Evil Empire, as well as the Gettysburg Address surmounted by the Stars and Stripes. But it was luxurious if overheated, and on this side had an impressive view of the river. While Lucy was busy in the bathroom, Michael took it in.

The scene was emptier than normal, since the night-cruise boats had been suspended. No reason for that had been given, but rumour ascribed it to fears of a river-based BA attack on the Houses of Parliament. As he watched, a couple of police boats, heading downriver, swung in towards the south bank, beaming searchlights. They were trained on the waste land where the Festival Hall, whose replacement was canvassed year after year and as regularly postponed, had once stood. The bathroom door opened, and he turned to contemplate a pleasanter sight.

They were in bed when the noise of helicopters, and then of distant gunfire, came faintly through the double-glazing.

'What do you think it is?' she asked.

'It could be BA, but ordinary criminal activity's more probable.'

'Is that how you see BA – as criminals?'

'I don't know. I've more important things under consideration right now.'

'That orderly mind again. You should aim for flexibility, and the ability to take two operations on board simultaneously.' She stroked his penis. 'As I do. Since you asked, the current mission is checking out local reaction to Perdrai's assassination. That means on-the-spot investigation. He thought of me because I was around when it happened.' Her fingers moved subtly. 'Would you say that's on-the-spot?'

'Yes. God, yes!'

Close together afterwards, she said: 'I only have three days. The great man can't spare me longer.'

'He obviously needs you. I've wondered . . .'

She laughed. 'I guess you would. Men usually do. It never crossed my mind to wonder about you being on the Rackham.'

'That's . . .'

'Different. Sure, sure. So is Aron. A Jew elected on the redneck vote. The lesser redneck maybe, but red enough. And also, being American-Jewish, although there's a liberal streak beneath the surface there's an anti-black layer below that. My virtue is safe from Aron. It has to be my efficiency that turns him on.'

'Can you persuade him the UK situation needs still more attention?'

'I'll try, but he has something of a butterfly mind. On the other hand, what stops you travelling my way?'

'Our bureaucracy is impoverished by American standards. Our junior bureaucracy, anyway. Or by European standards, for that matter.'

'Johann was talking about coming over. He wants to study possibilities of expanding their Virtual outlets, if the amendment fails.'

'Johann's not a civil servant. Frohsteig Wissenschaftliches Verkehrs can well afford their directors' travel expenses. I wouldn't be surprised if he skipped crappy flying and went by ocean liner, like the really big boys.'

'But if you took up Dieter's offer . . . Has he made one, by the way?'

'Not in detail, but it's an offer.'

She propped herself on an elbow. 'So tell me.'

'He reckons after Twickenham I'm a suitable promo image for western Europe. But there's something else as well. He thinks the time's ripe for getting rugby properly under way in Germany. There's been a build-up over the past decade, and he feels they could be really ready to go for it. He may be right – I've always thought they resented the French being in the major game and them not. He'd like me to organize a German national team, and then coach-manage it.'

'I guess that could pay better than the Ministry of Health.'

'Very much better.'

'Enough to fund a trip or two to the States – by liner, even.'

'Don't tempt me.'

She leaned in close, a nipple brushing his chest. 'You know, that was something I never expected to hear you say. I hope you don't mean it.'

Johann came to Sheaf by train; Michael met him at the station late on Saturday morning. He was carrying only an overnight bag, and they walked back to Georgian House by the short cut through the Cattle Market. Michael said: 'I'm glad you could come, though the means of getting here strikes me as a bit masochistic. I can't see why anyone would want to put themselves at the mercy of Southeast Rail when they can take a hire car.'

Johann shook his head. 'Nostalgia. Memories of coming down in half-terms from school. Leaning against the Aga. Granny T.'s steak pies.'

'At least you could have let me pick you up at Ashford.'

'And miss the run across the Marsh on the Sheaf Flyer? I saw two herons and a fox. Apart from the usual several thousand sheep.' He glanced at the empty pens they were passing. 'Is Wednesday still market day? And they're still sold on only to the abattoir?'

'Yes.'

'Wednesdays were the only days I remember feeling unhappy in Sheaf. I used to make a detour of this area.' He paused. 'How is she?'

'Anna? Not too good. She's come to a kind of acceptance now, but I'm not sure that's any better. Part of the time she still manages to pretend it's not happened, but the rest is deep misery. I don't know which is worse.'

'When Granny T. died . . . Grossvater Otto wanted to

come over for her funeral, but we talked him out of it. He's very senile, and you never know what he's going to say or do. Or when, or where. When he finally accepted having to stay at home, he took comfort in a phrase he kept repeating: '*Sie hat nie ein Kind verloren.*' She never lost a child. He was the youngest in the family, you know – only ten when the war ended. A menopause child, with two much older brothers. One was a Luftwaffe pilot, the other a Panzer officer: one was shot down over England, the other killed at Stalingrad. He still remembers what it did to his mother and father.'

'I think I understand. From seeing Anna.'

'To everything a season, and a time to every purpose. Not from Adam's point of view – he must have known what the odds were, and accepted them – but from hers it must seem so wrong. Monstrously wrong.'

'I wish I could understand why he did it,' Michael said. 'I don't suppose it would help, but I'd like to know.'

'He was a patriot. It's a passion that some totally lack, and some are driven by.'

'I met him in a pub, a few days before it happened. He created a scene because he couldn't have beer in a pint glass. Does that explain – justify?'

'Passion distorts, doesn't it? You have to be involved to find significance in little things.'

'He shot a man down in cold blood. On account of a half-litre glass?'

They had reached Friars Hill, and walked the last few yards up the cobbled slope in silence. Michael let them in by the side door. He had left Anna in the garden room, but had no idea where she might be now; he'd told her he was going to pick Johann up, but had not been sure she'd taken it in. He wasn't sure of any of her reactions any longer. But she was still where he had left her, sitting in the little armchair looking out of the window.

Johann had dropped his case in the hall. She turned and

smiled as he went towards her. He pulled her up out of the
chair to hug her.

'Beloved Orfant. It's good to see you.'

'And you, darling. What sort of trip did you have? And
how is everyone? How's Daddy's non-smoking coming
along?'

Their father had given up smoking five or six years ago.
Johann said easily: 'Fine. He's talking of cutting down on the
brandy now.' He released her, and looked at her. 'You're
looking great, Annie.'

'Am I?' She smiled. 'Anyway, you are, Joh'n. I've
been watching the birds. The starlings especially. They
are ruthless, but it's disarming in a way. They're so busy,
so . . . alive.'

The emphasis was deepened by the silence that followed.
Breaking it, Michael said: 'I'll get us a drink. Gin-and-T,
Anna? Jo'?'

She stared out of the window at the starlings, boisterously
scattering drops of liquid diamond from the bird-bath. 'It's
sleeping that's bad.'

'Can't you take something?' Johann suggested.

'A pill, you mean?' She shook her head. 'It's not getting
to sleep. I can do that. But I dream, and he's there, and then
I wake up in the dark. And he isn't. He's not there, Joh'n,
and he never will be.'

Maggie Bruton, the feature writer from the *Sunday Times,*
had sworn she would be down early on Monday morning.
Michael telephoned the newspaper when she hadn't arrived
by half past ten, and was told she should be there any
moment. It was a quarter to twelve when the vermilion
A-class Mercedes swung into the courtyard.

She was in her late thirties, not unattractive but somewhat
overweight, and considerably overdressed in a mustard-
coloured, fur-trimmed tweed suit and magenta silk blouse
and scarf. Her lipstick was also magenta. She offered no

apology for lateness. Michael said: 'I don't know how long you usually need, but we'll have to keep this one brief.'

She looked at him with a mixture of curiosity and hostility. 'Why?'

'There was some work I was able to do at home, but I have to be on the road this afternoon. I assumed we'd have cleared things by this time.'

'You're in Hospital Admin, right? Under Helen of Oz?'

'Yes.'

'I wouldn't have thought missing a day mattered. Or a week, for that matter. I thought we might have lunch together.'

He was already regretting having agreed to the interview, and was tempted to tell her to get out. On the other hand, his chief reason for agreeing had been the comment, when the Features Editor called him, that they would be doing a piece in any case. That had been accompanied by a benign smile, but the implication that non-co-operation might lead to less than friendly treatment was plain.

While he was hesitating, she added: 'I thought we might also have a chat about Adam Frodsham. He was your nephew, right?'

'I'd rather keep to sport.' She took a pack of low-hash cigarettes out of her waist-bag and scrabbled for matches. 'My sister is very distressed, as you can imagine. She doesn't read newspapers, but someone might show it to her.' Maggie Bruton lit up, still without looking at him. 'I can manage lunch, but I must be on the road soon after that.'

'I'm told the Dragon's not bad, for a small town.' Greed softened her expression into something approaching amiability.

'I'll book a table,' he offered. 'Perhaps you'll have a drink first. Gin and tonic?'

She actually smiled. 'Vodka, if you've got it. Ice, twist

of lemon.' She looked round the hall, her eye settling on a painting. 'Isn't that one of your sister's?'

'Yes, but . . .'

'Don't worry. Just demonstrating that I do my homework. You'll feel no pain.'

She was into her second large vodka when his phone buzzed. She nodded when he excused himself, and switched off her tape recorder. He went through to the landing before accepting the call. The screen stayed blank, but a voice asked: 'Michael Frodsham?'

'Yes.'

'Is this a secure line?'

'As far as I know. Who is that?'

'I'm afraid I have to remain anonymous, for the moment at any rate. It's about Adam. I'd like to see you. Soon.'

'If you can't tell me who you are . . .'

'Let's put it this way – you might just recognize me when we meet. I was at the funeral, but I wasn't wearing a balaclava.'

Michael paused. 'In that case, I don't think there's anything I want to say to you.'

'This is important, Michael. Too important for me to accept that sort of refusal. I can see you in London, or I can come down to Sheaf. Your choice.'

'My choice might be to ask for police protection.'

'What for? You're not being threatened. But I need to see you.'

The voice was reasonably cultured but carried a hint of the West Country: a warm burr with stony edges. He didn't want Anna to have to listen to it.

'All right – London.'

'Tomorrow.' That wasn't a question.

'Where in London?'

'You'll be picked up at Charing Cross, from your usual train. Obviously, you'll keep this confidential.'

'I'll have to tell the office I won't be in on time.'

'I'm sure you can think up something to satisfy them. Tomorrow, Charing Cross – ten fourteen, or as soon as your train gets in.'

When he returned to the sitting room, Maggie Bruton was on her feet by the door, inspecting a watercolour of Sheaf from the Flats. 'Sorry about that,' he said. 'Where were we?'

'Trying to work out how a dynamic character like Michael Frodsham became something as dull as a civil servant. But why might a dull civil servant think he needed police protection? I don't apologize. Audio-hyperaesthesia is a more useful talent than screwing your editor in contemporary journalism.'

'I've been getting a few crank calls.'

'Penalty of fame. But this crank's talked you into taking even more time off from that engrossing job at the Min of Health & Rehab.' When he said nothing, she shrugged. 'It's not relevant unless you say it is.'

He took her empty glass. 'The other half?'

'Smallish, if we're having a bottle of Chablis to wash down those Sheaf Bay scallops I've heard so much about.'

He brought her the drink. 'The Marsh lamb is good, too.'

'Great. Anything with that, as long as it's claret. Cheers.'

There was no one on the platform. The man who touched his arm in the station forecourt was in his forties, dressed in blazer and flannel trousers and wearing horn-rimmed spectacles. The glasses might indicate a more complex defect than myopia, but more probably an inability to afford laser treatment. The car which drew up a short distance from the taxi rank was also inconspicuous, a run-of-the-mill Ford. As Michael got in, he asked, semi-seriously: 'No blindfold? Or does that come later?'

He received no answer. The driver didn't speak either, but drove in silence down Whitehall and through Parliament

Square. They crossed the river and headed south by way of the Oval and Brixton Hill. Just before reaching the South Circular road, the car turned into quite a wide street lined with large, detached houses, which had once been impressive but now made up a slum of tenement flats. The only one retaining single identity carried a sign in broken neon tubing: Hotel Balmoral. From the appearance of people hanging around in front of it, and the noise, it seemed to have been turned into a shebeen.

They pulled up a little further along, opposite a hangover from the late Victorian suburban gothic movement: it had a facade of grey plaster, shattered in places to display underlying red brick, a badly degenerated stepped baronial entrance, and crenellation round the roof. Where there might once have been a front garden, a couple of coloured children squatted between abandoned cars, scratching with sticks in the dirt. The driver drove off when Michael got out. The other man spoke for the first time.

'Come on.'

He led the way up filthy, uncarpeted stairs to the second floor, knocked on a door and pushed it open. There was scarcely any furniture: a single bed, neatly made up, a deal table and a couple of chairs. Apart from peeling floral paper, the only decoration on the wall was the familiar St George's flag, fixed by safety pins. A blue-suited man of about sixty, with a greying toothbrush moustache, turned from the window and nodded to Michael's companion.

'I'll call when I need you.' He gestured courteously to Michael. 'Take a seat.'

The south-west accent was stronger without the distortion of a phone connection. Michael remained standing.

'You said you wanted to talk about Adam. I've only agreed because if I didn't you said someone might come down to Sheaf. My sister is in a bad enough way as it is. I don't want any more shocks for her. The one at the funeral was more than enough.'

'I'm Harry Porter. I wish you would sit down. I can't offer you a comfortable chair, but it'll be easier to talk if we're not eyeballing. I appreciate your coming in, and I'm sorry about the cloak-and-dagger bit. It would be nice to do without that – to be respectable and have proper offices with carpets, and a sexy receptionist and a drinks cabinet, but you'll appreciate that things are difficult. I won't keep you long.'

He took his own seat once Michael had sat down. 'Cigarette?' Michael shook his head. Lighting one himself, Porter said: 'I'm glad you don't. That performance in the France match was one of the finest things I've seen in a long time.'

'I'm sure you didn't bring me here to talk rugby.'

Porter smiled. 'Not really, but it does come into it. Rugby put you on the screens and into the headlines. It's Adam I want to talk about. He was very fond of you.'

'We were close when he was younger. Not over the last couple of years.'

'As I said, he was fond of you. He respected you. I know you didn't see eye to eye politically, but he hoped that would change.'

'Yes,' Michael said. 'I hoped that, too. One could try to make allowances for someone of his age.'

'But not someone of mine?'

'No.' Michael paused. 'You're not my kin, which makes a big difference, but you're also old enough to know better. As far as I can see, you, and people like you, have been responsible for my sister's son turning into a killer, and being slaughtered like an animal because of that. I can't even mourn him properly, because what happened was the due and proper result of his own actions. His directly: yours indirectly. What is it you want to say to me?'

It was an outburst whose unwisdom he recognized as he spoke. He was not only dealing with lunatics, but at their mercy. No one knew where he was, or was in a position even to start looking for him. Lunatics and, as recent events had shown, killers.

But Porter's response was mild. 'I wanted your help. And still do, unpromising as the prospect may look.'

Michael laughed. 'You mentioned rugby. It has its violent aspect. When I've been booted, I've booted back. But we don't carry Heckler-Kochs. Even if I approved of your political aims, I wouldn't fight for them.'

'We wouldn't want you to, at this stage. There are other ways in which you could help. But your attitude might change. Some of the best and toughest fighters started as pacifists. You're bothered that Adam executed Perdrai?'

'Execution is a judicial act. What he did was kill a defenceless man.'

'Perdrai,' Porter said, 'had signed eleven orders of arrest and committal on BA members during the past three weeks. Committal was to the Special Federal Institution in Lille, which is under the direct control of Euro Geheimes Polizei. These were people Adam knew, two of them close friends. We have to presume they are dead, following torture.'

'That's simply ridiculous!'

'The trouble with advanced communications is the illusion of information they give you. My great-grandmother lived all her life in the Forest of Dean. She went into Cinderford maybe twice or three times a year, and she could count on the fingers of one hand the number of times she'd visited Gloucester, fifteen miles away. She had very little idea of what went on outside the county, let alone in Europe or America. She knew she was ignorant of the wider world, and it didn't bother her. New York and Moscow were meaningless names. But what she knew about her village and her neighbours was solid knowledge.

'Today we see things happening on the far side of the globe, at the moment they're happening. That makes us think we're well informed. In fact, all the information we get comes through a few channels, and those channels are controlled. Basically, we're more ignorant than she was.'

'Most things can be controlled,' Michael said. 'Paranoia is an obvious exception.'

Porter stared at him, expressionless, and for a moment he wondered if he had gone too far. Then Porter stood up.

'I thought it was worth a shot, but I see I was wrong. I won't keep you. It looks as if we're both impregnable to argument.'

The sudden conclusion surprised Michael, and partially disarmed him. For the first time he could believe there was a man behind the posturing patriot: wrong-headed, destructive, dangerous, but also human. He said: 'I can rely on you not to bother my sister?'

'The mother of a hero and martyr commands respect.' Porter smiled. 'In any case, there's no way we could usefully employ her. Unlike you.'

Michael stood up, too. 'There's one thing.'

'What's that?'

'When you called me, I was being interviewed by a journalist. I went out of the room to take the call, but I think she eavesdropped on my end. She more or less told me she had.'

'Not to worry. Your pick-up at Charing Cross was monitored. The worst that could happen would be your getting taken in and questioned. If so, you can tell them the truth. You know nothing they don't know themselves, and this place will be abandoned within minutes of your leaving. We need to keep on the move. But thanks for telling me.'

'It wasn't on your account. I didn't want one of your thugs jumping to conclusions.'

'A sensible precaution. And logical thinking. It's a pity you can't see your way to helping us.' Porter pressed the quick-call button on his phone. 'I'll fix your return transport.'

* * *

Bad Dream

They had a bad weekend with Anna. Waking in the night, Michael heard her footsteps from the next room, pacing with the monotony of despair. When he went in to her, she looked at him in a hungry anticipation that crumpled as she recognized the irrelevant, living person where she had sought the unreachable dead. She let him take her to sit on her bed, and huddled close when he put his arms round her; but she was far away. He could feel the sharpness of her ribs against his arm. She was so thin.

She wouldn't let him get her anything, and wouldn't get into bed. They remained uncomfortably side by side, while for the thousandth time he tried to think of something to say which might help; and for the thousandth time failed. The night had turned chilly, and he put the coverlet over her shoulders. She looked at him as if he were a stranger – an intruder she couldn't even be bothered to resent.

Eventually she fell asleep, leaning against him, and he eased her under the covers. He stayed for several minutes, watching her sleep and praying she would not dream. But whether or not she dreamed, she must in due course wake.

Later he slept heavily himself. When he looked in on Anna she was asleep, but in a tangle of disordered sheets. He put the bed to rights as well as he could and went down to the kitchen. DD was beside the Aga, holding the coffee pot in a tremulous hand. He said accusingly: 'It's past nine.'

'I'm sorry. I overslept. Let me see to that.'

'I had a bad night, too. I heard you go in to her.' Michael poured coffee for them both. 'I didn't think I could do any good.'

'No. I couldn't, either.'

'Something ought to be done.' DD went to the fridge for cream, heavily laced his own mug, and offered the pot to Michael, who shook his head. 'I mean medically.'

'I've had a word with Sarah.' That was Sarah Dunhill, head of the principal Sheaf practice and Anna's doctor since before Adam's birth. 'There's nothing she can do without Anna's consent.'

DD shifted restlessly. 'But surely . . .'

'It's grief, not derangement. And in fact she wants the pain. No – that's wrong. She doesn't want it, but she can't bear to reject it.'

DD picked up his mug again. It was one of a batch Granny T. had potted in her early days of Sheaf and her marriage: thin yellow sheaves of corn ribbed a base of golden-brown. They had been exhibited at the Courtauld, and were collector's pieces. Coffee spilt as he carried it shakily towards the door.

'I'm going to listen to my music,' he said. 'But something has to be done about it. You must do something, Michael.'

His father had called most frequently from Frohsteig, but Johann also kept in close touch, and Dieter and Hildy called from time to time. Maria-Mercedes sent her love by proxy. When Johann got through late on Sunday afternoon, the call was non-visual and there was a weird background noise. At first, Michael couldn't make out what he was saying.

Johann repeated: 'I said, can you pick me up?'

'At the station? Where are you? In London or Ashford?'

'Neither. I'm airborne. I'll be arriving at Lydd – around five o'clock.'

'The airport? But there are no afternoon flights.'

'I'm using the company plane. How's Anna?'

'Much the same.'

'This is an impossible line. See you in an hour.'

Michael had never known Johann employ the Frohsteig jet; it was one of the features of executive life he tended to poke fun at. Driving back with him across the Marsh, with the light of a drab day fast draining into dusk, he received brief and noncommittal answers to his questions. All Johann would say was that he thought there was something which might help Anna, but needed to talk to her about it. Michael did not pursue the matter. Ahead, the silhouette of the little hill town stood sharp black against a darkening sky. Presumably he would know soon enough.

He had told DD of Johann's call, but not Anna. They found them both in the library, with Anna presiding over tea. The room was lit only by a single dark-shaded lamp, and she did not look particularly distressed as Johann went to kiss her. She expressed mild surprise at his being there, but didn't show it. Surprise required a belief in continuity, and she no longer had that.

Michael said: 'Let's go through to the garden room. It'll be more cheerful with a fire. I'll bring the tray.'

Johann's hand on her elbow steered Anna to the Queen Anne chair beside the fire. He sat her down and crouched beside her, looking up. Michael put another log on, and the fire blazed high. Her face showed white and drawn in its light. Johann took her hand in his, chafing it gently.

'It's great to see you, Orfant, but I've seen you looking better. Still not sleeping?'

She shook her head. 'I'm all right. You mustn't fuss about me.'

'You always fussed over me. Remember the time I fell in the canal, and you fished me out and cleaned me up? And bought me ice-cream on the way home, and smuggled me in at the back door and up to the bathroom because I was scared of what Maria-Mercedes would say?'

'That was a long time ago.'

Her voice was weary. Johann said: 'Look, Annie. I know I don't know how awful it is, and I know it's probably much worse than I can imagine. But I think maybe we can help. Will you listen to me – really listen?'

She nodded obediently. 'Yes.'

'Our research side has been doing some work on people in . . . emotional trouble. It's early days, but we've had positive results.'

'With Virtual, do you mean?' Michael said.

'A modified form of Total.'

He understood why Johann had been reluctant to discuss it with him in advance. What surprised him was that he should believe Anna might be willing to consider anything of that sort for a moment. Much middle-class contempt for Virtual was possibly affectation – an automatic refusal to see any good in a form of entertainment associated with addicts and drop-outs – but Anna's dislike was more solidly based. When they were children he had been ashamed of his own fondness for watching television, knowing how sincerely she despised it. Even then, she had seen no point in second-hand reality.

Growing up, that concentration on what she saw as the essential had turned first to her art, subsequently to Adam. All else was duty. She had been good at that: he did not recall the incident Johann had referred to, but did not query its validity. She was wonderful at looking after people. He doubted if anyone apart from himself guessed at the indifference which underpinned the caring. It was ludicrous to think that she, of all people, might find relief from her misery in some prefabricated pseudo-existence.

Johann said: 'Let me tell you about it.'

'It's very kind of you.' She managed a smile. 'I do mean that, Joh'n. But it wouldn't do any good. Really it wouldn't.'

'It will give you Adam.'

A shudder racked her body. 'Oh, no . . .'

Michael could no longer hold back. 'Leave it,' he said harshly. 'Those shoddy fantasies you peddle aren't going to help her. Let her be.'

Later he regretted the harshness. The proposal was well meant, and Johann could not be expected to take a detached view of the basis of his working life. But it didn't seem to have bothered him. Over whiskies, he said: 'It really is a major development, Mike. As you know, Total is a kind of pseudo-life which is external to the mind proper. There's interaction, but in a passive sense: walking into a dream made reality, as it were. What they're learning to do now is tie in with the mind's own creative function. Our makers and authenticators provide a story and a detailed framework, and the operand – the patient – builds on that.'

'There must still be a waking up,' Michael said. 'And surely that's the bit that's unbearable.'

'Perhaps chiefly unbearable because an ordinary dream is arbitrary, and can't be recalled. What's certain is that they've been getting clinical remissions – over seventy-five per cent with depression and even quite significantly with schizophrenia. Grief is a depressive illness. I wish I could persuade her to give it a shot. I brought the equipment over with me.'

That accounted for the metal case that had accompanied his overnight bag.

'She won't.'

'You may be right. But I thought it was worth a try.'

Waking in the night, he heard Anna pacing again. He was dead beat, and wondered if he could ignore it; it wasn't as if he could do anything to help. Hovering between rationalization and conscience, he became aware of a distant voice, indistinct but certainly Johann's. He doubted if he could do any better, but it freed him of his own obligation and he was able to turn over and go to sleep.

He was wakened by Johann. It was beginning to get light. Outside his window the abbey's outline was etched against pale blue. Johann, in his dressing gown, was smiling – in fact, grinning.

'Something to show you.'

They went into Anna's room. She was lying back in bed, with pillows heaped behind her. The helmet obscured much of her face, but the part that showed was transformed with joy.

Five

The Frohsteig building was not in fact so named: its title, in spindly neo-Deco lettering over the main entrance, was Thatcher House. It formed part of the Tottenham Court Road redevelopment of the early years of the century, the last major London office-building programme; it had been Euro-funded and was regarded by anti-Europeans as a monstrous bribe for the British government's final surrender to qualified majority voting. The name given to this, the centrepiece, had been seen as a contemptuous insult added to the injury.

Clad in innovatory rose-pink plastic, with antique-futurist towers at each corner looking into a piazza equipped with Fritz Lang fountains and abstract statuary, it had won not only the first Euro-Design Award, but major architectural awards throughout the world, including the United States and Greater Iraq. Time, though, had uttered a corrective verdict, and even more rapidly than usual. It had not helped that the cladding, like some earlier technological breakthroughs, had failed to match expectations, pitting badly under the gales of winters worse than anticipated, and randomly discolouring. The patchwork result gave the towers a mottled and irretrievably scruffy look.

This individual falling short was compounded by the economic disaster of the rest of the development, which even before it was completed had succumbed to the impact of an economic recession, and had now spent some years as one of the prime central-London slums. This did not trouble

Dieter, who explained that the price had been right, the position excellent, and the views over the surrounding squalor towards Buckingham Palace or the Hampstead heights were breathtaking, on a good day.

That was undeniably true from Dieter's own office at the top of the west tower, and the opposite window looked down into a piazza which had been renovated with Teutonic care. As Michael watched, ant-like figures crawled about their never-ending tasks of planting and tidying. Dieter finished his call, and Michael's attention returned to the man behind the Saarinen desk.

'I am sorry over that,' Dieter said. 'I said to Marilyn to hold calls, but she shows initiative. She knows you are here, and the call concerned you. I think maybe I promote her to central office.'

'Would she go?'

'Alas, probably not. Also, she speaks very little German. It is a charm for me, the British reluctance to speak foreign tongues, but commercially it presents a disadvantage.'

'The call concerned me, you say?'

'Yes. Earlier I have spoken with Rosbaud.' Michael nodded: Llewellyn Rosbaud, whose maternal grandfather had played a couple of times for Wales, was President of the *Grossdeutsche Rugby Verein*. 'He thinks a series of three games against an England XV is good – in Danzig, Bremen and Nuernberg. This can be in late summer, before your season begins. With good media coverage, it will be a stimulus to making a permanent German national team. So things will be easier for you.'

'I'm still thinking about it.'

'Good! But I hope you will not require too long to say yes. The moment is right for an announcement. Already you are a figure known in Germany. The Bruton piece – did you know it is reprinted in *Stern*? And the photograph of you making the last try was on the cover of *Spiegel*. It was very impressive.'

'It was an impressive effort by the cameraman. He was really in close, right up against the corner flag in fact. Getting between him and the Frenchman was like going through Scylla and Charybdis.'

The door had opened while he was speaking. He turned to see Hildy. She was wearing a deceptively modest black outfit, minimally trimmed with silver. It was high at the neck and below knee length, but the skirt had its usual split, providing a glimpse of silky golden thigh, and the silver trimming drew attention to an engaging thrust of breasts.

'You must sack Marilyn, Dieter. She tried to tell me you were too busy to see your little niece. *Mikey-Schatz* – what is it concerning whirlpools? Is that something improper for a young girl to know?'

Michael kissed her. Dieter smiled benignly. 'I thought you were busy filming through the day.'

'And miss a chance of seeing Michael? Especially when Onkel Dieter is going to take us both out for a seriously gross *Mittagessen*.'

Dieter shook his head. 'No.'

'Really sumptuous.' She went and leaned over his desk, putting her arms round his neck and giving him a long sensuous hug. 'If not the Trefoil, the Dorchester. Five courses, at least.' As far as she was concerned, Michael knew, it would be steak or lobster with salad, no dressing: she was a food disciplinarian.

'I shall be dining with Lufthansa,' Dieter told her. 'Not so good, but it cannot be avoided. I have a six o'clock appointment in Nuernberg. But I can spare you Michael.'

'Also your *Diamantkart*, which I hope is valid for either of them. We will not keep you from important business. Have you organized it for Anna yet?'

'Not yet. But it progresses.'

'Organized what for Anna?' Michael asked.

Dieter showed surprise. 'Did she not tell you?'

'No. Perhaps you'd better.'

'She comes to Germany, for Total. To the Brosser Clinic. It is an independent medical centre, but they work close with our research people.'

Michael was taken aback, and slightly confused. He remembered Johann saying that Total was essential for long-term treatment, and that long-term treatment was advisable where there were indications that depression might be endogenous rather than contingent, but he had not realized this was so serious or imminent a possibility. It was one thing seeing her helmet-and-gloved, quite another to envisage her in a cocoon, wired and intubated, her remoteness become absolute separation.

'Is that really necessary?' he asked.

'It is, if we wish her to become truly well. Michael, the Brosser is the best place that we have, I promise you. It is in the Steigerwald, a mountain behind it and a lake before. You will see no place more beautiful.'

'Does the landscape matter, to someone in a cocoon?'

'But you will see them when you visit, as I am sure you will wish.'

Dieter spoke patiently, earnestly, above all rationally. Michael wondered if his own surprise had resulted from simply blanking out a prospect which so deeply repelled him. Anna was the one who mattered. 'Let me get this right,' he pressed. 'You've discussed it with her?'

'Johann has. He called her yesterday, in the afternoon. They talked a long time.'

Michael had stayed the night in London, and not seen Anna since the previous morning. 'And she agreed?'

'Most willingly, happily.'

It was not something Michael could seriously doubt. He had seen the look in her eyes as she prepared to put on the helmet – an anticipation not just of joy, but of salvation – and the sad bewilderment when she took it off. It had been an unnecessary question. And much as he loathed what it involved, it was necessary to consider the alternative: that grinding agony from which there was no relief.

'Do they get complete cures – without residual addiction?' he asked.

'Did Johann not tell you that?'

'Yes. He did.'

Hildy put an arm round him. 'You will get her back, Mikey, and healed of this wound. And meanwhile her shadow-life will be all of beauty, with her beloved Adam. That is so much better than those tainted fantasies in which your little half-sister plays her part. Come, we will go and spend Dieter's money.'

She turned back to Dieter, put a slow questing hand inside his jacket and came out with his wallet. She fingered through to find the plastic card she wanted. He sat smiling as she took it and with equal deliberation returned the wallet, then rewarded him by kissing her fingers and pressing them against his lips. She smiled herself, with seductive assurance. '*Küsse dich. Danke schön, Onkel-liebling.*'

The organization of the demonstration at Adam's funeral had been, as Michael had suspected, an exception reinforcing a rule: BA's uprising came at the wrong time, in the wrong place, and at half cock. It followed a statement in the Commons by the Prime Minister, Jim Palin, that an Order in Council had been issued making reasonable suspicion of membership of Britain Awake! sufficient ground for arrest and detention, and was coupled with temporary suspension of habeas corpus. The next day, Palin addressed a meeting of the Southwest Development Board in Bath: the assault was on the Assembly Rooms, where he was speaking. After a brief struggle, the military detachment responsible for his security was overpowered. The local police, as at the burning of the Christmas Pudding, stood by. Bath was generally regarded as being somewhat anti-Federal, but that was probably a special fix. The flag of St George was raised in the centre of the city, and 'Land of Hope and Glory' raggedly sung to celebrate the victory.

What they had not reckoned with was the speed with which the squadron of helicopter gunships and a second wave of troop-carriers moved in from Melksham. They recaptured the Assembly Rooms and recovered the Prime Minister, shaken but safe. The soldiers put down the rest of the rebellion within a couple of hours. Casualties were light, and almost entirely confined to BA activists.

Succeeding disturbances in Leeds and the East End of London, and sporadic demonstrations elsewhere, were dealt with just as firmly. Press and television voiced outrage and contempt. The *Times* leader was headlined: 'A Wretched Little Business'.

The following Saturday was DD's eighty-eighth birthday. In recent years he had made a show of ignoring the occasion, but this year changed his mind; he told Michael he wanted to have a party.

'I remember my eighteenth,' he said. 'Worst bit of the war – winter before Alamein. I got a weekend pass, and my mother baked a birthday cake out of carrots. T. might have made something of it – T. could make something of anything – but my mother couldn't brew tea without burning the water. Now I'm eighteen years into injury time, so I'll have a party. Nothing fussy, Michael, but no carrots.'

The guest list he provided was inevitably small, since most of his contemporaries had long since been buried in the cemetery on Sheaf Hill. One name surprised Michael.

'Julian Souter?'

'Yes, I think so. A twat in some ways, but he seems to mean well. He's given me one or two market tips which haven't done badly.'

Souter was the youngest partner in the long-established firm of Barnes, Dickson & Turnbull, Solicitors, who had handled DD's legal affairs for more than fifty years. He was short and red-faced and had a puffed-out look, vaguely reminiscent of a pouter pigeon. Since he chattered a great deal in a rasping voice and frequently wore a green pullover, Anna had nicknamed him The Budgie.

His wife was a tall, coldly smiling woman, who dominated him. They lived, childless, on the outskirts of the town, in a mercilessly neat and clean modern house from which he could be seen emerging in the morning in stockinged feet, taking shoes from a plastic bag to put on in the porch. Their cleaner had regaled the social grapevine with the information that the hall featured a notice board, on which wifely instructions for his household chores were pinned daily.

Souter had taken over DD's affairs the previous year, when Jim Dickson retired, and had first visited the house to see him after Granny T.'s death. Two things had surprised Michael: that he had addressed his grandfather as DD without being offered or seeking permission; and that DD had appeared not to resent it. With Dickson – senior partner in the firm and twenty-five years older – it had always been a scrupulous 'Mr Dorigny'.

Michael's father arrived from Frohsteig with Johann, and Hildy came down from London. He brought presents from Dieter and Maria-Mercedes: a jeroboam of '97 Branntwein, and a blue and crimson silk smoking jacket at which DD snorted derisively. Michael produced for Anna a box of the cigars she had invariably given him; she wept when he handed her the gift tag to write.

'I'm hopeless, aren't I? Can't get anything right any more.'

He held her for a moment. 'It'll pass, love. You're going to be better.'

She shook her head, but said: 'Do you think Johann will have a date yet – for the Clinic?'

The day was fine, a burst of spring, and they had opened the conservatory doors to let people spill out on to the terrace and lawn. DD tackled his presents with small-boy enthusiasm. That even extended to the bedroom slippers Michael had found – his current set gaped to reveal bony yellow big toes – but Michael was under no illusion that they would replace the old ones. His champagne flute held in a twitching hand, DD said: 'Extreme old age isn't as bad as I expected. All that stuff about it only being better than the alternative . . . I must say, I'm enjoying this more than the one seventy years ago, when we wound up down the bloody shelter.' He surveyed his guests with satisfaction. 'Very kind of you all, very kind. But at my age one can be frank, rude even. The best present is one I've given myself. I'll go and get it.'

He set off unsteadily across the lawn towards the pottery. He'd been there on and off during the past several days, and yesterday Michael had been astonished to see the kiln smoking for the first time in years. He'd wondered if he should comment, but decided against it. When DD returned, he was proudly brandishing an object.

'What do you think of it?'

It was a pottery mug, a bit misshapen but not bad for an old man with Parkinson's. The base colour was matt black, and the painted image on the side stood out boldly. The pale flabby face was also somewhat shakily painted but, despite two striking additions, unmistakable as that of Joachim Mischendorf, the current German Chancellor. The embellishments were a Hitler lock of hair and a Hitler moustache.

A moment's embarrassed silence was broken by Johann laughing: 'Very good, DD. Spot on in every way!'

Mischendorf had given an interview on the Euro television network following the Bath incident, in which he had not only excoriated BA terrorists, but hinted at identifying them with the British generally. He talked of a national arrogance which had outlived any possible justification: the English in particular should realize they were no longer imperial masters but merely a sulking and trivial minority in the European Federation. They must learn this lesson, or expect to have it taught.

'Not bad, is it?' DD asked fondly. 'Not bad for eighty-eight.'

Except for Anna, the family made a late night of it. Even DD stayed up until near midnight, when he retired even more unsteadily than he had entered, but still under his own steam.

When the doorbell rang just before eight the following morning, Michael answered it in his dressing gown. A sergeant and police officer stood there.

'Hello, Parsons,' Michael greeted the sergeant. 'We're all late starters today, I'm afraid. What can I do for you?'

Parsons was thick-set and grizzled, close to retirement. He looked Michael in the eye, but the effort was plain. 'I'm sorry, sir. I'll have to ask you to let us come in.' He tapped his chest. 'I do have a warrant, if you'd like to see it.'

'A warrant for what? What are you talking about?'

'Well . . . it's to search this property, for materials relating to a prohibited organization.'

It must be a belated follow-through on Adam, presumably a consequence of Britain Awake! being proscribed. Michael was confident there was nothing to find: he'd checked Adam's room thoroughly. His concern was for Anna. 'My sister's not been well, and still isn't . . .' he said.

Parsons raised an apologetic hand. 'I don't think we'll need to upset Miss Frodsham, sir.'

The two of them made straight for the garden room, and Parsons stumped across to the fireplace. DD's birthday present to himself stood where he had tenderly placed it, in the centre of the mantelshelf. Parsons lifted it.

'I'll have to take this, sir.' He nodded to his constable. 'Check the pottery for any more, or anything similar.'

Michael asked: 'But why? This is ridiculous.'

'Instructions. I'm sorry, sir.' He hesitated. 'I think I ought to warn you. There may be a charge against Mr Dorigny.'

'What charge?'

'Aiding and abetting an illegal organization. It's covered under the Order.'

Johann was coming down as the police were leaving. Still scarcely believing it himself, Michael told him what had happened. In silence, Johann put the kettle on the Aga and measured out coffee. Taking mugs from the rack, Michael said: 'It must be connected with Adam. Some bureaucratic lunacy . . .'

'I'm not sure.'

'It has to be.'

'They didn't search the house, did they?' The kettle whistled and he filled the coffee pot. 'You said the sergeant went straight to the fireplace and took the mug. And then sent his constable to the pottery – checking in case DD had done more than one, I suppose. They knew what they were looking for.'

Michael was beginning to think more clearly. 'Are you saying DD was informed on – by someone at the party?'

'It looks like that. Unless he's been going round Sheaf, boasting about it.'

Michael shook his head. 'He wouldn't have done that. It was his surprise; remember how pleased he was with his little joke? And he's not been out of the house since.'

His father appeared while Johann was pouring coffee. He was agitated by the news.

'Oh, God! That's awful. I didn't like it at the time, but . . .'

'It's surely not serious,' Michael said. 'A technical offence. They can't do worse than caution him.'

His father shook his head. 'I wish I could believe that. We had a farmer near Nuremberg last year who put an American flag up over his barn. He was obviously mad, but they sent him to prison for three months. He was younger than DD, but not that much.'

Michael suppressed an impulse to say: 'But this is

England!' Instead he said: 'Anyway, I don't think there's any point in mentioning it to him at this stage.'

His father said: 'Perhaps he can be talked into staying in bed. I'll take him coffee up.'

When he'd gone, Johann said: 'It might be a help if we could work out who did the informing. Do you know of anyone at the party with an official tie-up? Or semi-official – or ex? What about the old chap with the side-whiskers . . . Awkright?'

He had been the only guest within a decade of DD's own age; a widower, crippled by arthritis, who had been Chief Constable of the county before the office was abolished by a Euro ruling.

'It's not possible. Not Bill Awkright.'

'Mike, we need to keep . . . our minds open.'

'Awkright's more anti-Europe than DD himself!'

'Appearances can be deceptive.'

The comment struck home unexpectedly. That was true, he realized, even in the context of family. Johann was the least Teutonic of the German branch, but he was still the son of Maria-Mercedes, who from time to time displayed a distinctly Valkyrian aspect. Anger flickered among the embers of shocked disbelief. He thought again of his father's ready acceptance of DD being faced with a prison sentence. Living over there had inured him to authoritarianism.

He remembered a visit to Germany when he was about twenty, and being struck, as he crossed a park in Baden on his way to the casino, by the freshness and charm of a young mother, pushing a pram along an adjacent path. Their glances had met, and he'd felt strangely pleased that her beauty was safeguarded by her maternity: that all her thoughts were concentrated on the child – her first, he felt sure.

Then she had raised a hand from the pram handle to gesture towards the grass on which he was walking and said, in a harsh accent: *'Das ist verboten. Strengst verboten!'*

National characteristics survived internationalism, much as one disliked the idea . . . He thought of Canny Yates, who'd taught Modern History at school, quoting a comment on the British infantry of the first World War – that they were lions led by donkeys – and saying: 'At any rate, better than the Huns: donkeys led by hyenas.' He'd laughed with the rest – Canny was respected, and somewhat feared – but had been shocked.

'It might be a help to know who it was,' Johann repeated. That was when Hildy appeared, seeking an explanation. She looked very attractive in a swirling yellow housecoat, but her expression, as she listened, turned grim.

'It was a stupid thing to do. I am very fond of DD, but he should know better, at his age.' The prank seemed to bother her more than the treachery which might render it serious. 'If *Grossvater* did something like that, against the British Prime Minister, we would call it rude – *ungebildet.*'

Use of the German expression underlined her resentment. Could the hostility run so deep that she herself could have turned informer? He told himself it was impossible – monstrous even to imagine she could be capable of such a thing.

But the suspicion, even though immediately rejected, would not go away. It had been Johann, he remembered, who had broken the embarrassed silence after DD produced the mug, but his laugh, even at the time, had seemed forced. 'Appearances can be deceptive.' And it had been Johann who'd proposed Awkright as a candidate.

Michael's father came back into the kitchen. 'I've got him to stay in bed. I took him his *Telegraph*. He's feeling a bit under the weather after last night, anyway.'

Hildy, her smile back in place, said: 'Poor old DD. It was the port, I think.'

'I feel it might be a good idea to get on to Dieter,' Johann said, 'he might have some useful advice.'

Hildy came and pressed herself against Michael. 'Don't

look so bothered, *liebchen*. It will be all right. Is there still coffee?'

Michael shook his head. He felt ashamed of himself; the moral line between treachery, and unjustifiably imputing it to others, was a thin and wavering one.

'I'll make some fresh.'

It was a further indication of Anna's retreat from life that this morning, as with so many of late, she stayed in her room, engrossed in the pretence of Adam. Michael brought in logs and set and lit the fire, a chore she had previously jealously guarded as her own. DD had got up, but only to go to his study, out of which drifted the massive masculine beat of Gregorian chant. Michael was fixing Martinis when Johann came into the garden room. He looked happier.

'I think we're in the clear.'

'Are you sure?' John Frodsham asked. 'What did Dieter say?'

'He called me back, just now. He got on to Paul-Ernst.' He explained to Michael: '*Ober-Kommandant* Paul-Ernst Leipziger, who owes him a favour or two. He's with the *Sicherheitspolizei*, and carries weight. A bit of a pain in the arse, but efficient. The case is being filed under Trivia. No action to be taken.'

'You mean he can fix things like that – from Germany?' Michael enquired.

'Apparently. I'm afraid DD doesn't get his mug back. The Sheaf police have been told to break it up and dispose of it.'

'I'll tell him I knocked it off when I was making the fire.'

Hildy asked: 'And if he wishes to see the pieces?'

'He won't. He's always had a horror of broken pottery.'

'Or decides he will make another? Several others, maybe?'

'I doubt that too, with his present attention span. But

I'll sabotage the kiln to be on the safe side.' He lifted the pitcher of Martini towards Johann. 'Thanks, Jo'. Ready for a drink?'

'More than ready. One other thing: Dieter agreed it might be a notion to find out who did the informing, if only as a precaution for the future.' He took the glass Michael handed him. 'Apparently, it was Souter.'

Michael was surprised. They had talked, after he had gone, about the man's gratuitous affability. 'The Budgie?'

'A somewhat larger bird, I feel: one that might easily take off an incautious finger. A parrot, at least, maybe a vulture. I gather he's set himself up as an information source for the security forces. His position as a solicitor lends itself to that.' He sipped his Martini. '*Das schmeckt!*'

The plane was half-empty, and Michael found himself the sole occupant of a row. After the usual, minimally edible meal had been served, there was an option of film or Virtual. The former gave a choice of a thriller or a tear-jerker based on the life of Princess Grace of Monaco; the latter offered safari, off-piste skiing or tropical cruising. He decided on a book instead, but had read only a few pages when a tall uniformed figure came down the aisle and stopped beside him. The gold bands on his sleeve identified him as the skipper.

'Mr Frodsham? Rory Kay. Am I interrupting you?'

Although it was an American airline, his accent was British. Michael shook his head, closing the book. 'Not a bit.'

Kay looked to be in his middle fifties, greying but handsome; his body language projected laid-back amiability but also authority. 'Mind if I sit down? I noticed your name on the passenger list, but until I saw you I couldn't be sure it wasn't another Michael Frodsham. I thought you'd be in luxe.'

Michael shrugged. 'My Civil Service ranking doesn't rate luxe.'

'I think we could manage an upgrade. I have discretion.'

'Thanks, but I'm fine here.'

'I saw the video of the France game. Great stuff.'

'Thanks again. But I'm surprised it was shown in the States. Or did you catch it on one of your London turn-rounds?'

Kay smiled. 'I've a contact in England who picks up things he thinks I'll like. Such as that. I also take the *Telegraph* and the *Spectator*, and a couple of others.'

'How long have you been living in America?'

'I haven't totted it up lately. More than twenty-five years.'

'You haven't lost your accent.'

'That happens in the first year, if it's going to happen. Otherwise you stick with British. I remember before I left England someone talking about a buddy of his who'd been twenty years in Manhattan. He said: "And whenever he ties one on, he stands in the middle of the room reciting Rupert Brooke – and his four kids lie around with their fingers in their ears groaning 'Aw, pop . . . !'" At least, I don't recite Rupert Brooke.'

'And when . . . ?'

'When I retire?' Kay grinned. 'It's not a sensitive subject. I have some flexibility, but it's due within the next few years.'

'You'll keep the British connection?'

'We're coming back.'

'Your wife's British, as well?'

'No. She's the reason I went over in the first place. But we have a deal, and part of it is retiring to England. The kids will make up their own minds about what they do: they have both passports so it's no problem.'

'There have been a few changes in a quarter of a century.'

Kay nodded. 'I've noticed. We get over on holidays.'

'We probably weren't in Europe, when you left.'

'No, I don't think we were.'

'And at the moment things aren't looking too bright.'

'I've noticed that, too. Even from Virginia. The business in Bath got full coverage in the States.'

'But you're still planning to come back?'

There was a pause while coffee was offered and declined. Kay finally said: 'Some things don't change: a pint of beer in a pub, the smell of wood smoke on an autumn evening, or wet grass in May. OK, so they can put up what looks like an English pub in Virginia, and serve the beer warm if you ask them nicely, but even when your eye and tongue can't tell the difference you know it's veneer. And you can smell wood smoke in Vermont, and sometimes the weather in Washington State could be mistaken for English. But they're just not the real thing. It's the difference between Virtual and living.'

'I gather there's a lot of opposition to Virtual in the States. Aren't they talking about banning it?'

'Yes. And on that I'm American. Don't misunderstand me. After twenty-five years, I know they're right on quite a few things. But I'm still coming home when my contract expires.'

Lucy met him at the airport, and they took a taxi to her apartment. She'd not said much about it, and he'd envisaged an anonymous pad in some large block, but it proved to be the first floor of an elegant colonial house in Georgetown, looking on to a garden of neat lawns and magnolias in blossom. Michael made appropriately admiring noises.

'Not bad for an uppity black broad, though I say it myself. I can't afford it, of course, and I guess I was a fool to take it on. If Aron loses in November, I'm going to have to hope I find some Republican sucker to take it off my hands.'

'Do you think he might lose?'

'He ought not. They're going to find it hard to pull off a right flanking move, with him making like Teddy

Roosevelt. What I am going to do right now is pour us a couple of scotches, and then I guess you may want to freshen up. Tonight I'm taking you out to dinner at a little place I know.'

'Zodiacal?'

She smiled. 'No. Not when you're the guest. French. If a Brit can stand a demonstration of French superiority.'

'So long as they confine it to cooking.' He checked his watch. 'Even if I take two showers, that seems to offer a few hours before we eat.'

'You could rest up, if you're tired from the flight.'

He put his hand against the fullness of her breasts. 'I don't think I've ever felt less tired.'

At the end of the evening, in bed again, she said: 'I've been worried about you.'

'Why? Things are going well. Dieter waving bags of Euros under my nose. And I'm quite enjoying the minor celebrity role. I owe this trip to it. It's a routine liaison with opposite numbers in Federal Health Administration, but I've jumped a queue. My boss thinks she may be able to use me in some of her own manoeuvres, and wants to keep me sweet.'

Lucy reached across him for her drink. 'It wasn't your career I was thinking about. It's what's happening in England I don't like.'

'Some of it I don't much like myself.'

He told her about the aftermath to DD's birthday party. It had not seemed wise to refer to it on the phone, though as recently as a few weeks ago the notion of surveillance wouldn't have crossed his mind.

After he had finished, she said, 'That's what I mean. It's not a good situation.'

'Things will settle down.'

'I hope so, but that's not how the local scuttlebutt figures it. There are whispers of a really big crackdown coming.'

He didn't want to talk politics. 'Do you know what makes me feel bad?' Her hair brushed his face as she shook her head. 'My own reaction, at the time. We didn't know who it was who'd informed on DD. And my first impulse was to blame them.'

'Them?'

'Johann – Hildy.'

She thought about it. 'I can't imagine any way I'd suspect family of two-timing over something like that, not so long as anyone else was living on the planet. But we're black. My parents, when they were young, may have been fooled for a while by the Martin Luther King and White Liberal combo, but this is a different generation. We've settled for reality. Maybe my father would have joked about being 'an uppity damn nigra', but he wouldn't have meant it seriously. We've learned to accept it's a tough world out there, and one that's not going to change this year or this decade – maybe not this century. It's something the Jews managed to live with for a couple of thousand years, and we can if they could. Maybe one day we'll find a homeland, and a chunk of planet to be boss-man in, but considering what came before that for them, it's not exactly something to look forward to.

'At that, we're doing better than those heavy feminists of twenty, thirty years back. We're acceptable, some of us, and if we make it we live well. Some of our black brothers – well, most of them – may be stuck in fenced-off ghettos with trigger-happy guards making sure they stay right there, but that's economic, not racial. So we're told. And the Jews in old Europe had ghettos too, didn't they? Not with armed guards – just a pogrom now and then.

'So OK, we're disadvantaged, but what's special about that? And what we have in return is what the Jews always had: loyalty. Not the big stuff MLK promoted, but small-scale, and all the stronger for it. We're cynical about plenty of things, but not about kinsfolk.'

Michael took the glass from her hand and put it on

the bedside table, a good reproduction of a serpentine gilt console. He touched her without urgency. Temporary satiation, but with renewal of appetite guaranteed: a good feeling. He said: 'I see what you mean, but it doesn't make me feel any better.'

'And I guess I can see how it might be different, if stuff like race got in the way. Or is that nationalism? I can't myself figure races among white skins, but maybe that's down to insensitivity.'

'I doubt if it's anything so fundamental,' Michael said. 'Anna and I were thrown together when our mother died; we'd always been close, but we got closer. Father was away a lot, which was all right. I remember defending him once, to Anna. I said it might be worse for him than for us, her dying. Profound thinking, for a six-year-old. I remember thinking something like that while I was saying it, and feeling proud of myself.'

She smiled, fingering his biceps. 'Self-satisfied, even then.'

'Sure. Priggishness is buried deep in the English psyche. But that meant there weren't any excuses when he re-married. Anna was more openly resentful, but I was pretty bad about it too. And that extended to our half-siblings when they started arriving. I thought I'd adjusted to it. I really like them both, Johann especially.'

He enjoyed the feel of her hair, as she nodded. 'A boy with charm.'

'And yet, twenty years later, I'm prepared to think the worst of them, on no evidence. That's nothing to do with nationalism – nothing so excusable even as Adam's anti-Germanism. Just old-fashioned jealousy. Pretty demeaning, wouldn't you say?'

'Not if you're willing to take an honest look at it. How is Anna, incidentally? When . . . ?'

'They'll have a bed for her next week. She's due to go in the day after I get back. She resented Germany even more

than I did when we were little, and now she can't wait to
get there. One of the minor ironies.'

Lucy snuggled close. 'That's life, massa.'

After Michael had got through business – officially an
exchange of views on the economies of hospital administration, unofficially the furtherance of a brief from Helen
Rackham to sound out the latest US position on Virtual –
Lucy showed him the sights: the White House, the Capitol,
the Air & Space Museum. They had salad lunches in a small
cafe which had a stream running through to a pool with a
white marble fountain, before going on to Arlington. The
Vietnam Memorial, and more marble – what looked like
an infinity of it – but sombre black. He touched one of the
names, the hard edge of the lettering softened by generations
of questioning fingers.

'An impressive monument to America's last major war.'

'Last, or maybe just latest.'

'That's only electioneering, surely.'

'Sure, it's electioneering. Aron senses a national mood
– frustration with years of economic stagnation, combined
with amnesia over body bags. America flexing its mighty
muscles again. And something to take our minds off the
Hispanic administrations in California and New Mexico;
from those agitations for independence. But it's not just
that. You know he has cousins in England?'

'I'd heard.'

'His family split when they left Poland during the Hitler
years, but they've kept a strong link going. Did you ever
read the book he wrote as a junior congressman? *Strategic
Error?*'

'No.'

'His thesis was that the biggest mistake the US made
in the twentieth century was pushing Britain towards the
European union. We threw away that unsinkable aircraft
carrier for a trade advantage that didn't work. I'm not

103

sure he doesn't see himself as the man who could win it back.'

Michael turned his back on the mind-numbing lines of names. 'I've heard Adam talk that way, now and then – about the possibility of our long-lost cousins riding to the rescue. What Aron needs to realize is that the overwhelming majority of us don't want rescuing, even without a war – a war that would be fought on our patch of ground, not America's. The US may have been cheering us on from the sidelines, but we gave up that aircraft carrier status voluntarily, and with no regrets.'

Michael was booked for a mid-evening flight the following day, and after lunch Lucy took him to see the ghetto barrier: he had expressed an interest when she was in England, but hadn't expected her to remember. The high metal fence circumscribing Washington's slum area was punctuated by watchtowers equipped with searchlights, infra-red and laser monitors, and at intervals by checkpoints where vehicles were examined by bored and hostile-looking guards in riot gear. They stood near one of these; it was a chilling sight.

'I'm glad you brought me,' he said. 'At least, we don't have anything like this.'

'You could add "yet" to that. This is America, the land of the best and the worst. And also of the future.'

It happened very fast. At one moment there was just a truck standing at the checkpoint, with guards desultorily inspecting its contents; then an eruption of figures from around it – bursting out, spilling forward, brushing the guards aside before they could reach their weapons. The black men, in ragged jeans, mostly shirtless, were yelling indistinguishably as they headed towards them. He tried to reach Lucy's arm, but by the time he made contact the mob was swarming over them.

Six

The Army captain looking after him seemed young for his rank – still in his middle twenties, Michael guessed. He was conventionally handsome in a heavy-jawed fashion, and his uniform looked as if it had been ironed on to him. He had a southern accent, Texan possibly, and was economical with words, answering questions briefly, and volunteering no unnecessary information. When Michael sought it, he was laconically told explanations could wait for his official debriefing. He was sirred punctiliously.

They took a lift to the top floor, where he was escorted about fifty metres along a corridor to a room labelled Specops G2. It was on the outside of the building, and the view of city lights against a black sky reminded him of time elapsed. The room was pleasantly furnished – desk and executive chair, but also two easy chairs, a red leather sofa, and a coffee table with a drinks tray. Moreover, the man who came from the desk to greet him was in marked contrast to the other, who saluted, and smartly withdrew. He was late fifties, with grey hair closer to civilian than standard military length, an amiable, slightly squashy face, and bushy eyebrows that were still black. He grasped Michael's hand strongly.

'Ike Haddon. Glad to meet you, Mr Frodsham. I'm sorry it has to be an occasion such as this.' He indicated an armchair, and took the facing one. 'Can I offer you a drink? Scotch?'

'Thank you.' He watched Haddon pour large measures

into heavy crystal glasses, accepted water and refused ice. 'There's nothing to apologize for.'

Haddon shook his head. 'It calls for an apology when a guest in our country gets roughed up by a mob.'

'The response to that was impressive. I imagine it's a standard drill, but I couldn't believe how fast your chaps came out of that helicopter.'

Haddon grinned. 'We do our best.'

'In fact, they didn't have time to damage us. The medical check-up wasn't necessary.'

'They weren't planning on damaging you. The procedure is to drag you into the ghetto, strip you of anything of value, and then look for a ransom. Theoretically we have a police presence inside, but in practical terms we're limited to punitive reaction. It wouldn't be easy to recover an individual. As far as the check-up is concerned, you are a foreign national; we needed to establish you were presently in good shape, if only to make sure we don't get hit by a civil suit later on.'

'And Miss Jones?'

'Sure, she's fine too. Not a foreign national, but we still take care.'

The scotch was good, a single malt. Looking at the night sky, Michael said: 'I've missed my plane.'

'Unfortunately, that is so. Something else we regret. We've booked you on the same flight tomorrow – will that be in order? And tonight we're putting you up at the Grand Hyatt, unless . . .'

'That won't be necessary. But thanks.'

Haddon checked his watch. 'I'd like at least to give you and Miss Jones dinner. She's accepted, as long as it's OK with you. She had something to attend to, but we're scheduled to meet with her in about an hour. Does that suit?'

They chatted; he was an easy man to talk to. He came of an Army family, Michael learned: his grandfather had fought in Normandy and Korea, his father in Vietnam. He had two younger brothers serving, and a son at West Point. His wife's family had been Army too. His home was in Manassas, with a view of a Civil War battlefield, two daughters at high school, a couple of horses and three Labrador dogs. His wife bred and judged that breed.

He went on to talk more openly than Michael would have expected about local problems. The ghettos were a scandal, and something needed to be done: the difficulty lay in working out just what. The virtual alienation of Spanish-speaking Americans in California and New Mexico added to the pressure. He suggested, frankly, that the proposed Amendment banning Virtual could have a political purpose in echoing the Pope's denunciation of esping: neo-Catholicism was rife in both states, and this was a useful sop to Hispanic sensibilities.

Eventually the subject of conversation switched to Michael. Haddon put questions but only in a general way. He asked about his work, but accepted hospital administration as an answer without pressing for details. He also asked where he lived, and observed warmly: 'You're a lucky man. That is a truly beautiful township.'

'You know it?'

'My wife and I visited, not long after we married. We stayed in the Neptune.' He chuckled. 'I like that notice on the wall: "Rebuilt 1380". And that bar with the fireplace you could roast an ox in. We holidayed in England quite a bit in the early years. I guess we both fell in love with your country. Then the children came along, and enforced different priorities. Maybe when the girls are in college, we'll get back again.' He paused. 'If the situation permits.'

'Things are a bit tricky at the moment,' Michael said, 'but it'll pass.'

'You think so? I hope you're right. Foreign troops on English soil – that bothers me.'

'Fellow European troops. Not exactly foreign.'

'Is that how the majority of English people see it?'

It was Michael's turn to hesitate. 'There's some resentment, in some quarters.' The question made him uneasy, but Haddon's affable manner seemed innocent enough. 'It isn't easy to work out how serious it is.'

Haddon nodded. 'It's even harder for us, as Americans – getting a fix on something that's three thousand miles away and under increasingly heavy censorship. And it's going to be more difficult still, from now on. The latest word is that all Americans may be banned – no new visas issued, current visas cancelled.'

Michael was startled. 'I hadn't heard that.'

'May I ask you not to mention it? It's classified.'

'No, of course,' Michael promised, privately exempting Lucy from the undertaking. 'This would apply just to Britain – not Europe generally?'

'That is our understanding.'

So they could meet in Germany, or France; more difficult, but not insuperable. Haddon topped up the glasses, and sipped his appreciatively.

'Beats bourbon or rye. Those English beers were even better, but even supposing I could get them they'd be a no-no these days. You need to watch your gut, if you want to stay in the Army. Do you mind if I call you Michael?'

'Of course not. Go ahead.'

'Michael, there's something I'd like to put to you. It's the sort of thing that could be awkward with some people, but I read you as a man who takes a laid-back view of situations. We're increasingly limited on information from the UK, as I've said, and denial of information is hard on the military mind. It would be helpful for us to have a source keeping us posted on the local situation. Very helpful.'

Michael took his time about responding while Haddon waited with no sign of impatience. He said finally: 'I don't think you told me what your present job is. The

sign on the door – Specops. Would that be Special Operations?'

'Sure.' Haddon leaned back, hands clasped behind his
head. 'Branch of military intelligence. Routine stuff.'

'Which makes this a routine proposition to me to act as
a US agent. I'm not interested.'

'It depends what you mean by agent. We're not looking
for anything heavy: no microphotography, site surveillance,
analysis of troop movements – nothing like that. Nothing
more, in fact, than reports on the scene in the street by a
man in the street. Local colour, local reactions. It wouldn't
be much from you, but it would mean a lot to us. And it's
worth money to us. Payments into a Washington account.
And we can fix it you get access to the account by arranging
for you to make regular visits here.'

Despite himself, he was intrigued. 'How would you
do that?'

Haddon grinned, the grin of a conspiratorial schoolboy.
'Too easy. You came over this time for a meeting on hospital
administration, but my guess – my informed guess – is that
you had an undisclosed agenda. Your department deals with
Virtual, and everyone wants to know what the other side is
up to. We can give you something to take back that will
whet the appetite. You won't need to ask for a repeat trip:
you'll be sent.'

'The answer's no.'

'Time to consider?'

'I've considered.'

Haddon got up from his chair and went to his desk. He
wrote on a notepad, tore off the top sheet, and handed it to
Michael. It was a London telephone number.

'You can throw it away,' Haddon said, 'or you can
put it in your organizer. It's a safe contact – in reverse
order the number can go down under Books: that's a
bookshop in Chelsea.' He consulted the time again. 'We
ought to be moving. There's a realtor's convention in

town, and that sonofabitch maitre d' could let our table go.'

His flight was delayed, but only by an hour. He thought of Captain Kay, and speculated on the possibility of him skippering this flight too: possible, but unlikely. And even more unlikely in the future if Americans were to be banned from entry to Britain. There would be a ban on American airlines too, presumably. Kay would have to do without his warm beer, and pink roast beef at Simpson's.

The lounge where they were sitting had been decorated as a lunar landscape. That was pure nostalgia – how long was it since NASA had been wound up? Ten years . . . fifteen? Untwinkling stars, authentically positioned, dotted the ceiling dome, and a blue-and-white earth was full in the east wall.

Lucy said: 'I'll miss you.'

'Yes. I'll miss you too.'

There was a silence, which she broke. 'What is it? Something's wrong.'

He fiddled with his glass. 'That was a good dinner last night. Generous of the US Army to lay it on. And I like Haddon.'

'He's OK. Tell me what's wrong.'

'Before we joined you, he made me a proposition.'

She did her best to make a joke of it. 'I wouldn't have figured him for a fag. Or you as a probable target.'

'He made it sound like nothing much, but basically he was trying to recruit me: as an agent.'

She paused. 'You sure?'

'The offer was concrete. Money payable into a dollar account. He also said he could arrange further trips like this. I believed him.'

She put a hand on his. 'What did you say, Mike?'

He looked at her, and she looked levelly back. Her beauty seared him. 'It's not my kind of thing. Not even for the sake of further trips like this.' She said nothing. 'How are you feeling? No ill effects from yesterday afternoon?'

'No. I'm fine.' She smiled. 'I wouldn't have thought you'd need ask.'

'It could have been coincidental. The report of a foreign tourist being attacked might have been put through to Haddon as a routine item. The rest could have followed naturally: him doing his apology and reassurance stuff, and then the offer arising spontaneously out of a pleasant chat over a couple of large scotches, and our getting on so well together.

'But the more I thought about it, the more unlikely it seemed. That rescue was too prompt, too good. The chopper hovering right overhead, troops at battle alert swarming out to get us . . . And the ghetto boys were kid-gloved. It was nothing like the manhandling you get in an everyday maul on the rugby field. I'd guess they were acting under instructions too. Wouldn't you?'

Lucy didn't answer. He took his hand away. 'Just as you were: to put me in the right spot at the right time. I didn't work that out till this morning. *Post coitum veritas*, maybe. Of course, I didn't want to believe it. I tried to tell myself the whole thing was too crazy: setting up something so elaborate in the hope of recruiting a low-level civil servant in hospital management. It doesn't make sense, does it? But if someone had told them about my German connection, it begins to look more reasonable. After all, Frohsteig Wissenschaftliches Verkehrs are the biggest producers and researchers into Virtual in Europe – in the world, probably.'

'Did he ask you about them?'

'No. It's not the way it works, is it? Softly, softly, catchee flunky. "Oh, by the way, Mike, there's a small extra item on the agenda. Something we'd like you to do for us the next time you visit with your father. We're confident you'll feel happy about this." No need to mention the account with Riggs Bank, or the possibility of details being leaked to the right quarter in London. No need at all, because it's staring you in the face.'

In a low voice that fuelled his anger, and at the same time devastated him with a sense of irretrievable loss, she said: 'I've known Ike a long time. I think I know him better than any white guy, except for one. He promised me there would be no pressure, and there would be total back-up and protection. As good as my own, or better.'

'We'd be in this together, you mean? Frequent fucking, courtesy of Specops, and expensive dinners laid on to keep the libido from flagging. Good wines – if not French, top-quality Californian. Something to laugh about in our Darby and Joan years. And meanwhile you were prepared to go along with the play-the-sucker line. I ought to tell you he didn't blow your cover. He even gave me a London contact number, to throw me off the scent.'

The cross he had given her at Christmas rested against the darker cleft of her breasts, the yellow stones flickering with her breathing in the lounge's pseudo-lunar light. Her hand caressed it, let it go, moved forward . . . and he wondered if she would touch him again, and what he might do if she did. But she let it fall to the table. In a frozen voice, she said: 'That's not the way it looked.'

'I'm sure it isn't. Viewpoints are the problem, aren't they? They're a lot more important than screwing. Item one: as you told me, twenty-first century American life can be tough on coloureds. Even when you make it, against the odds, you can't rest easy. You need to keep both eyes open, like the Jews. And, like the Jews, group loyalty is your main defence. In which respect, Whitey doesn't qualify any more than the Gentiles did.

'Then there's item two: you're an American black. DD talked to me once about a girl he knew before Granny T. She was from a Jewish refugee family, living in Hampstead just after the war. That was soon after the news of what the Germans had been up to became official. They'd had

112

cousins, uncles, aunts murdered: the girl's own grandfather stayed behind and wound up in Auschwitz. They hated Hitler with an intensity DD couldn't begin to comprehend.

'All the same, they ate German, dressed German, thought German. What eventually fixed him was something as trivial as a radio programme. The family had the German passion for *Kultur*, and were avid listeners to the BBC Third Programme. The BBC were making a big thing of a new translation of *Faust* they were broadcasting, and she was wild with enthusiasm. This, she told him, would at last teach the English to appreciate Goethe. DD got up and left, took the tube back from Belsize Park, and picked up Granny T. in a queue for the Salad Bar at Lyons' Coventry Street Corner House. They were married within three months.

'Hildy was quite right: Americans don't take little countries like England seriously. They're OK for a vacation, but not the sort of place where real people live.'

'I'm sorry. I'll never be able to tell you how sorry.' She stood up, moving with that bodily grace which would always take his breath away. 'Have a good trip, Mike. A good life.'

He had a day with Anna: Johann had arranged a twenty-four hour delay on admission to match Michael's American hold-up. Given an edited account of the attempted kidnap, he shrugged his shoulders.

'People herded into a ghetto, with armed guards keeping them behind fences . . . whenever I get pissed off with Europe, I must remind myself to think of America. What about Lucy? She wasn't hurt?'

'No, she's fine.'

It was a bright day, but cold. Anna was looking no better physically, but seemed strangely wrapped in calm. She said she would like to go to the cemetery, but refused his offer to drive her there. They walked, taking the short cut past the school, where the gardens of the hillside houses were brightening with crocuses and daffodils and flowering currant. At the top of the steps in the field leading up to the cemetery gate, she stopped. He thought she might be tired and offered an arm, but she was looking at the paddock below the cemetery. There were sheep in it.

'Do you remember Prince?'

Michael nodded. Prince had been an ancient horse, retired from a local riding school and provided with this patch of ground for his old age: a chestnut with a white star on his chest and one white foot. They had come up here as children to stroke and marvel at the velvet of his nose, and to bring him treats. He had been particularly fond of bread and jam.

'What happened to him?'

'He died,' she said, 'in the first winter you were away at school. Heart, I think. He was over forty, people said.'

That was the winter after Mummy died, the winter before Maria-Mercedes met his father. He said: 'I never asked, did I?'

She shook her head. 'And I never told you. I was sorry when he died, but glad in a way. I used to hate thinking of him up here when there was frost and snow and gales.'

'He had a sort of shelter. That shed with the galvanized iron roof.'

'He would never use it. He used to stand out in all weathers.' She pointed. 'Look.' At the far end of the paddock, two tiny lambs huddled close to a ewe. 'The first I've seen this year.'

Adam's grave was raw still. Anna's retreat from life had not stopped her ordering the stone, but the earth had not yet settled enough for it to be laid. She took dying daffodils from the jar, and replaced them with sprigs of mimosa. At the foot of the grave lay another floral tribute: a red-and-white wreath which had been regularly but anonymously renewed. It bore no message, but to Michael's eye it had BA stamped all over it.

Anna looked from the grave towards the paddock. 'I used to lie awake at night, and think of Prince out in the cold and rain. And then I pictured being old myself – not out in a field, but sick, maybe poor. And alone. I thought I could imagine what it might be like. But we never can, can we?'

But she smiled. 'I'm glad I saw the lambs. And he's not here, I know that. This isn't real.'

He knew, sadly, what she meant. Reality waited for her in another country, inside a steel and plastic cocoon.

Michael had a brief call from Helen Rackham, telling him she wanted him at her place that evening. She put it as baldly as that, with no sop about coming round for a drink. Since she'd recently launched a new crackdown on expenses, with particular reference to unnecessary use of taxis, he started to ask directions from the Docklands tube station, but she cut him short. The office car would be outside the main entrance at five thirty.

Her house was as characterless as he would have expected: a yellow brick box with reflector windows. Security was represented by the police car parked opposite. A Pakistani girl with a Birmingham accent showed him through a hall chilled by several prints of Utrillo snow scenes into a room where the Deputy Minister was busy at a desk. She let him stand for two or three seconds before glancing up and nodding towards a chair. It was reproduction William and Mary, and more comfortable than it looked.

He knew she would have been given an explanation for his absence from the office the previous day, but she made no reference to Anna. She put questions about his American trip, pertinently and precisely. At the end, she said: 'So you didn't pick up much. Did you get an impression they might be holding back?'

'I wouldn't know. If they were being reticent, it might be because they still don't know whether there's going to be a ban on Virtual. But the probability of that is high.

115

Aronheimer's committed to campaigning for prohibition, and I get the impression the Republicans are uneasy about the mileage he's getting out of it. I would think they'll go along.'

'You don't think their Virtual Producers' Association lobby can hold the line?'

'Frankly, no. It's the same puritan surge that made alcohol illegal, nearly a century ago. The opposition's running scared. They may get over that before the amendment gets ratification at State level, but I think it will go through Congress.'

She said, restlessly: 'All in all, a bit of a wasted trip.'

Wasted was an irony. He reflected how different things would have been if he had taken Haddon's proposition, and come back with information which would have kept Helen happy. He reflected also that this evening he had passed the point of no return as far as making an official report on the incident was concerned. Why hadn't he? He had nothing to gain from not doing so – no hope, or desire, of seeing Lucy again.

There would, on the other hand, have been a lot to gain the other way round. He could visualize the delight in Helen Rackham's face, contemplating what she might do with a situation like that. And, of course, he had very much more to lose here. The story, it occurred to him, could be as easily leaked from the other end – either through the British Embassy in Washington, or the bigger and more important Euro Embassy. He felt a tingling of cold sweat at the thought. Even if he denied everything, suspicion would stick.

Nor was it possible to rule out actual evidence, from hidden cameras and recorders. Telling himself Ike Haddon wouldn't do that sort of thing was a non-starter. Ruthlessness went with the job. The only hope there was that Haddon could be thinking he might still change his mind and take the bait.

Helen Rackham shrugged. 'Well, that's it. I've a feeling

our trans-Atlantic contacts may be fairly sharply wound down in the future anyway.'

Remembering Haddon's remarks about a possible ban on Americans, he ventured cautiously: 'Any particular reason for that?'

'None I can pass on,' she told him crisply. 'Personally, I wouldn't have many regrets. I can't stand their moralizing, especially about things like Virtual. All this nonsense about it being morally degrading. It's far less pathogenic than drugs – or alcohol. If in fact it's pathogenic at all. I often use it before I go to bed.'

He was surprised, both by the fact and by her admission of something it was fashionable to snigger at, but made no comment.

'Sailing,' she said. 'I grew up in a boat family. You can get some good sailing out of Perth: we took a few long-distance trips to Indonesia. It offers the best combination of discipline and pleasure I know. I'm too old for it now, and the English Channel's not the same – and I don't have the time. But the glove-and-helmet take me back.' She looked at him with a slightly contemptuous smile. 'It's a much better relaxant than whisky, Michael. Or even rugby.'

He hadn't really been expecting to be offered a drink. As she stood up to give him his dismissal, he said: 'Yes, Minister. I'm sure it is.'

Hildy remained London-based, and it had become usual for them to meet for lunch once a week in a wine bar close to Leicester Square, convenient both for the studio and the Ministry. They drank white wine, and she devoured undressed salad with cold meat. On their meeting following his return from America, she chattered volubly about a number of things, chiefly the fascinatingly bitchy aspects of her profession. He was content to listen, conscious of her prettiness and vitality.

He himself was eating the house ham-and-cheese pie;

famous, if the proclamation on the blackboard was to be believed, for forty-one years.

She paused to look critically at his plate. 'More calories there than leaves in Vallombrosa. It will be necessary to diet before next season, Mikey.'

'If there is one. I may hang up my boots.'

'Even if you do that, I do not wish a fat *Stiefbruder*. We all have a duty of discipline – to not offend others, especially our nearest and dearest, with grossness. How is Lucy?'

'She's fine.'

'You gave her my love?'

'Yes. She sent you hers.'

'When does she visit London again?'

'I'm not sure. With the American election hotting up, it isn't easy for her to get away.'

She took a sip of wine and a draught of Malvern water. 'Something is wrong. Tell me.'

He thought of Lucy, in the airport lounge. He said, sharply: 'Nothing's wrong. What are you on about?'

'You are only just back from Washington, from Lucy. To say nothing about it means something is wrong.'

Michael laughed. 'I've not had a chance to get a word in edgeways since I sat down.'

Hildy pouted attractively. 'I have been talking too much maybe, but because I observe the hunch of your shoulders when I come in. The body language of men is written in capital letters. But OK, then. Talk, and I'll listen. Tell me about Washington. Tell me about Lucy.'

He did his best to do so, concentrating on topography. It wasn't all that difficult, but he was aware of being dull and wooden, and of Hildy appraising this. She cut him short on the Air & Space Museum.

'I cannot bear such places. To fly in a machine is so boring, when one can fly in the mind. I am glad you had a good trip, and that Lucy is well. Listen, this next weekend

I am free. I thought I may come down to Sheaf. Will that be all right?'

He said warmly: 'Of course it will! There's only me and DD in the house now, rattling about like a couple of shrivelled nuts. We'll be delighted.'

'Age has shrivelled DD quite nicely. You are not shrivelled at all.'

The *Evening Standard* headline proclaimed: IRISH BOMB-SHELL. Underneath: 'Paddy Puts The Boot In'.

The rotating presidency of Europe had come recently to the Irish Union, where for some time political power had lain with Belfast, though Dublin remained the capital. The president, Paddy McGuire, was himself an Ulsterman, who had entered politics after making a fortune in the Euro-funded reconstruction and development which had followed the unification of North and South, and Northern Ireland's consequent secession from the United Kingdom.

This was McGuire's first speech in the Euro Council, and he made great play with the benefits which had flowed from the Irish experience. It might be worthwhile considering extending them. Ireland was at peace, after long travail, and looked with compassion across the Irish Sea to where Scotland and Wales lay once more under an ancient yoke after the failed experiments of devolution. Freedom mattered to them too: freedom within the security of pan-European harmony. What the English seemed to mean by freedom, on the other hand, was the maintenance of an out-dated colonial dominance: they resented the notion of merely equal status with their European neighbours. Their even closer neighbours on the island of Britain had a right to be protected from this intransigence. It was an obvious case for invoking the subsidiarity principle. He would be proposing to the Council that Scotland and Wales should be admitted as separate and independent members of the Federal Union.

Peter Graveny tapped Michael on the shoulder. 'I'll have a scotch, while we're still part of the same country. What do you think of that load of pig-shit?'

'Do you think we're meant to take it seriously?'

Graveny watched carefully as the barman double-pressed the optic; it was the boy Adam had abused over the half-litre glasses. 'One thing I learned early in life was never to trust the Irish – man or woman, North or South, drunk or sober. Nor the Scotch, except when they're distilling. And the Welsh even less. We'd be better off without the lot of them, except it won't keep the buggers out.'

'He'd never get it through, surely.'

'Why not? We're not liked by anyone. The French, Germans, Italians would all love to see us screwed. And there are enough Welsh and Scotch nationalist Euro MPs to make it look good even as far as Britain itself is concerned. Odds on, I would say.'

'But nationalists are only a small minority at Westminster, and the United Kingdom can't be dissolved without the consent of Parliament.'

'How old were you when Maastricht was pushed through? A schoolboy anyway, so you're excused. I was of mature years, and all I did was fume and rant and get drunker than usual. I was very clear-headed about it, if I say so myself. I could see what was in it for the businessmen, and the civil servants, and the politicians: that lovely gravy train steaming down the hill towards them. I knew them for the shits they were, and nourished a fine contempt for their greed and self-interest. But I didn't do anything about it. I wasn't an Adam. And it's too late for the Adams now, too bloody late altogether. Do you really think consent of Parliament means anything, or has done for twenty years? Drink up, and have another North British.'

On Saturday morning in Sheaf, Johann called him.

'Mike, I got your message. Sorry I was missing. One of

those bloody company dinners. Anna's fine. I spoke to Stern yesterday afternoon.'

Julius Stern was Medical Director of the Brosser Clinic.

'Has she been cocooned yet?'

'Yesterday morning. All's well.'

'I thought I might try to get over.'

'I'd be delighted. So would Pa. But you realize it won't be a very rewarding visit as far as making contact is concerned? She stays under completely for the first two weeks.'

'Yes . . .'

He told himself the sense of loss was irrational – that what mattered was Anna being free, for the time being at least, of the misery he had found it so hard to witness. His unease, and restlessness, probably stemmed from that other loss which he had tried, with no great success, to put out of his mind. He was tired of imagined dialogues in which everything improbably came right; and of petty emotional victories in which anger boosted self-esteem. He was even more weary of his own weakness in surrendering to such pointless indulgences.

Johann's image was starting to break up: the local connection had been intermittently on the blink for more than a week. He said: 'I'll think about it. Give my love to Father.'

As he switched off, he heard the whine of a vacuum cleaner upstairs. Janice had been more than willing to give him an extra hour preparing a room for Hildy. She had been thrilled when she learned Hildy was an actress in Virtual, and Michael suspected had gone hot-foot to spread the news through the council estate. But she had confided to Anna that she had subsequently vetoed the programmes she allowed her husband and son to esp in that respect. Soft porn was permitted the former and probably blind-eyed as far as the latter was concerned, but embracing Anna's half-sister in her undies was off limits for both.

DD was equally excited by the prospect of her visit. He

had been a great man for female grandchildren – Michael had noted the difference without minding it, Granny T.'s affection being the more valuable – and Hildy's early appearances at Sheaf, as a toddler, had coincided with Anna's withdrawal into her passion for Marcus Reddaby. He had made much more of Hildy than Johann or, subsequently, of Adam – though lingering resentment against Reddaby might have played a part there.

At any rate, he now recalled an early-teen passion of Hildy's for shell-on prawns, and was determined they must have some for her. He was prepared to go and get them from the fishermen's co-operative on the bank of the Trug, but Michael said firmly he would go himself. DD was increasingly uncertain on his feet, and the expedition involved treacherously steep steps down to the Flats. Actually, the suggestion suited him. They had found an obliging widow to take over the cooking from Anna, but Michael preferred to handle it when he was down. Prawns, apart from conforming to Hildy's calorie-counting, would provide an easy starter to their meal.

Winter, as was becoming commonplace, had reoccupied the citadel of spring. He returned from the fish shop against a wind whipping hard across the Flats, bearing more snow than sleet, and at the top of Cerdic's Cliff, with his Barbour hood up, found himself bumping into a figure coming the opposite way. His apology was pre-empted by a lengthier one from the other party.

It was the first time he had encountered Souter since DD's birthday. The Budgie must have been made aware that his calculated leak had produced no result, and perhaps been warned about tangling with an influential family. Michael was not surprised to find him more effusive than ever, especially in his inquiries about DD: a man, as he said, of the old school.

The awning of Sheaf's high-quality ironmonger's shop offered a protection from the elements which was also conducive to prolonging conversation. Souter spoke of the new European president's suggestion of splitting up the United Kingdom, which had clearly ruffled his feathers in the right direction. It would never happen, of course, but the threat of it might be beneficial in damping down anti-European sentiments.

His chubby face contorted improbably into an intimate smile. 'One doesn't blame the young for being misled, any more than one should blame the old for clinging to outdated prejudices. The responsibility lies with our generation, doesn't it? We're the ones who must do what we can to keep things moving forward. I've been paid a great honour, Michael, in that respect: I've been asked to form a local branch of the Carolingians.'

The *Sodalitas Carolingiana* had spread rapidly through the Federation over the past ten years from its birthplace in Vienna, but until recently had made little headway north of the Channel. Its present rapid expansion was seen as a middle-class reaction to the excesses of Britain Awake! Souter's own references to the misled young and the outdated old were plainly deliberate, a combination of defiance and warning. He was not, Michael realized, someone whose contemptibility should lead one to disregard an underlying boldness.

He laid his hand lightly – weakly even, but with positive effect – on the dripping sleeve of Michael's Barbour. 'I think you could be a very useful member, Michael. Quite apart from your fame on the rugger field, you're the kind of person we need.'

'I don't think I spend enough time in Sheaf to get involved in local activities.'

'Commitment is more important than activity. Think about it.' He peered up earnestly into Michael's face. 'I shall ask you again.'

It was a good evening. Hildy was at her liveliest, and DD

burst into senile blossom, roaring with laughter at her jokes and drinking more wine than usual. His tremor seemed less in evidence. When Michael brought coffee to the sitting room, he discovered his grandfather bringing a tray from the sideboard. It held three crystal thistle glasses, the Waterford jug, and a dusty bottle with a peeling label. He thrust the jug imperiously at Michael.

'We haven't any Highlands water, so the tap will have to do. Let it run at least half a minute.'

When he next got back, the pair were giggling. DD said: 'And your audience – all those masturbating males?'

'Why not, darling? I perform a service, but I am not touched.'

'No, I suppose you're not.' He chuckled, and beckoned to Michael for the jug. 'Power without responsibility . . . as Baldwin said, the prerogative of the harlot throughout the ages. Or was that Kipling? So my youngest grandchild is a virginal harlot – a *demi-vierge!*'

'Yes, it is power. Shall I tell you something, Grandfather? I enjoy the knowing that I have it. In fact, it's quite exciting.'

They were both half-drunk, as was Michael himself. DD's interest diverted to the dusty bottle.

'A Deveron from Speyside. Must be five years since I last sampled this. No more mature, of course, but it was more than twenty years old when it came out of the cask. Taste it by itself, to get the pungency. Then water, half and half.'

He poured measures into the glasses, and watched Hildy as she sipped the undiluted malt.

She smacked her lips. 'Heaven!'

DD nodded approval. 'Better than Virtual, eh?'

'Much, much better.'

He launched into a panegyric on whiskies past, and went from that to more general reminiscence, hinting of devilry sixty or seventy years gone. It was long after his normal bedtime, but he seemed tireless. Michael was conscious of the drag of fatigue – the previous night's sleep, like many recently, had been badly broken – and wondered if he might leave them to it. But he realized that was out of the question, and shook himself awake. Not long after, DD abruptly stood up.

'That's enough. I know when I'm boring people.'

'Beloved DD, you couldn't. Not ever.'

'When I find I'm dead-beat from talking, I must be.' She rose from her chair and kissed him. 'Hildy, you've done me more good than you will be able to imagine until you too are very old. I shall sleep well, and all the better for hoping to be spared another few hours to see you at the breakfast table.'

She smiled at Michael, as his footsteps retreated down the corridor. 'He is so sweet, but talks so much. When I wanted you to myself. And that terrible malt whisky, tasting of furniture polish. I think maybe I am a great actress, after all.'

'You must be tired.'

She fixed him with a direct stare. 'No. But I think you are.'

He looked at his watch. 'It's after midnight.'

'So, your carriage has turned into a pumpkin. But fortunately your bed is near. First, I want to show you something. I will be quick. Sit down, and have a proper whisky.'

He assumed she had gone to fetch something from her bedroom, but she was away longer than he had expected. She returned very quietly; he looked up to see her standing in the doorway. She was wearing a costume whose pale blue colour might have served, in a more conventional dress, to proclaim the innocence of her blonde beauty.

The styling, though, was the reverse of conventional. Beneath her breasts, cupped and tantalizingly lifted by the flimsy silk, flesh was exposed to display not only her midriff but most of her stomach. Thin vertical bands which accentuated the slimness of her waist narrowed from their divergent curve towards a junction only just supra-pubic, while lower down the dress frilled high against the luscious cream of her thighs.

She smiled. 'Well?'

'Incredible.'

'It is the costume from my latest epic. I am a barbaric princess, on a far planet. The customer is a space captain with a mission to civilize the natives. He tries to be severe, but I come, and look into his eyes, and sway a little forward to brush his chest with mine . . . and against his will his hands find the simple knot that unties the halter from my breasts, and touches them – gently, then fiercely – and they go on seeking, lower, lower, until he, the brave space captain, falls to his knees . . .'

She walked forward slowly in little silver slippers, and he felt the shivering anxious joy of lust rise and possess him. In reality, in flesh, she presented the script she had just outlined, and he followed it; to the letter and beyond. Past the scent she was wearing, her smell was sweet and pungent.

With fingers in his hair, she whispered: 'This! I have wanted it always. My sweet, sweet half-brother . . . Always. Since being a child in pigtails. Forbidden, but I knew I must have it.'

Her fingers twisted and pulled, pain accentuating desire. He was sick and lost, out of control in a way he had never been before. He stood up, and felt her mouth open wetly to his, her tongue probing deep. His hand went down to rip the gossamer shield from her thighs.

He could not believe it when she sharply pulled away from him.

'Nein, *Stiefbruder*. Forbidden. No more.' When he tried to seize her, the body which had clung to him was rigid in rejection. 'No. No!'

'Hildy, please . . .'

'Poor Mikey. Sad for you now, but maybe later you

126

will be glad.' She drew away, and he could see her eyes again; she was smiling, fondly, cruelly. *'Demi-vierge,* DD called me. Such an old-fashioned word, but true perhaps. Maria-Mercedes once called me that.'

She touched his face gently, impersonally. 'You are tired. Go to bed. I will forgive you for destroying my little costume.'

She held its tatters carelessly against her as she walked away from him.

Seven

S tern was short, nearer one metre six than one seven,
and squat. He had thick black hair which had receded
conspicuously, a pallid skin and large, brown eyes. His right
hand seemed to be permanently fixed in his trouser pocket.
He spoke English well, but volubly.

'As you will appreciate, Mr Frodsham, your sister's
admission for treatment was not merely voluntary, but
actively sought by her. The treatment itself would normally
be preceded by an in-depth psychological and psychiatric
evaluation, which would occupy several weeks. In view of
the degree of her depression and the self-evident nature of
the onset precipitation factor, I agreed to waive that stage.'

Heinrich had driven Michael and Dieter up from Frohsteig
in the Mercedes: Johann was away at the Warsaw office.
They had come through pelting rain, which had eased as
they got into the hills. By the time they reached the sign
indicating *Klinik Brosser – Virtualisches Heilverfahren*,
the grey of a clearing sky was yielding glimpses of pale
yellow, and his first sight of the Clinic showed it framed
by blue lake, snow-topped mountain and the dense green
of the pines through which they had been driving for
ten minutes or more. An arch of deeper blue hung over
all.

Their approach, from the side, revealed the extent and
depth of the complex. The front, facing the lake, though
obviously of recent construction, was architecturally archaic
in the classic Bavarian style: viewed head-on it could have

been a typical though over-sized hunting lodge, wooden-built, deep-gabled, with carved and painted ornamentation. At the rear a large area, roofed and walled in plexiglass, connected with three single-storey extensions, the two on either side much longer than the central one. Between and surrounding these extensions there were lawns, ornamental flowerbeds (many already rich with colour), clumps of evergreens, and water in varying manifestations of stream and fall and fountain.

Stern had been waiting for them in the hall, presumably alerted by the call Michael had noticed Heinrich make as they entered the approach road. He approached them smiling, through a not unpleasant gloom: the hall was high and heavily beamed; the paintings on the walls were mountain views and waterscapes, interspersed with several stuffed eagles. At the foot of a wide sweep of stairs, a stuffed bear stood with its head to one side, its pose quizzical, but deferential.

They were served coffee and cake in the area between the house and the extensions. One side of this was largely occupied by a swimming pool; the other, where they were sitting, had been laid out as an orangery. Fruits gleamed gold and green and yellow among glossy leaves, separating smaller spaces holding rustic chairs and tables. It looked as if the roof over the pool had been designed to open, and there were sun-blinds, presently furled. At the moment the pool was covered, and no one else was present.

The coffee was excellent, the cake a sticky, over-rich confection of biscuits and chocolate. Pressing this on Michael, Stern introduced it as: 'An indulgence of mine. It is from a recipe of my grandmother, who used to make it for me as a small boy. That was in Israel. She went there, having survived Belsen, and here I am, in Germany. Things change. Good cake, do you agree?'

He nodded. 'Very good, indeed.'

'As I have said, it is customary to make a preliminary

evaluation. That is not, however, important from a medical risk standpoint. We are not talking about a procedure which involves risk. Virtual Total –' he pronounced it as German, softening the V and emphasizing the final syllable of 'Total' – 'has been scrupulously investigated, over many years, and been shown to be, under proper administration, entirely non-injurious.'

Michael said: 'I gather some Americans have reservations about long-term use.'

Stern nodded. 'I suspect the real reservation of the Americans is related to Total itself, basically an objection to Virtual; and is not so much scientific as emotional. But I would agree with them, as far as long-term use is concerned – not that it is necessarily or even probably damaging to health, but that it has not been sufficiently tested. Although, as you know, some institutions have used it long term and no contra-indications have emerged, except in a few isolated cases where the physical maintenance system was almost certainly at fault.' He shook his head decisively. 'There could be no question of that here.

'We run no programmes longer than for three weeks at a time. After that, the patient is returned to a pleasant and active life –' he spread his hands to embrace the pool, and the gardens and woods beyond the plexiglass – 'which includes expert counselling. As far as traumatic depression is concerned, it is not uncommon, even at that early point, to get a remission which justifies discharge. If not, a week or two later the patient takes a second course. Sometimes a third. We have not yet found it necessary to authorize a fourth.'

Stern's right hand had gone back into his pocket. With the other, he waved towards the table. 'Would you like more cake? Or coffee? Then I propose we first show you a little of our technical side.'

A door opened into a corridor with three more doors, and

Stern electronically keyed open the middle one. That led to a second corridor, where he opened a door on the right, disclosing a room where two young men, one scarcely more than a boy, and a woman of about thirty, sat at desks equipped with keyboards and VDU systems. Each was wearing a Virtual helmet, and had a glove available.

'Material from Frohsteig is tailored here to the individual before going back to Frohsteig for final checking,' Stern explained. 'It represents quite a late stage in dream-making.'

'You do call it dream-making? I would have thought you might have a more technical term.'

Stern shrugged. 'It serves. The process is not identical with dreaming, but closely related. One observes some rapid eye movement, but far less than in true dreaming – presumably because REM is linked with mental creativity, and this is a more passive operation.'

What was appearing on the screens seemed haphazard, certainly lacking any obvious interconnection. Michael tried to follow the set-up behind the desk nearest to him. A pre-technology farming scene with figures in nineteenth-century costume, long-horned cattle, a glowing autumn sky . . . birds in flight over a long level stretch of water . . . a small room with people talking in front of a massive ceramic stove . . . a face in close-up, a woman with dark auburn curls, warmly smiling . . . yellow-winged butterflies spiralling up between broken marble columns . . . water again, under moonlight this time . . . a soaring swallow . . .

Stern had been watching him. 'Flight is considered to be an important factor in therapy.'

Dieter commented: 'I have wondered about the eagles in the hall.'

'That is window-dressing, but yes. The bear guarding the stairs also: it signifies the bringing together of human and animal in a non-threatening way. A bear in the wild can be very threatening indeed, but here we deal with myth. Bears are valuably used in our dream-making. Water, in many aspects, is an important therapeutic tool also. We are not exactly post-Jungian, but regard him as the most useful of the early twentieth-century subconscious-mind theorists.'

'My sister . . .' Stern regarded him sympathetically. 'Water, birds and butterflies, bears – I'm sure you're right about the therapeutic value, but that wasn't what she was promised. It was her son's death that was destroying her. She asked to be admitted here in the hope of getting him back – of having that illusion, anyway.'

'And we give her that; as well as the birds and bears. They are only part of the background, he is the foreground.'

'How?'

Stern pointed to the younger male. 'One of our apprentices. Not quite as young as he seems – he has been with us more than a year. And he is still only in the foothills of Alps which he must climb to be a programmer. If you had the time to spare, Mr Frodsham, I could explain, but not here and now, not in this day or a hundred such. Basically, what our technique depends on is the readiness of the individual to be fooled – to fool himself, herself. The human mind looks continuously for significance and recognition. A child sees itself as the centre of the universe, an illusion which commonly returns in old age, invariably with senility.

'When I was very small, I was taken to a dog show in Tel Aviv. I escaped my parents and they had to hunt for me. They found me embracing a dog whose pen carried a sign: "Dangerous! Do not approach!" It did not much resemble our family dog, but it represented dog for me. And perhaps having that illusion, therefore having no fear, made me safe in that situation.

'As far as your sister is concerned, we have data relating to her son: still photographs and videos, records of dress, minor possessions. The videos register characteristic bodily movements and gestures: the style of walking, for instance, which scarcely changes throughout life. We have voice samples, from which speech can be synthesized into dialogue of our choice, into which she will enter because that is her heart-felt wish. You understand that in Total, unlike Virtual, there is a direct cortical input. Using that, we have the ability to fuse the imaginative talents of our practitioners with her need. It is an effective combination. Come, you will wish to see she is well cared for.'

Her room was in the west ward. In the long extensions, access corridors ran adjacent to the central wing, so the rooms all looked outwards – towards gardens, the forest, a sweep of mountainside. The room itself was small, but by no means cramped; as well as the bed there were a couple of armchairs, a shower and toilet cubicle, and a table and chair additional to the bedside table which formed a base for nursing care. A nurse stood by this, in crisp black and white uniform; she bowed to Stern, who smiled acknowledgement.

The walls had a number of pictures – seagulls above a quiet harbour, a skein of geese over marshland, salmon leaping – and there were fresh flowers in hanging vases. A window looked out over the carefully tended gardens.

Michael said: 'It's very nice. But . . .'

'What?'

'I was wondering why all this is necessary, for unconscious patients.'

'They go to sleep here, and wake up here.'

'Fresh flowers . . . ?'

'It might be required to bring a dreamer back early. It has never happened, but we think it best to be prepared, just in case.' He smiled. 'I am Jew and German. Thoroughness is important to both.' His look deferred to Dieter. 'The Clinic owes much to Frohsteig Verkehrs, who not only provide basic research but have funded nursing care most generously. That, to be frank, accounts for your sister being admitted without reference to our waiting list, which is very long. But her treatment thereafter is not special. All our patients are treated equally – with the greatest care.'

Michael had not yet looked properly at Anna. He overcame his reluctance and went to the bedside. A ripple mattress vibrated gently underneath her, and a single sheet was drawn up to her shoulders. She was breathing easily and steadily, and that part of her face not obscured by the helmet seemed calm and untroubled. The end of a feeding tube protruded from a corner of her mouth, but even that did not look especially ugly. He would have bent and kissed her, except that the translucent plastic of the cocoon prevented it. He noted it was shaded faintly green.

Again, Stern seemed to read his mind. 'The window receives much sunshine. Normally, curtains are kept drawn, but the nurse has opened them for your visit. The cocoon's plastic has protection built in against the remote possibility of a curtain being accidentally left open, involving risk of sunburn. We take every precaution, Mr Frodsham.'

'I'm glad you decided to come over,' Johann said. 'Whatever I could tell you about the Clinic, seeing is believing. Anna's peace of mind is being taken care of, but there's yours also. How did you get on with Julius?'

'It was reassuring. He seemed to know what he was about, and to take it seriously.'

Johann laughed. 'Seriously is right. Jew and German, and thoroughness is important to both. He has his little catch-phrases. Anyway, I'm glad I got back in time to see you. Apart from Warsaw being a bore, as usual.'

'What were you there for?'

'Oddly enough, an enterprise somewhat similar to yours: checking out a Total set-up. But in no way resembling the Brosser Clinic. No individual rooms, with picture windows and paintings on the walls. This has cocoons in underground dormitories, rows of hundreds, like sardines in a can.'

'Would there be any connection with something my boss mentioned, a while back?' Michael asked.

'Your Rackham lady. I'm not sure. What did she say?'

'She was talking about purpose-built clinics for Total addicts. She didn't say anything about cocoons wall to wall.'

'Well . . .' Johann hesitated. 'That is coming up, too. But this particular effort comes under Economics rather than Health.'

He said incredulously: 'Not the hibernating workers?'

'Then you've heard of the project?'

'Rumours of rumours. We dismissed it as American black propaganda.'

'It's classified *Geheim 2A*. Not to be disclosed without senior authority. Don't tell Dieter we've been discussing it.'

'If you think—'

Johann deftly secured fresh glasses from a maid passing with a tray. 'He takes things too seriously. Maybe not the *Ding an sich*, but the prejudices of the civil servants who've done the commissioning. One sees his point: they are the paymasters. But any security requirement that may have existed has just about run out. I gather there'll be an official announcement over the next month or two.'

'Let me get this right. We are talking about the same thing? Redundant workers being put into Total hibernation, as a means of dealing with the unemployment problem?'

'Roughly speaking, that would be about right.'

'But it would be impossible, from any standpoint. Unthinkable. For one thing, the Federal Commission on Human Rights wouldn't stand for it. Slave sleep, even with pleasant dreams laid on, is fundamentally no better than slave labour.'

'Where does slavery come in? You weren't thinking in terms of compulsion, were you? The FCHR have been kept informed, but since the whole business is voluntary and Total clinics are absolutely legal, they wouldn't need to take it into consideration anyway. It's a matter of personal choice. If someone opts for a winter of sweet content, for himself and his family, rather than rough it out in the cold hard world, surely he's entitled to do that? Virtual addicts do already, and no one makes an issue of it.'

'But this would be creating addicts.'

'Not according to experts who've been consulted, including the top people in Virtual psychology. Addiction is a special characteristic. These will pass six blissful months in the cocoons, and gallop out raring for spring. Meanwhile, they're well cared for. The notion of sardine rows may seem horrifying, but that's in the eye of the beholder. Apart from optimum nourishment – the food intake's been precisely calculated for maximum health maintenance – the new series cocoons have built-in muscle exercisers. Everything's being taken into account: oral hygiene, hair cutting, nail paring. They'll come out healthier than they went in.'

'And what about those who don't fancy the prospect, despite the propaganda and promotion which I'm sure will also be laid on?'

Another girl appeared, tempting them with canapés. Foie gras, Michael realized. Johann waited till she had moved away.

'As I say, it's voluntary. No pressure, no reduction of normal benefits; nothing like that. They can enjoy an ordinary freezing winter on the bread line, if that's what they prefer. But I don't think many will.'

'You may be surprised. I can see why Anna thought she needed this, and I hope Stern's right about its value in relieving depression, but nothing would get me into one of them.'

'My dear Mike, you're suffering from a not uncommon extension of the pathetic fallacy – attributing sensitivities to the insensitive. The try-out will be in Poland, and they've done extensive field research on the prospects. The usual

Gadarene swine factor is projected to apply. With less than thirty per cent take-up in the first couple of months, it would be likely to fail. But once that critical point is reached, social pressure will push acceptances close to ninety-five per cent. And initial soundings suggest a probability of forty plus per cent within a week of launch.'

'It sounds crazy.'

'Certainly not that. I've also seen the projection for cost benefits to the Federal economy over the first five years, and, believe me, they're impressive.'

Maria-Mercedes bore down on them like a battleship on errant frigates, faultless in lines and trim and bearing. After scolding her son in rapid German, she turned her commanding, empty smile on Michael. He wondered what his father had ever seen in her, apart from physical beauty: maybe that had been enough. It was the reverse consideration, in any case, which should inspire speculation. It had been she who, for her private inscrutable reasons, had picked out the humble English widower with two children.

'The von Grenzendorfs will like to meet you, Michael. They are a distinguished family – from the Almanac, you understand? Their money is in land. A million hectares, perhaps.'

She delivered him to a couple in their fifties, a nervous, expensively dowdy woman and a small wrinkled cockerel of a man, who democratically elected to be addressed as Beate and Friedrich. Friedrich had, he explained, learned about the game of rugby during an exchange year in Oxford. He had watched occasional matches in Germany; the nearest town to their principal estate had a team. He was delighted to learn that Michael was to take on the task of creating a German national side.

'It hasn't been decided yet.'

'But you have been asked, yes? And I am sure you will not refuse the challenge. The English always accept challenge. As we do: there is cousinhood in this.'

Beate contributed, in a clear, birdlike voice: 'It angers us that so many people do not understand the English. This proposal to take away your territories in Wales and Scotland—'

'They're not English territories. We're all part of the United Kingdom, a much earlier union than the Federation. And I don't think the proposal needs to be taken very seriously.'

She put a hand on his sleeve; it, too, was birdlike, faintly clawing. 'Perhaps you are better without them. Excellence can sometimes be pulled down by the inferior – racial excellence above all. How Germany has suffered!'

Her husband nodded agreement. 'Italians, Slavs, Turks, French – with the freedom to come and go as they choose, to soil our land. From the beginning, there is trouble from them, but it becomes continually worse. We are no longer safe in our beds. When you make this team for us, you must choose only Germans – *echt deutsch*.'

Maria-Mercedes rescued him in due course; but not, he realized, out of any thought that rescue might be required. She replaced him with a young married couple, who looked suitably deferential to the million hectare plus estates. Michael saw his father unattended, and went to him. He had seen him briefly on arrival at Frohsteig, but not since visiting the Clinic. His father asked how he had found Anna, and he told him.

His father nodded. 'Johann said it was excellent. And anyway, anything Dieter is behind must be sound. The company have put a lot of money into it, you know.'

'Yes, I know.'

'He's taking me up there when she comes out of treatment.' He hesitated. 'I feel bad about this.'

'What could you possibly have done to prevent it? You couldn't put a limit on her love for Adam. Even less could you have prevented him turning assassin.'

'Parental guilt isn't rational.' His father smiled painfully. 'Especially when you know it has a rational basis.'

It was not a subject they had discussed, or ever could without pointless embarrassment. Most if not all the No Entry signs in a relationship were presumably there for a reason. He switched to talking about golf, for which he knew his father had developed a late passion.

'You never played at Sheaf, did you? It's not my game, but the course is meant to be very good. As you know, it offers a good view at least, if that counts. Sand dunes and Sheaf Bay, and a glimpse of France on an exceptionally clear day.'

'I must bring my clubs over, and try it out.'

'DD and I would be delighted if you did. It's lonely, with just the two of us now.'

'Hildy told me she'd been down.'

'Yes.'

'I'd be glad if you could keep an eye on her, Mike. I worry about her a bit. One does, about girls. This stuff she does – I know it's not as bad as it sounds, and I know about the generation gap. I remember my father getting steamed up over television programmes I took for granted as a teenager. But one can't help worrying.'

Michael said, more sharply than he'd intended: 'Did you worry the same way about Anna?'

'She was never involved in anything like that.'

'About her and Marcus.'

'I didn't like it – didn't like the man. But . . . Hildy's the baby of the family. I never saw Anna in that light. From when she was very little, she seemed responsible. After you were born she looked after you almost as much as . . . as your mother.'

'I know. I remember her being pretty good with your second batch too, when we visited.'

It had gone bad again. His father said: 'It's difficult to explain – I suppose anything is, that matters. We're bound to look at things differently. Georgian House, for instance: it's been your home from birth, the only one you've known. I came to it as an adult, and an outsider. I was there for several years, some of them very good years. Then afterwards . . . I was an outsider once more. Granny T. did her best to get past that, to make me feel at home, but I always felt DD was disapproving.' He hesitated. 'I still do.'

It was probably never possible to accept that the person who had been in the truest sense a towering figure, a giant who lifted and carried and knew the secrets of the universe, could be riddled with doubts and uncertainties.

'But you will come to Sheaf, and play a round or two?'

'Yes.' The tone carried no conviction. 'I look forward to that.'

Michael had mentioned the impending interview to Helen Rackham prior to the meeting, and she had nodded consent. He had presumed she would be irritated, and expected either disapproving silence or sarcasm when it was time for him to withdraw. But she anticipated the moment, interrupting a discourse by Sylvia Perenaike on new guidelines for drug dispensing to look at her watch.

'Time you were off, Michael.' She had switched, wholeheartedly as usual, into smile mode. Looking along the table, she added: 'The department's star is due to shine again this evening. And on Bert Benedict, no less. We'll get through the rest of the agenda fast, so we can all go home and watch.'

Beside him, Peter Graveny muttered: 'I doubt they'll be showing Bert Benedict at the Eagle & Lamb, but best of luck, mate.'

Although it was less than ten minutes' walk, the television company had sent a car for him, a long luxurious AudiPlus, driven by a girl in eye-catching, skin-tight black uniform with the company's logo on her trousered thighs and even more prominently displayed across her breasts. She did not attempt conversation during the brief ride, which was nevertheless a noisy one: the AudiPlus had an executive bray-hooter and she used it to the full. Drawing up outside Twenty First Century Tower, formerly Centre Point, she darted round smartly to let him out.

'Reception will clue you, Mr Frodsham.'

Within a couple of minutes of presenting himself at the desk, a lift door pinged open and another girl high-heeled across the echoing pseudo-marble floor towards him.

'Wonderful to see you, Mr Frodsham. I'm Millie. We'll go right up.'

Millie's voice was thin but musical, with a rising inflection on end words. She herself was tiny, scarcely above a metre fifty, and delicately proportioned in a neat, navy blue dress. All Benedict's assistants, Michael had heard, were of much the same physical specification, and the soberness of their outfits was presumably also meant to contrast with the great man. Unlike the chauffeuse, she chattered her way up to the seventeenth floor; about nothing in particular, but amiably.

The BB Show, she explained, took up the whole of this floor, and had extensions above and below. She led him to the hospitality room, which provided a view up Oxford Street. She offered a wide range of alcoholic drinks and when he excused himself on account of the early hour, reeled off an alternative list of specialized mineral waters, soft drinks, teas and coffees. He told her coffee would be fine, and she spoke briefly into her phone.

To Michael, she confided: 'We always offer drinks on arrival, but you are so right. Much better wait till you're nearly due on. BB has a hawk's eye for excess alcohol. He won't let anyone on camera who might possibly be under the influence. Did you know he breathalysed a junior cabinet minister once?' Michael did, but showed appropriate surprise and admiration. 'It's the one thing he has a strict rule about. Apart from that, he's a pussy-cat, most of the time.'

He appreciated the final qualification. Benedict's reputation in interviewing celebrities was as a man who could draw out the best in his subject without ever falling into dullness or letting them do so – someone whose percipience and wit could spice up insipid virtue. He could do it with no need of the snide factor: an early nickname had been the Hello Man, derived from the feel-good colour magazine of the turn of the century. On rare occasions, though, he took against an interviewee and inflicted mental and emotional mayhem with equal precision. The ever-present possibility of this happening was said to account for a good percentage of his enormous viewing figures.

With this in mind, Michael had made up his mind to back out if he detected signs of antagonism in the run-through. It had been done before, and Benedict had accepted the withdrawals without malice. He always had a standby interview on tape, and the news of someone funking confrontation was regarded as another badge of merit.

When he was taken through to Benedict's private lounge though, he found the atmosphere totally affable. Switching off a monitor screen, Benedict said: 'Michael! Great to see you.' He chuckled richly. 'You'll forgive my not getting up.'

The chair in which he sat bore a close resemblance to the amply proportioned leather throne he used on camera, and Benedict in the flesh looked even vaster than in his screen persona. His weight was popularly said to be in the two-hundred kilo region, and Michael was prepared to believe it. Flesh bulged and swelled under the red silk trousers and gold shirt. He was tall with it: standing, he would comfortably top two metres. An enormous hand grasped Michael's with surprising firmness.

'Sit, laddie. Have a drink and a peanut.'

The gin and tonic Michael had eventually requested was waiting on a small table beside the chair facing Benedict's, in a tall frosted glass capped with a split half-lime. Next to it was a plate of canapés. Benedict's chair nestled close to a larger table, with a jug and crystal glass of iced lemonade, and a much bigger plate of titbits. Releasing Michael's, his hand went blindly to the plate and scooped up several items indiscriminately. Chewing, he reached as automatically for the glass, and drained it.

'I love having athletes on the show. Any athletes, but sprint runners especially. You know I once wanted to be a sprinter?' He laughed uproariously. 'I was only seven or eight, but it was comic even then. Fatboy, boy and man! I've not lain down to sleep for five years, but they tell me that's not a long-term problem. I go to the best physicians, and the very best gives me three years, at the outside.'

Millie had sketched an outline for the interview, which Benedict followed closely in the run-through. He was easy and good-humoured, needle-sharp at picking up nuances. While he talked and listened, he chewed and drank unceasingly; both plate and jug were replaced with fresh ones at regular intervals. Once the macabre initial impression his bulk created had subsided, Michael found himself warming to the man.

Finally, Benedict said: 'OK. Gonna be good. I have the gut to have the feeling. So we go our separate ways to make-up, and meet again –' he glanced up at a shadow clock taking up most of the ceiling – 'in just over half an hour. Take a shower, if you like. I always do. I'll show you my shower-room some time. It goes to the Elephant House at the Zoo, in my will.'

The actual interview picked up the atmosphere of camaraderie and deepened it. He solicited a couple of rugby anecdotes which Michael had told before, but never, he was sure, as effectively: both Benedict's lead-in and his well-timed interjections helped point them up. He made a joke about Michael possibly abandoning England to give aid and comfort in *Mittel-Europa*, but converted it into an inoffensive jibe at the Germans: would they be able to scrum down in lederhosen without splitting their pants and exposing their limitations? They had passed the commercial break and Michael was feeling completely relaxed when, without change of expression or intonation, Benedict said: 'And Adam Frodsham, who shot the High Commissioner, was your nephew, I believe. A prominent member of the illegal organization, Britain Awake! Do you have any sympathy with his views?'

Adam had been mentioned during the run-through, but briefly and sympathetically, and the subject quickly dismissed. Michael felt shock, the outrage of betrayal, but with it a determination to stay cool, not to be intimidated. He said: 'I was very fond of my nephew, but I didn't share his views.'

'As far as you know, he was the only member of your family who had contacts with BA?'

'I'm certain of it. He was very young, and the enthusiasm of the young can lead them astray.'

Benedict smiled hugely into the camera zooming for close-up. 'Nothing and no one ever led me astray, but I can't claim too much credit for that. It's one of the few benefits of gross immobility. The only one, in your family, you say? What about you yourself, Michael? Are you saying you've never had any contact with BA?'

Michael recognized the classic cross-examination prelude to a knock-out: putting the question to which you already had a damning answer. He could guess where the information came from, too: the source had to be Maggie Bruton, and her eavesdropping at Georgian House. He had the sense neither to lie nor prevaricate and did his best to keep a level voice, but he felt himself flushing.

'I made no contact with them. They contacted me, after Adam died.'

'After your nephew was shot dead, that would be, right? After he'd murdered the Federal High Commissioner. Would you describe the contact?'

'They phoned me, and asked me to see one of their representatives.'

'At your home?'

'No, in London.'

'And you agreed?'

'Yes.'

'Now, why would you agree to a request like that – from an illegal organization which, you've just told us, you blamed for leading Adam Frodsham astray?'

'Because I thought they might come down to Sheaf, if I didn't. There was that implication. And I wasn't prepared to risk further distress to my sister.'

'So you accepted their invitation to go to them. What happened?'

'Nothing much. I was met at Charing Cross station, and taken to an address in south London. I met a man who asked if I would support BA. He didn't specify how, because I refused point-blank to have anything to do with them. He didn't argue, and had me taken back to the station.'

'That was all?'

He controlled a tremor. 'That was all.'

Benedict's own right hand, as had happened several times during the broadcast, went to where the food bowl had been, hovered briefly, then lifted authoritatively. He said, very quietly: 'And did you report this meeting to anyone – to the authorities?'

'No.'

'Why not?'

'For the same reason that made me agree to it in the first place. I wanted my sister left alone.' Benedict remained silent. 'And there wasn't anything of significance to report. The man I saw told me nothing, except that the house where we met would be abandoned within minutes of my leaving. I saw no reason to doubt him.'

The silence continued. Michael tried to anticipate the supplementary questions which, he now saw, cried out to be asked. For the moment, though, silence was Benedict's weapon. Michael saw the full-moon face staring at him, and had an almost overwhelming urge to talk . . . to explain, justify. He fought it, in a mute battle of wills. Then, with enormous relief, he became aware of the studio light winking for end of broadcast. Meticulous observance of timing schedules was another thing on which Benedict prided himself.

Benedict finally spoke, shaking his gigantic head. 'That was a great game you played for England, Michael. Pity about the other stuff.' He turned in monumental dismissal to smile into the signing-off camera. 'So, good night, folks.'

Even before the studio director gave the cut signal, two trim girls in sober blue were hurrying forward with snacks and lemonade.

Reactions to the broadcast varied. DD referred to it only as something he'd missed: he'd forgotten the time, listening to Handel. Helen Rackham mentioned it in passing, with an air of studied neutrality. Peter Graveny said: 'Bad luck, mate – what a bastard!' He looked as though he might have gone on, but Michael offered no encouragement. One of the girls in the office chattered innocently about watching the show with her family, and wasn't he *big*; and another, usually talkative, blushed and said nothing. On a routine visit to the Norman Hospital, Mary Dwyer made no comment, but poured him a stiffer shot of Irish.

Johann called him from Germany, where a dubbed version of the BB Show stood high in the ratings.

'He feeds the Germanic obsession with food and fatness: something even grosser than our own self-caricature. The gag about lederhosen went down well. *Amüsant, aber nicht ernsthaft*. Treacherous, though. Our Shakespeare got that one wrong: never trust the overweight. But you handled him beautifully.'

Hildy called too, from the London studio. Semi-nude

figures in weird costumes came and went in the background, and there was a pervading tinkle of twenties music. It was their first contact since her weekend visit to Sheaf, and she launched into commiseration. How could that fat swine do such a thing, to her beloved *Stiefbruder*? The degenerate pig! All those little girls dancing attendance, but it was well known in the business that in private life it was little boys who looked after him. Michael was not sure whether he detected, behind the loquacious sympathy, a note of excitement. *Schadenfreude* was also a good German word. She asked if he would like her to come down to Sheaf, and he said yes, but not just yet. He was busy at the moment.

Everything was filtered through self-dissatisfaction. He resented being tricked into the situation, but it was his stupidity in not anticipating it that weighed more heavily. As did his reaction to Benedict's query about not reporting the meeting with Porter. He still wasn't sure why he hadn't, but knew his attempt at justification had been feeble.

It was almost a relief when, six days after the broadcast, he was called in by Federal Security. The address was in Egerton Gardens, a set of three terraced houses converted into one. There was a single small lift which groaned up to the third floor, where an elegantly furnished room looked down across a high wall at an Elizabethan manor house, whose park must once have encompassed this expensively built-up area.

He was interrogated by two men – a thin dark cockney in a double-breasted blue suit and a small podgy man in tweeds with a more cultured accent. He speculated as to which was in charge: the latter did most of the talking, but the one in the blue suit gave a greater impression of authority.

The tweedy man, who introduced himself as Andrew Percy, repeated Benedict's question: why hadn't Michael reported his meeting with the BA representative to the authorities? His answer didn't, to his own ears, sound any more convincing than it had before, but he got through it.

Percy nodded, and said: 'All right. Take us along from the beginning. From Adam Frodsham's death.'

A recorder had been pointedly switched on. They listened, with occasional requests for clarification – chiefly from Percy, but it was the other who pressed for details relating to Porter. He could get no idea how he was doing. They were courteous, but his hands were sweating.

There was a pause when he finished. Percy looked at his companion, then back to Michael.

'You committed a major technical offence, Mr Frodsham, as I'm sure you realize. We for our part realize you were under considerable stress at the time. And as you say, you were not withholding valuable information. Valuable in your estimation, that is. It really would have been wiser to let the proper authorities be the judge. I hope we can rely on you to see it in that light in future?'

'It won't happen again.'

'But if it should . . .'

'If they contact me again, I'll let you know.'

'Good.' He put an arm on Michael's shoulder as they stood up. 'Thank you for coming in. I know you're a busy man. That was a great game, by the way. I'm looking forward to a repeat performance next year.'

'I doubt if I shall be playing next year.'

'I hope you're wrong there.'

Both men were smiling. As they reached the door, the blue suit said: 'You have an American friend, I believe? Lucy Jones – on Isak Aronheimer's staff?'

'Yes.'

He realized he ought not to have been surprised; it would have emerged from any routine check-up.

'Do you plan to see her in the near future?'

The link with the earlier conversation was plain, as was the implication. He shook his head. 'No. I have no plans for that.'

*   *   *

148

In Sheaf the sun was shining, the magnolia bursting into white-cupped, near-Oriental beauty. He thought about Lucy, with resignation rather than either bitterness or desire. 'If she be not fair to me, what care I how fair she be?' The quotation evoked dust dancing in a sunbeam in a sweltering class-room, and bored, adolescent incomprehension concerning any aspect of sex beyond the maddeningly physical . . . The misery had grown less, he told himself, and the end, if not yet in sight, was imaginable.

Walking up from the Flats with a crab to dress for supper, he encountered Souter and was granted a dubious greeting. It didn't matter, though, what the Budgie thought or did: he was in the clear. He congratulated himself on that, negotiating the cobbles on Friars Hill, aware of self-doubt, even self-disgust, but refusing to let them surface.

DD came to him in the kitchen, while he was tackling the crab. He began: 'While you were out . . .' His voice seemed very weak; he paused to draw gasping breath.

Michael took his arm. 'What is it, DD? Are you all right? Let me . . .'

He shook his head. 'They called, from Frohsteig. Johann did. It's Anna.'

'What about Anna?'

'She's dead.' He shuddered as Michael reached and held him. 'Anna's dead, Michael.'

Eight

M ichael remembered Granny T.'s funeral, almost exactly a year ago, and the house brimming with people; this afternoon only family were present. Granny T., of course, had been a considerable figure in Sheaf, known and loved by generations younger than her own, while Anna, even prior to Adam's death, had been reclusive. From Adam's birth, in fact. A few locals had attended the ceremony and might have expected to be bidden back, but Michael had no heart for it. The Frohsteig contingent was there in force, apart from Otto, now bedridden.

Numbness still covered Michael like snow, paralysing any will to act, turning voices without warning into meaningless echoes. The shock of her death had been as great as Adam's, but the loss was of a different order of bitterness: he mourned Adam again, and more sharply, in grieving for Anna. Beyond that, grief for Anna was grief for the childhood they had shared. There was a picture above the chimney piece in the sitting room which they had jointly pleaded with Granny T. not to put up. It had been painted by a friend of hers whose skill in portraiture was limited – the garden background was reasonably well done, but the two figures were awkwardly posed, with faces which, though recognizable, bore inhuman, mask-like expressions.

Anna had titled the picture 'The Aliens Have Landed', and for years after it had been the subject of their appeals to have it thrown out, or at least relegated to the obscurity of Granny T.'s bedroom. That might have been possible after she died, except that DD had made it plain he wanted no changes in his domestic surroundings. By that time too, old embarrassments had been outgrown and familiarity had engendered tolerance.

With a glass of whisky in his hand, Michael studied the scene for the first time in many years. Anna wore a white dress, embroidered with poppies, which she had insisted on having against Granny T.'s advice. She had quickly come to dislike, even hate it, but had stubbornly worn it through an entire summer rather than admit her misjudgement. He was in short grey flannels and a prep school blazer. He had not really been entitled to wear it because he was not yet enrolled at St Edward's, but they had bought it in Canterbury the previous week and Granny T. wanted him immortalized in it.

His face stared back at him as on that morning when, a window of sunshine having been seized in a day of scudding clouds and showers, it had gazed at the camera the artist was using as an aide-memoire. (Better at least, they had agreed, than the dreaded boredom of sittings.) He wondered, would a better painter have seen behind the stiffness of the smile, and registered some hint of the pain of the recent past, and the desperate fear of what lay ahead?

It had overwhelmed him the evening before, after Granny T. had read to him in bed. Daddy, so soon to become and forever remain Father, was away in Germany: a fact whose only significance then was one of distance, though that was bad enough. It seemed obscurely connected with being sent to boarding school, along with the bewildering misery of their mother's illness and death. She, who he was sure would not have let it happen, was no longer there to prevent it.

He had thought he was crying too quietly to be heard. Perhaps Anna had just looked in on him on her own way to bed. At any rate, she had hushed and hugged him. When he went on sobbing (in part out of fear she would leave him if he stopped), she had slipped into bed beside him. He had

151

fallen asleep, and woken in the night to the sharpness of her knees against his back; she had been painfully thin at that age, too.

Johann, coming to stand beside him, said: 'I used to dislike that picture.'

'We loathed it.'

'It was a sign of your really belonging – to Sheaf, to Georgian House – and that they belonged to you. I was jealous.'

Michael said in surprise: 'I never knew. After all . . .'

'We had Frohsteig, and the Schloss? True. But we didn't have Granny T., except on visits – as guests – and we didn't live in our father's home.'

'He never thought of it as that.'

'Didn't he? It was very obvious he didn't think of Frohsteig as his home. He doesn't now. Poor Papa. And I didn't have Anna, either. She was wonderful to me, but I was always conscious of the short-term basis. What I had was my beautiful indifferent mother, and a father lost between two worlds.' He laughed. 'Amazing I turned out the balanced responsible person I am, wouldn't you say?'

'You had Eton, of course.'

'Did you mind? That was Mama's doing. Her English connection had to be the biggest and best – well, the dearest and snobbiest.'

Michael shook his head. 'No, I never minded that. I've always felt a bit sorry for Etonians. They remind me of Sir Walter Elliot's obsession with the Baronetage. The inferior Old Etonian lets you know he went to what he calls that little grammar school at Windsor in the first five minutes of conversation; the better types wait for half an hour. I must say, you're an exception proving the rule.'

'Maybe because I'm a foreigner. Or because Maria-Mercedes does more advertising on my behalf than I could conceivably want.'

Michael looked at the picture again. The spray of apple

blossom Anna was holding had been painted in afterwards, which perhaps accounted for the particularly unconvincing angle of her elbow. As if the poppies on the dress weren't enough. He said: 'I still don't understand. She never had a serious illness – not until Adam was killed at least, and then it wasn't physical. A heart attack – at her age, and with no history of heart trouble? Even if one believed in people dying of a broken heart, it doesn't fit. She was in the cocoon, under Total, reunited with her beloved. At peace. A phoney peace possibly, but real to her.'

'Dieter said the p.m. revealed an aneurysm of long standing. It wouldn't produce symptoms, and with a good health record there was no occasion for the sort of check-up that might have revealed it. She went to the Brosser with a clean bill of health from her doctor here. Physical processes are slowed down during Total, but the clock goes on ticking.'

An obsolete phrase, though the wall clock by the door was ticking right now, staccato and sombre – as it had ticked on the morning of the photograph for the picture, and through a couple of hundred years before that. He turned away.

Johann said: 'It would have popped whatever she was doing, wherever she was. What we need to remember is that she was at peace. As you said, it was real to her. She died in the middle of a joyous dream. There's not much chance of either of us getting so lucky.'

The rest stayed overnight, but Hildy went back that evening. They had scarcely spoken to one another during the day. She came to say goodbye.

'I am sorry.'

'Thank you,' he said automatically. 'We'll all miss her.'

'About Anna, of course – but also about you. *Ich bin ein schlimmes Mädchen, aber* . . . It was not fair.'

'No, I don't think it was.' He looked at her, fetching in black, with just one piece of jewellery: a diamond-studded arrow pinned to the curve of her left breast. 'But at a guess I would think you'd done it before.'

'*La séduction demi-vierge?* Yes. It is an indulgence, like a drug. But one should not involve a friend.'

'I wasn't a friend though, was I? Something rather closer – and wasn't that precisely the point?'

'Mikey darling, you cannot shame me more than I shame myself. Not just that, but also knowing it was bad with you and Lucy. I hope perhaps that part is better now.' He turned away from her. 'Since she sent flowers for Anna.'

'What?'

'Didn't you see them? The yellow tulips.'

'I didn't look at any of the cards.'

She checked the time. 'My train is in ten minutes, and tonight I have a working dinner. Will you have lunch again, sometime? To show you forgive your shameful little half-sister?'

'Some time.' He accepted the kiss on his cheek. 'I don't know when.'

The others left the following morning. Janice came in to do the beds and clear up, and after that there were only himself and DD in an otherwise conspicuously empty house. Michael fixed lunch – pâté and bread and cheese – and afterwards DD retired for his nap. When he got up, it would be to go to his room and his music.

He thought of going up to the cemetery and finding Lucy's tulips, but could not bring himself to do it. Any message she might have sent, written in a stranger's hand, would be more painful than he felt like bearing. Presumably Interflora still operated, even though the long-expected ban on Americans in Britain had come into force the previous week. There had been exceptions for Americans of long residence and, as a cultural concession, for staff and pupils of the American University in Liverpool, but all other visas had been cancelled. He had not tried to work out how he felt about that: numb came closest.

Instead, he wandered through the house. He had no specific purpose but came eventually to the little room beneath the eaves which had been Anna's. She had moved into it after yielding her previous, larger one to Adam, on his fourteenth birthday. This was part of the earlier Tudor house, with a ceiling crossed by crooked beams. It was as she had always kept it, neat and almost bare. The one adornment to the white walls was a set of Chinese paintings on rice paper, depicting scenes of mysterious ceremony. They had spent an afternoon once, arguing their significance – a feast, a wedding, an enthronement, a scene of birth and a scene of death, and two more obscure occasions – and their probable sequence. Those were the only pictures she had kept after giving up painting herself.

Her desk stood under the window looking out to the hills north of Sheaf, and beside it was the Edwardian bureau where she had kept her few private possessions. A subconscious realization that the task of going through them was one only he could properly tackle was probably what had brought him here. The drawers too would be tidy and in good order. If it must be done, there was no point in delay. He was nerving himself to start when he heard the distant ring of the doorbell. It couldn't be anyone that mattered, he thought, and ignored it. After a few moments, it rang again, and for longer. Reluctantly he went downstairs.

At first all he noticed was the bulky hooded duffel coat, a badge the itinerant young had recently resurrected from more than half a century ago. A student begging, probably, braving the local ordinances against that activity which were rigorously enforced within the citadel of Sheaf. He was fishing in his pocket for money when she spoke from under the hood.

'Do I rate a cup of tea, Mike? It's been a long trip.'

'English tea,' Lucy said. 'Eventually hypocrisy pays off. I've genuinely been missing it.'

They were in the garden room, and he had put on the standard lamp against an afternoon that had turned sombre. She sat in the Queen Anne chair in a pool of light, darkly beautiful against the yellow upholstery and no less lovely for being dressed in a faded blue sweater, tattered jeans and scuffed trainers. Looking at her was enough, but questions hammered up through his contentment.

'I don't understand. How did you get here?'

'It's not that hard. The ban only applies to Britain. And it's only strictly enforced at English ports and airports. People have got in through Edinburgh. I decided not to take a chance on that and went for Paris, which is a whole lot nearer anyway. There's no ban on Americans in mainland Europe, at least not yet. All I needed after that was to keep a low profile at the Tunnel. That was easy too. I've always known there was life after Gucci.' She sipped from her mug. 'Easier maybe than life after English tea.'

'But once you were on this side of the Channel . . . you're illegal now.'

'Sure.' She smiled. 'I took a chance you wouldn't turn me in.'

He thought of Souter. 'Someone else might.'

'So what can they do, except deport me?'

He said, slowly: 'I don't know. Things are changing, and some things are being concealed. I've been told horror stories I didn't believe. I still don't want to, but I'm not as confident they're all lies as I used to be.'

Lucy nodded. 'Things are changing, all right. I made sure there were people back home who knew where I was heading, and could be relied on to make a noise if I didn't surface at the right time.'

'Ike Haddon?'

'Among others.' She paused. 'We can talk about Ike later. I want to say how bad I feel about Anna. You know me, and family. I don't see how I could bear it, losing one of mine.

156

And I do know between you and Anna it was more than just special.'

'How did you know – that she was dead?'

'From Johann. He worries about you.'

'Does he know you're here now?'

'No. As I say, me they could only deport. It didn't seem a good idea to have a Euro citizen involved, though.' She looked at him. 'Except you. I was ready to take a risk on your account.'

The invisible bridge joining their eyes was more real than the room about them, and more demanding. He held the contact as he walked across the Persian carpet to where she sat, though it seemed more that the contact was holding him. She rose as he reached her, into his arms.

It was Lucy who eventually broke away. He tried to hold her, and she shook her head against his face. 'I have to talk. And not like this, not yet. Sit down, my love. Please.'

He found himself doing a strangely childish thing. He sat on the floor, beside her chair. Her hand was on his head, strong fingers in his hair. He thought of Hildy's fingers, teasing, tormenting, and turned that thought away. Lucy said: 'I'd like you to meet my mother sometime, before we all die. I don't know if you'd like her, but I guarantee you will be impressed. One thing you have to understand is that black people can be very different, even if we all look alike. My father's side, they came up early. Keep the lighting real low and his grandfather would have passed for middle-class, even before World War II. Poppa was second generation college-educated. He could probably have made Ivy League, but his father had gone to NYU, and he stayed loyal. That's where they got together. Momma's family came from Harlem, and not rich Harlem either. When they met, she was slinging hash in a greasy spoon.

'Least, that's what she says. Really, she was waiting on table at the college refectory; she never believes in spoiling a story for want of a little embroidery. Thing is, she was very unsuitable, and when he took her home his folks made that plain. You English with all that middle-class snobbery have got nothing on your average middle-class American black. Far as I can tell – and quite a bit of it comes out of what used to be the enemy camp – they used every trick in the book to save their precious boy from this sassy bitch from the big city.

'They ought to have won. Poppa's a great guy, but he was a good son. Like, obedient? Had my mother been the littlest bit unsure of what she wanted, for the both of them, she would have been eased out, and he'd have married the one they had in mind, eldest daughter of the attorney who handled Granpop's business affairs. But she decided she knew best, and went for it the simplest way by getting pregnant. That turned out to be brother Joshua, who's just gotten an award for the Pentagon replacement building. Both maternal grandparents are dead, but the other two bust with pride every time he gets a notice in the *Washington Post*.'

Her fingers tugged, not roughly but with authority. 'I'm the youngest, but I guess I take most after her. What I'm trying to do is say sorry, but I need to explain things first. I know what's best for me, which is sharing with you till the Lord blows the whistle. And I'm arrogant enough to think it's best for you, as well.'

He heard himself making a sound – sigh, groan – of consent. She said: 'OK, I ought not to have set you up with Ike. But I do know Ike. I wouldn't trust him with your life if I didn't trust him with mine. There would have been some risk, sure, but we'd have been in it together. And I was winning you over to travel my way, just like Momma did.'

He turned his head to look at the curve of her knee in the ragged jeans. 'You didn't get pregnant.'

'No.' Her leg moved against his head as she laughed. 'Not that I didn't consider that. Or don't still have it in mind. Can I say sorry now?'

'It doesn't matter.'

'Everything you said at the airport that night was right. You whupped me good, and I had to take my whupping. But I guess my mother's blood runs too strong. I still knew what was best for us, even if I'd figured a wrong way for making it happen. When Johann called me, about Anna, I knew nothing was going to stop me coming to you.'

He did not speak immediately, at ease in the security of physical contact. At last, he said: 'How long can you stay?'

'Till tomorrow. I reckon I've earned the night.'

'Longer than that. Please.'

'You said it: I'm illegal.'

'No one saw you arrive. No one would know you're here, in a house as rambling as this. DD needn't know, even. I could smuggle you up to the top floor before he wakes from his nap.'

'And, as I said, I took precautions. If I don't make contact with Ike tomorrow, he's liable to start hunting for me. That could get embarrassing.'

'Call him from here.'

He felt the shake of her head. 'Not secure. Nothing in England is secure now, and there are other people to consider. I may take chances with us, but I can't with them.'

'You're really going back tomorrow? You came all this way, to tell me that?'

Getting out of the chair, she helped him up too and stood before him, eyes intent on his. 'Come back with me.'

'I wish I could, but even though the ban's one-way still, visas are definitely out for the ordinary citizen, and scarce as gold bricks for anyone else. My boss has decided there's no future in American connections. I could try working on her, but I can't see any way she would buy it. Or I might put on my other hat, and go to Dieter. But I can't see even Dieter getting me an American visa in aid of promoting rugby. And if he could we'd be talking months, if not years.'

She put her hands on his waist. 'I'm not talking months, or years – I'm talking now. And I'm not talking visits. I'm talking US residence. All you have to do is marry me. The US government insists on that one, and so do I.'

He thought she was joking, but her look had no jest in it. He said: 'That's not possible. You know it's not.'

'I don't think it would have been, while Anna was alive. But it is now.'

'There's DD.'

'He doesn't need you. The person that mattered to him died a year ago. He's happy enough wrapping a blanket of music round him. But if it matters to you, bring him too. Ike will swing him a card, as dependent relative.'

'He couldn't leave Sheaf. He's an old dog.'

'It's a younger one I'm concerned about. Mike, I hear things. There's trouble enough now, but it's going to get worse. The Atlantic link is flimsy, but for the moment it's still there. It may not be for long.'

'There are always rumours.'

She looked as if she were about to say something, but checked herself. 'You're right. They may just be rumours. But I believe them. What it is – I want you, and I don't think we have too much time to play with. I'm not allowed to live here, so I want you to come to me. Simple stuff.'

There was the sound of a door opening upstairs. DD would be looking for a cup of tea.

'The simple stuff's always the best,' he said. 'Most of me, the me that's looking at you now, wants that more than anything in the world. Yet if it got what it wanted, it couldn't live with itself. You're right about the difference with Anna being dead, and you could even be right about DD. But I couldn't leave Sheaf, either.'

Michael wanted to drive Lucy to Folkestone, but she vetoed it. Federal troops were a heavy presence round the Tunnel mouth; if they picked her up they could do no more than expedite her return to the United States, but things might be more difficult for him. She stretched against him, yawning. Neither had slept more than a fitful hour or two.

'I still haven't abandoned hope of your changing your mind.' He shook his head; there was light at the window, a hint of early sun behind the bulk of the old monastery. 'Yeah, I know. But let me dream. And I'd sooner leave you here, in Sheaf, than walk away from you into that Tunnel.'

'I can't believe you're going.'

She smiled. 'You didn't believe I was coming, either. It's an unpredictable universe, thank God.'

DD, who had been delighted to see her, was up early and breakfasted with them; his understanding was simply that she had planned to come for Anna's funeral but been held up by a flight delay. If he'd heard about the ban on Americans he obviously dismissed it as just another confusing triviality of modern life. Michael was pleased to see him happy, but could have done without his chatter.

Lucy let him walk her to the station, through the cattle market which, since this was Tuesday, held only empty stalls and ranks of parked cars. There were two or three people in the booking hall, but no one he knew. Unforgivably, the Sheaf Flyer was on time for once. She whispered: 'Glad I came?'

'You know I am. I just wish—'

She stopped his mouth with a kiss. 'I'm glad. I hate this part, but in that respect we're no worse off than we were two days ago. And in every other, we're so much better. Maybe it's Momma's blood talking again, but I feel confident. Political crises don't last forever. Maybe in a couple of months the two sides will back down and we can get on with normality. Believe just one thing, Mike, if you believe nothing else: the first Washington-London flight that's open to Yanks will have my name on the passenger list. You believe?'

'I believe, but it's not important. If it's OK for you to

come here, it'll be OK for me to go to you. We won't argue who travels which way.'

He walked back to the house in a confusion of both mood and thoughts. Even if he hadn't been light-headed from satisfied lust and lack of sleep, it would have been difficult to accept the reality of the past twenty-four hours. Wrenchingly bitter as it had been to watch her waving hand diminish and then be lost at the bend in the line beyond the level crossing, euphoria predominated. In an ugly world, something which had been wrong was triumphantly right again.

He heard DD's voice as he let himself in, raised and annoyed. Pursuing it to the garden room, he found him in front of the console phone. DD turned to him, almost accusingly. 'These bloody things! I can't see why anyone needs to see who they're talking to, anyway. Some nutcase of a foreigner . . .'

'I'll see to it, DD.' He took his place in front of the screen. 'Can I help?'

'Mr Frodsham . . . it was you I wanted.'

He looked balder on the screen than he had at the Clinic, and paler-skinned and fatter. Michael suppressed his antipathy: it was not his fault Anna was dead. He said: 'How can I help you, Dr Stern?'

'I wanted to say . . .'

'Yes?'

'It is a terrible thing, terrible. But . . .'

Stern was struggling against incoherence. Michael thought of the man's bland assurance during his visit to the Clinic, that assumption of control which seemed to verge on mind-reading. He was not a man who would find it easy to accept failure, even if the failure was something for which he was not responsible. This outburst, the evident collapse of his sense of authority, was surprising, but not really out of character. Even the fact of it coming more than a week after Anna's death fitted in. 'I am Jew and German: thoroughness is important.' The more rigid the personality, the more total the collapse. Michael could understand that, but it didn't make either Stern or his distress more palatable. Anna had been his patient, and Anna was dead. It was not something to hate him for, but distaste was not unreasonable.

Keeping his own voice controlled, he said: 'Thank you for calling. I know it was nothing you could help. Dieter . . .'

'Will you come, Mr Frodsham?'

He was taken aback. 'Come where?'

'Here. To the Clinic. I cannot talk to you –' he gestured wildly towards the screen – 'like this.'

His distress was clearly extreme. Michael reminded himself of the deference he had shown to Dieter, the fulsome acknowledgement of what he and the Clinic owed to Frohsteig. He had taken on the treatment of a close relative of Dieter, and the patient had died. He must have been sweating over it, to a point of near desperation. The reaction was almost pathological, but in the abstract one could feel sorry for him. One didn't live, though, in the abstract. Michael had a sudden, almost physical recollection of Lucy – her scent, taste, touch. But one could try to be charitable.

'If you want me to come and see you, yes, of course. The next time I visit Frohsteig.'

He had no plans for visiting Frohsteig in the near future; by the time he did Stern would have made peace with his unhinged conscience.

'No! Soon . . . please. As soon as possible.'

'I'll see.'

'This is important.' The man's face was distorted, possibly near weeping. 'Please!'

It was becoming insupportable. Michael said: 'I'll check my diary, and see what I can manage. I'm sorry, I must go now. I'll get back to you as soon as I can.'

He clicked off the call before Stern could respond.

On the Marsh the lambs were near full-grown, both they

163

and the ewes overdue for shearing. That did not matter much on a day like this, with an east wind sharp under a grey sky, but they would be hot if the sun came out. Michael remembered a shearing contest on a farm near Nutarge, when he was about ten, and the bronzed figures of the Australians wrestling with the awkward, greyish, woolly creatures, clipping them with astonishing speed and precision into thin, white, pot-bellied beasts, and gulping down innumerable cans of Castlemaine. One of them had paid close attention to Anna, just sixteen and beginning to be noticed by the opposite sex. He had seen her respond and been jealous, and not sure of the object of his jealousy.

That was a long time ago. It must be more than ten years since the Australian shearers were banned. The shearers now were local, or from France or Spain, and they didn't go in for shearing contests or drinking lager by the gallon. This year, it seemed, they hadn't come at all.

Fields gave way to trafficless roads and empty plots, the skeletal remnants of the dream that had heralded Ashford as Europe's city of the future. The Sheaf Flyer drew into its humble side platform and shuddered to a halt. Michael opened the door of a carriage which had been old when he was young, and entered the echoing vault of the station, vaguely aware of something missing: there had been no announcement of arrival, or instructions about changing platforms for the main-line trains. He realized something else – that the platform was empty apart from two men with Heckler-Kochs. Not in uniform, he noted, and then saw they were wearing white armbands with red lettering. Three letters: BLA.

Belatedly the speakers uttered, though not in the customary bored tones of Southeast Rail. A sharp, bossy cockney voice said: 'This is an official announcement. This station has been taken over by the British Liberation Army. No one is permitted to enter or leave the premises without authorization by the local BLA Commandant. Members of the public must not occupy the platforms, but go at once to the refreshment area. Stand by for further announcements. Britain Awake!'

The men with armbands marshalled them into the refreshment room, normally almost empty but crowded now. The people already there seemed to have settled into an uneasy acceptance of the situation. The buffet was doing a heavy trade, and he joined the queue for coffee. A ginger-bearded man in front of him was garrulous. He lived in Headcorn and worked in Canterbury, and had been here over half an hour.

'Neat stuff,' he said. 'You've got to hand it to them. Took the place over without firing a shot.' He sounded excited. 'Somebody doing something at last – taking action!'

Michael said: 'I'm not sure what they think they're going to do with Ashford station, now they've got it.'

'Last stop before the Tunnel, right? I was talking to that bloke.' He indicated a BLA man. 'They'll take over the next fast train from London, load up with explosives, and make the driver take it on through to the Tunnel entrance. They're going to time-fuse the explosives and abandon it. They reckon the blast will be big enough to put the Tunnel out of action for months, maybe permanently.'

'And then what?'

'We'll be an island again, right? If the bastards want to come over here after that, they'll have to walk on the bleeding water.'

'It sounds a large order,' Michael said. 'I hope their execution's better than their security.'

'What's that mean?' The tone and the thrust of beard into Michael's face were hostile. 'What you on about?'

'Someone seems to have been talking a bit.'

'Well, it doesn't matter now, does it? Train's due any minute. They know what they're doing. They took over the station all right, didn't they?'

A whisper in the north turned slowly into the high-pitched

rumble of an approaching express, and the rumble built into a roar. Michael waited for the change in pitch which would signal braking, but it didn't come. The roar continued to build, and as it reached a crescendo the shriek of a through-train whistle was added to the din. Then the pitch did change as it hurtled judderingly on southwards, at top speed.

It was still audible, fading in the distance, when a different roar grew in the sky. The helicopter gunships came in low, spraying the platforms with machine gun fire. Before he flung himself to the floor, Michael saw one of the men in armbands spin round and fall outwards on to the track.

Helen Rackham was unusually twitchy. Michael came in for questioning round the table because of his involvement in the Ashford incident, from Sylvia Perenaike in particular. She hadn't been back to her home in Wolverhampton for several days, and communications with that region were down, but she'd heard there had been an uprising there too, and was worried about her family. There were rumours of civilian casualties.

Helen overrode her brusquely. There would be a government announcement later in the day. Meanwhile, they had the latest drug-control implementation proposals, and their relationship to hospital management, to consider.

Coming out, Graveny predictably suggested the Eagle & Lamb, but Michael had a valid reason for turning it down.

'My German uncle is giving me lunch.'

'And a German uncle is not a monkey's uncle, *ja*? *Schnell, schnell*, not what the hell. That was a right cock-up at Ashford, wasn't it?'

'Just about sums it up, I would say.'

'Do you think they had any chance at all of pulling it off – blowing up the entrance to the Tunnel?'

'Not the slightest.'

'So why try something on you can't possibly get away with?'

'I don't know. How do you figure nutcases?'

'I'm not so sure they are nutcases. What would you say the BA aim has been, all along? Yes, OK, to go back on every commitment over the past thirty years and take us out of Europe, but I'm talking ways and means. There's never been a worthwhile resistance movement that shied away from the prospect of reprisals. Provocation is its own justification. A bloodstained flag or two makes the point better than any number of street-corner rallies. You can win by losing.'

Michael thought of the man with the ginger beard. He hadn't spoken to him again, but had seen him as the bodies of the BLA man, and of a woman civilian who'd also been killed, were stretchered away. His expression had lost its cockiness, but in its place there was anger.

'I didn't want to upset Sylvia,' Graveny said, 'but my information is that it's still going on in Birmingham. And in my own region, I've heard they actually came out on top. Liverpool's under BLA control.'

'Temporarily, maybe.'

'What isn't temporary?'

Central London at any rate seemed calm and unconcerned. His taxi driver said nothing about uprisings but, recognizing him, talked rugby all the way to the Frohsteig building. He found Dieter away from his desk, staring out at Hampstead. He seemed abstracted, but came over to embrace Michael.

'How are you, Michael? And how is DD?'

'He's fine. All well at Frohsteig?'

'At Frohsteig, things are well. Though we are in grief still, all of us. What else is possible?'

'I had a call from Stern the other day. He sounded disturbed.'

'Disturbed, yes.' From his height he looked down at Michael, frowning. 'What has he said?'

'He told me he wanted to talk to me – wanted me to go to the Clinic. I said I would, but I don't know when I'll be able. He made it sound urgent.'

167

Dieter shook his head. 'No. It is not urgent.'

'It might seem so, from his point of view. I got the impression of an extremely conscientious man, and with Anna dying . . . even though there was nothing he could have done . . .'

'Certainly,' Dieter said. 'A conscientious man. And with that Jewish conscience. I think maybe he came back to Germany because he could not live in the Israeli empire, and that problem with the Arabs that goes on and on. But some things, when you run away, run with you. But it is not urgent for him now, not any more. Anna dying was not his fault, but guilt does not need a reason to come, and after it comes does not reason well. He had drugs, and the knowledge to use them. He used them, yesterday, to kill himself.'

Michael felt less shock than he would have expected. He remembered the face on the screen; agitated, pitiable but not likeable. There had been enough to mourn, without trying to wring out tears for a stranger. Instead he thought of Anna, with renewed desolation.

'A bad business,' Dieter said. 'These are bad times.' He indicated the television screen incorporated in his desk. 'Have you heard? There was a newsflash, a little time before you got here.'

'What about?'

'The British government has asked for full Federal support, after the attack on the Tunnel. England is placed under martial law.'

Like Stern's suicide, it was a shock that did not really surprise.

Dieter surveyed him soberly. 'I think perhaps we must abandon the rugby project, for the present.'

He restrained an impulse to laugh at the incongruity of the remark, so typical of Dieter. 'I think you're probably right about that.'

Dieter gripped his arm. 'We will go to lunch. Thank God there is always food, and also wine.'

168

Nine

M ichael woke to a rattle of hailstones on his bedroom window. Outside the monastery's silhouette was harshly black against a sky dark with heavy cloud, rather than residual night. He recalled a television programme from when he was on the edge of his teens, a projection based on the old global warming hypothesis. It had fascinated him with the promise of hot summers and mild damp winters, of a sub-tropical Britain in which monkeys and parrots chattered and squeaked through jungly forests; only to alarm him later with a threat of oceans swollen by melting polar ice. The sea level, a speaker had said, would rise by anything up to two metres. He'd watched the programme here at Sheaf, half excited, half terrified by an image of the sea bursting through the dunes at Oxbow Sands, racing north across the Marsh to seize the town in that ancient embrace – turning it into an island again, with waves battering the foot of Cerdic's Cliff and tall-masted ships riding less than a cannon-shot away.

All that was as remote and unreal now as Tennyson's *Parliament of Man*, which had also fired his imagination in an otherwise deadly boring class on Victorian poets. A new ice age was back at the top of the prediction pops. Intellectual fashions apart, the hail, giving way now to beating rain, was real enough. It was some consolation that this was not an office day, and his first appointment, at Brighton General Hospital, not until the afternoon. Although he was later than usual, there was no sound of DD moving about. He was perceptibly slowing up, and sleeping longer.

His mind turned to a more recent and happier memory. Lucy, at this hour, would be asleep, with family photographs crowding her walls and yesterday's clothes scattered over chairs and dressing stool. How long before he could hope to see her again? Her notion of the political crisis subsiding fairly quickly seemed over-sanguine after the declaration of martial law. He told himself to hang on to optimism: darkest hour before the dawn, and all that. But this morning's dawn was dark by any standard.

He roused himself eventually and was on his way downstairs to make coffee when he caught a glimpse of white in the tray of the fax machine on the landing. He switched a light on to read it: the message was brief.

'Please cancel/postpone outside appointments. Your presence is required at the Ministry, 1200 noon.' It was signed simply: 'Helen Rackham'.

God damn her! was his first reaction – laying that on at such ridiculously short notice. If his appointment had been early, he would have been gone already. He wondered about ignoring it, then checked the transmission time on the fax. 2239: it had been lying there over nine hours. Something else which had been bothering him came into focus: it was missing the Ministry heading, any heading in fact. The originating line showed a number he didn't recognize, probably her home fax.

He had a scratch breakfast while organizing a more leisurely one for DD, and headed for the station. The late start, compounded by the usual vagaries of Southeast Rail, got him to the Ministry just after twelve fifteen. The doorman, a lanky laid-back Jamaican called Gilbert, emerged from the shadows where he had been enjoying his pre-lunch joint to intercept him as he headed for the lift.

'Oy there, Mr Frodsham. You wanted in the Eagle & Lamb.' Michael looked at him in query. 'Mizz Rackham said to tell you. They all there.'

He found them in the snug, behind the main bar. They

were sitting round an assortment of drinks at the battered Victorian table, with Helen presiding at the far end. It was an occasion so out of character that it would have been no more of a surprise to see her handling a pint of bitter, but it was iced orange juice she put down as he approached.

'Michael, better late than not at all. That gives us a full complement. Grab a stool. Half of Adnam's?'

As though they were old drinking buddies – how had she known that? He took the drink the barman brought and raised it. Helen went on: 'So we'll waste no more time. You may be surprised by this.' Her gesture took in the pub interior with a mixture of explanation and contempt. 'I wanted an unofficial word, and it seemed more appropriate than the boardroom. Especially since –' she looked at her watch – 'I've not been entitled to preside over anything in the Ministry for the past twenty-one minutes. My resignation from office was effective as of noon.'

Michael did not join in the murmur of surprise, though he was startled. He would always have seen a dramatic resignation as on the cards should it further her career, but it was difficult to see what she could hope to gain in the present circumstances.

Ignoring the murmur, Helen said crisply: 'I've appreciated the co-operation I've had from all of you over the past eighteen months, even if I've not always shown it. I feel you're entitled to a few words of explanation of whatever's going to be put out in this evening's news. Actually, not being a member of cabinet, I've not been much better informed than the rest of you on what's been happening at government level. Things have been kept close to the chest, for obvious reasons.

'Apart from being less than fully informed, I've been a bit short on general comprehension. Possibly my original nationality has had something to do with that. This European business has been developing over half a century – you've grown up with it, and into it. But when I first got here – from a background where my grandparents never stopped talking about England as the home country and always watched the Queen making her Christmas address . . . late at night, and a hot night buzzing with bugs . . . even then, I had to come in through the aliens channel. I suppose no one's more a foreigner than a time-traveller from the past.

'Maybe I was marrying the past when I married an Englishman. The marriage didn't work, but I stayed in love with the country. I was puzzled, mind you. I thought a lot of pretty good things had been lost, and a lot more were at risk. But I told myself that an alien, even a friendly alien, wasn't the best judge of that. I couldn't be expected to understand the European idea as it deserved to be understood.'

She drained her orange juice. 'I probably still don't. It could all be nostalgic sentimentality – I liked my grandparents better than my parents, and I loved those Christmas gatherings, despite the heat and the bugs. But when we reach the point of calling in foreign troops – beg pardon, fellow-Euro troops – to suppress a revolt which whether or not it's crackpot is most definitely indigenous – then I guess it's time this time-traveller checked out.'

She flashed an unsmiling glance around the table. 'Thank you for listening. No handshakes, no embraces. Carry on drinking. It's on my tab.'

She headed briskly for the door. Peter Graveny signalled the barman.

'Large Scotch, in that case. Michael? You have to hand it to the lady for jumping to it. Result of all that kangaroo watching as a child, probably. My guess is she's packed and ready for the early Quantas flight to Sydney.'

'You think she's going back to Australia?'

'What else? And why not? She'll have kept her passport, and it's a nice safe spot. Better than this one. There's a rumour civilian traffic through the Tunnel's been suspended. Keeping the lines clear for the military, I suppose.'

*   *   *

Bad Dream

On Friday evening, Michael had an optimistic shot at calling Washington. The newscasts had been reassuring, stressing prospects of an early return to normal. It was an optimism echoed in the High Street by an ex-Army colonel who lived in the Square, Sheaf's particular oasis of gentility. He said he'd heard controls were already being relaxed, including communications controls. The difference between the military mind and the civilian, he suggested, was taking the long view and keeping your finger off the panic button. Michael declined his suggestion of a pint in the Dragon, and watched him stride off cheerfully in that direction, his Dandy Dinmont regimentally alert at his heels.

For a few seconds in which he heard the double-bleep of the network taking his call, and subsequently a wait tone, Michael felt optimism might have paid off; but these were followed by the familiar dispiriting crackle and the screen message: 'Contact not made.'

DD was querulous at breakfast next morning, and later wandered aimlessly through the house, apparently in no mood to be soothed by early baroque music. Michael asked if he felt like accompanying him to the cemetery, and was brusquely refused: he would be making that trip soon enough and, thank God, on a one-way ticket. Michael went alone, picking up an arrangement from the flower shop on the way. He could have cut flowers from the garden, but didn't feel like making the effort.

The day was sunny but bitterly cold, with a whistling wind from the north-east that encouraged him to step out. He wasn't sure which was the stranger feeling: that he had so recently walked this way with Anna, or that they never would again. In the paddock, the lambs that had momentarily cheered her were half-grown. Even if their hour of reckoning was imminent, all they knew right now was sunshine and green grass, and a fleece protecting them from the icy blast.

He laid flowers on both graves, noting the absence of a red

and white wreath on Adam's. Souter, also encountered the evening before, had mentioned it. The presence and regular renewal of the wreaths had been reported: the offending item had been removed and the Carolingians had organized a cemetery watch in the hope of apprehending the person responsible. They hadn't caught anyone so far, but the observation was continuing.

The chubby red face had pouted into a frown. 'I'm afraid the most likely explanation is that our chap didn't take full precautions against being spotted. I'm looking into that.'

'Or else you have a mole.'

He took it seriously. 'I'm checking on that, too. But at least we've put a stopper on that particular bit of subversion. I'm telling you about it, Michael, because of your link with the deceased. Must have been galling for you, things like that going on.'

Michael's instinct was to reply that political use of a grave was as contemptible in the Carolingians as it had been with BA; it was an indication of how things had changed that he found the urge easy to control.

Souter put a hand on his arm, and this time he felt the impress of his fingers. 'Have you given any more thought to joining us?'

'I've been too busy to think of anything but work and family.'

'You should make the effort. You might find it a help. It was a pity about that Benedict interview. People who really know you would never believe you might get mixed up with a criminal organization, but it's best to be completely above suspicion. And I think I ought to warn you that membership of the Sodalitas may not always be an option. The bandwagon's beginning to roll, and once it's really under way climbing aboard may not be easy.'

On his way back to the house, Michael thought about what he could put on the table for lunch. There had been grumbling about the monotony of a diet of bread and cheese and pâté from DD, who despite an affectation of indifference to food had always had a more than warm regard for his stomach. Granny T. had been culpable in that, though her love of cooking had not been an adequate excuse for his assumption that indulging his appetite represented her highest form of self-expression. On one of DD's birthdays, Anna, an impudent fourteen-year-old, had promised him a special surprise, blindfolded him, and led him to the kitchen, to show him where in fact it was. He had been puzzled, barely seeing the point of the joke.

Then, when Granny T. died, Anna had taken on the role, with equal diligence if not quite her scope. It was not a duty Michael felt himself capable of assuming, even if he had thought it proper to do so. DD, though, was an old man. He wondered about an omelette, with mushrooms perhaps. DD was fond of mushrooms, though he would undoubtedly complain about them being tinned.

Opening the front door, Michael heard his voice from the direction of the garden room, raised in cackling merriment. He speculated that this might be another staging-post on the road to senility – DD talked to himself a lot these days – then heard a second, quieter voice. He found DD in one of the bergère armchairs, leaning forward, hands clasped and elbows on knees, towards Hildy who was curled up on the sofa.

'Hildy,' Michael greeted her, 'a pleasure I didn't expect.'

DD scowled at the interruption. Hildy rose and came to kiss him. 'Mikey! Ought I to have warned you? Darling, so sorry. You know me, and how hopeless I am at planning anything.'

'You mustn't sell yourself short. I think you organize things very well. It's me and DD who are getting slack. Can you make do with an omelette and a glass of wine for lunch?'

'Positive heaven, except I will not let you have the trouble, when I come with no warning. It is fixed. We have a table reserved at the Dragon, and I pay – no argument. They have renewed my contract and I am filthy rich.'

'I'm not sure . . .'

DD interrupted angrily: 'Let the ungracious sod stay here and eat his leathery omelette, Hildy. I'm coming, and I won't quibble about your picking up the bill. A granddaughter who's the loveliest girl I've seen in decades, and who offers to buy me lunch . . . I may not die happy, but this is a good moment on the run-in.'

When they got back to the house, Hildy insisted on making coffee, having brought some with her from London. It was Viennese, and DD, who had been known to devastate dinner parties with denunciations of the obscenity of adding fig to a beverage he loved, praised it without stint. Hildy flirted with him and he reciprocated enthusiastically, more alert than Michael had seen him for weeks. But despite that, and the caffeine, he eventually began to nod, and Hildy cajoled him into letting her take him up for his rest.

'He is sweet,' she commented when she came down. 'So also is *Grossvater* Otto, but much duller.'

'Less responsive?'

'Don't be so severe with me, Mikey. Even if I deserve it. No, it is not that. Sex is not the only excitement. When it has gone, there will be other things, I hope – to be still as *schlagfertig* as he is would be good.'

'*Schlagfertig?*'

'Quick-witted. But when the translation is literal – ready to take a blow. And ready to give one also. God, I hate to see him mastered by tiredness. I hate old age more than anything. I hope I die before it comes to me. But I suppose everyone says that.' She turned, in a whirl of skirt. 'I will make more coffee. There is something we should talk about.'

He wondered, while she was absent, what she might have in mind. He was sure of one thing – that he was not prepared to discuss Lucy with her – but he no longer felt raw and aggressive in her company. The more some things mattered, the less others did.

Hildy poured coffee, lacing her own thickly with double cream, her only dietary weakness. Stirring it in, she asked: 'Dieter has told you, about Stern?'

'About him overdosing? Yes. I can't feel too much about that. It's not his fault Anna's dead, and I suppose an overactive conscience is better than none.' He paused, wondering if she might take that as a dig. 'But I can't pretend I'm grieving. I didn't warm to the man.'

She shrugged. 'I scarcely knew him. He was at the Christmas party, of course. So was one of his assistants, Berthold Gegener.'

Michael nodded. 'Swooning at your feet. I remember. I saw him again at the Clinic, but only fleetingly.'

'He's a nice boy. He wrote letters to me, after I came to London.' She saw Michael's eye on her. 'Nice letters. He is an innocent.'

'And you wrote back. Also innocently, but with just a hint that there might be life beyond innocence. Real life.'

Hildy smiled. 'You think you know me, and perhaps you do a little bit. Better than Berthold, yes. But it is only a little bit, Mikey. Do not believe you know me truly.'

'I don't fool myself about that. No one knows anyone truly. As far as most are concerned, a pragmatic view is enough. No need to pursue things further, no urge.'

A flicker of her eye took the point, and a quick smile denied resentment of it. 'I had a letter yesterday from Berthold. He was shocked that Stern has killed himself. Not just shocked – he cannot understand it. He thought he knew Stern – as a friend, not just boss. He has been living with Stern and his family, in fact. And Stern has talked to him, since Anna died. Berthold had never known him like this – so dreadfully unhappy. He was experienced as a medical: he had lost patients before.'

'Not many who were closely related to his principal sponsor, probably.'

She was silent a moment. 'Berthold thinks – he thinks Stern thought there was something wrong, at the Clinic.'

'Wrong?' He felt a choking sensation, a stab of unreasonable fear. 'In what way, wrong? To do with Anna's death?'

'Just wrong, he says. You understand, it is nothing Berthold himself knows, or suspects. The suspecting is about Stern's death, not Anna's.'

'Have you spoken to Dieter about it?'

She hesitated. 'No.'

'Why not?'

'I did not want to trouble him. With the supposings of a young man. Dieter is busy always. Also . . .'

'What?'

'Dieter is his sponsor, too – his employer. Berthold has written to me, in confidence, because he is worried. If I tell Dieter and it is only his foolishness, he may get into trouble. You must not think me unfair in everything.'

'You're telling me, though.'

'Because it concerns Anna. She was my sister, also. When I was little . . . she might have hated me because I was your father's child, but it was not so. Even after Adam came, she gave me the love she could spare.'

'Yes, I know she did that.'

'And Dieter can be touchy, about the company. He seems as though he stands high above all problems, but these things are of great importance to him – more important than anything in the world. He has created the business, from the beginning, and made it big.'

Michael shrugged. 'You know him better than I do.'

The initial panic anxiety had subsided. Berthold was very young, possibly unbalanced. His calf-like devotion to Hildy had most likely been mirrored in his attachment to Stern. Hero-worshipping the older man could, on Stern's death, have triggered an emotional crisis in him. It didn't have to have a rational basis.

It was Stern who had fed Berthold the idea of there being 'something wrong' at the Clinic. He could only have referred to a technical failure or an error in clinical procedure, something which should not have happened, or had been done badly. Any responsibility for such shortcoming was ultimately Stern's; and it looked as though he had accepted it, and passed sentence on himself. Digging him up to echo it would serve no purpose for anyone.

A similar, irredeemable finality applied to Anna's death. No amount of probing or condemnation would bring her back. But in her case there was at least the consolation of knowing that she had died persuaded she had recovered her lost love. It was a serenity not one in a million was likely to know. More through her strength than his own, he could believe now that he and Lucy might eventually share a life, perhaps a long one; but even if that came about, it would one day fall to her to close his eyes, or him hers.

He said: 'There's not a lot one can do, is there, since you don't want to bring in Dieter? Nothing that would help anyone.'

'It might help Berthold if we talk with him.'

'We?'

'I will be happier if you are with me.' She smiled, without guile. 'My big brother.'

'*Stiefbruder*.'

'Yes. Even so.'

He wondered if it was as simple as that, or could be. Her humiliation of him smarted less, but forgetting it, or what it had told him about her, was another matter. Yet he did not have to trust her, and whatever her motivation, there was no point in getting involved, even as far as arguing.

He said: 'If you think it will do any good.'

'So – when?'

'I've a lot on my plate at the moment. And I'm sure you have commitments.'

'None that I cannot break.'

'OK.' He drank his coffee and stood up. 'I'll see what I can work out, and let you know.'

Peter Graveny called Michael on Monday morning from his car. He had his carphone bracketed on the dashboard: even when interference wasn't breaking up the image it bobbed up and down, inducing nausea.

'Still at home, then? Thank God there are some of us who take our responsibilities seriously. What would the hospital service be like if everyone skived off? Better not answer that, come to think of it.'

'I'm picking up an appointment I lost when Helen summoned us in for the short goodbye. A woman called Wright, and her rights are something she stands on heavily. I made a suitably crawling apology, but there can be no excuse for letting her down. Last time it had to be afternoon; now it's eleven forty-five precisely. Buggers up the day, but I gather that's the idea.'

'She probably fancies you.'

'That would be daunting, if true. She's close on two metres tall, and built to match.'

'That'll be it, then. She needs a scrum-half for a quick touch-down. I was wondering when you were likely to be up in the Smoke next.' Graveny had a fund of outdated colloquialisms. He frequently spoke of people as 'bods', an expression Michael had only otherwise heard as a boy, on the lips of a deeply wrinkled RAF officer left over from World War Two.

'Wednesday, probably.'

'Good. Keep lunch open. My grapevine has yielded some bonzer gen. How are you with lamb?'

'I like it. And half a minute's walk to Cerdic's Cliff

gives me a view of several acres of the animal, on the hoof. Marsh lamb.'

'It's not bad, either. But I'm talking something special – something from outside, and not brought in through Customs either.'

'If you're saying New Zealand . . .'

'I'm not. I'm saying Icelandic. But I'm not saying it twice, and I hope you won't repeat it. The patron owes me a favour, which I reckon will stretch to a second portion for an old buddy.'

Icelandic lamb, always of high repute, had acquired an otherworldly snob esteem since Iceland, in response to prolonged political and economic pressure from the Federation, had responded defiantly through a trade arrangement with the United States which included an American defence guarantee. So its lamb was not just a prohibited import, but one from near-hostile territory. Never cheap, its ounce-for-ounce price had risen to eclipse that of caviar. Michael asked: 'Can you afford it, on our kind of salary?'

'As I said, a favour owed. Are you on?'

'They might get raided. Yes, what the hell – I'm on. Any news of Helen, by the way? I suppose it's too early for a postcard of the Opera House.'

'Not a word. What does seem odd is that they still haven't named a successor.'

'The PM is probably too busy sorting out his back-benchers. That anti-Federal fracas in the House on Friday must have bothered him.'

'Maybe he's running short of pliable shits. It's a hard world. I've got the underpass coming up, so I'd better break off before I break up.' On the screen he was breaking up already. 'Wednesday, from the office, twelve thirty. I won't say where we're going, in case Customs descend on you with thumbscrews.'

The doorbell rang as he was coming away from the console. The postie, a gnarled and more than slightly nutty woman in her late sixties who had somehow defied compulsory retirement, glared up the steps, holding out a package. Her peaked cap dripped rain on a small sharp nose. He thanked her, and reached for the package.

'It's all wrong,' she said. 'Federal regulations says a house got to have a letter box measuring thirty by eight centimetres minimum, or else an outside box with an aperture of the same dimensions.'

It was a point she had raised before, and he answered it as patiently. 'That's true. It's also true that houses granted historic status at the date the regulation was brought in are exempt. And all the buildings inside the citadel of Sheaf have that exemption, including this one.'

'Bloody citadel,' she said. 'Bloody Sheaf. Burning it down was the only good idea the bloody French ever had.'

She thrust the package at him and stumped away across the courtyard, splashing through puddles. Michael looked at what he'd been given. It was addressed in block capitals in an unfamiliar hand. There had been reports of cranks to the right of BA reviving that other old terrorist custom, the letter bomb, but there was no reason to think he was a likely target. The date-stamp was Paris, which made the threat even more improbable. He closed the door and tore open the wrapping.

Inside was a DVD; he checked the envelope again but found no covering letter. In the sitting room above him, the wall-clock chimed a half-hour: nine thirty. He needed to allow an hour and three-quarters for Brighton, the roads being what they were, and there might be difficulties with the hospital car park. He didn't relish the thought of arriving even a few minutes later than the time appointed by Sonia Wright. But his curiosity had been roused. He went to the book room, to the muffled accompaniment of Gluck from DD's study, and slipped the disc into the machine. That would be sufficient to establish what it was: watching it could wait till he got back.

Lucy burst smiling on to the screen. 'Love laughs at mail censors as well as locksmiths. Leastways, I hope and trust it does. I won't go into ways and means, but if a black lady weighing one hundred and thirty-five pounds can slip through the mesh, I reckon something this size ought to have a good chance.'

He gazed at her image hungrily. She was wearing a dress he hadn't seen before, of silvery material. She ran her hands down, from neck to thigh.

'How's that for honesty? Some girls may get peaky from love-sickness, but I fill out: three pounds extra since I saw you last. Doesn't mean I don't miss you – doesn't mean I don't worry over you. And it certainly doesn't mean I'm giving up on hauling you over here. I mean to have you. I'm not saying a true Brit like you is going to enjoy turning Yank – not right away, at least – but concentrate on the fringe benefits. And you get to keep your racial identity. You don't have to turn black as well.'

She rattled on, not inhibited by the camera but not playing to it, as Hildy would have done. She talked easily, about everyday things: a meal she had had with an old girlfriend, her cat Luther. Later, after a fractional pause, she was more serious.

'I don't think I told you my maternal grandpop was an evangelist. Took the Baptist word all over Alabama, Georgia and Mississip. He had biceps like a steelworker; when he put the believers under the water they knew for certain they were in the power of the Lord. He converted folks by the score, hundred, thousand probably, to something they had no notion of taking up when they went into his tent. I've never seen myself as wanting that kind of power – to change people's way of looking, make them see things my way. And I still don't, with people that don't matter – strangers. OK, I work in politics and I'm professional at my job, but it's not serious with me. If Isak doesn't get back into the White House, I'll be disappointed, sure, but I'm not going to weep and tear my hair. I won't lose sleep.

'I guess I stand back some, and that even goes for family, much as I love 'em. Brother Joshua's got himself in deep shit lately, with a girl in his partnership. It's going to be a messy divorce. Momma and Poppa are fighting alongside his wife, Tildy. So's my sister. She's sworn she won't speak to Josh again if he goes through with it. She probably means that: we're a strong-minded bunch. I'm not saying I'm neutral – I like Tildy, and the kids, and the girl's high-yaller with the sort of pretty that won't last – but I'm striking no attitudes. It'll sort itself out with no help from me. Or not, as the case may be.

'One reason is, I remember my grandpop got himself into the same sort of trouble, in his day. Baptized this sweet kid who was on vacation from New York, and couldn't stop himself giving her a little post-baptismal attention. She got pregnant, and he had to give up the ministry. They went back to NY, he worked as a street cleaner, and my mother got born. It worked out, the way things do.

'But you and me is something I'm not prepared to leave fate to work out, not while I can do a little working out myself. I want us to be together, and in a place where it's reasonably safe – safe as anywhere can be in a mayhem and murder world – safe for us and those three, four Anglo-piccaninns. The business I'm in, you get to know how things can be fixed, and get to know the fixers and the friends of the fixers. All you have to do is get your honky hunk to the US Embassy in Paris, and I guarantee the rest will follow.

'Yeah, I know about DD, and you're right, he wouldn't transplant here. But you worry too much about him. Sure, he's old, but he's not as dependent on you as you think. Within twenty-four hours of your leaving, the Frods-Hams will whisk him over to Frohsteig, where he'll have his son, and that sexy granddaughter, and *Grossvater* Otto to reminisce with. They can put schnapps in their beer, and sing along to "Lili Marlene".

'What matters is relationships, living relationships not dead ones. DD had his with Granny T. – a great one from what you tell me. All he's doing now is passing time in the waiting room. He doesn't really give a damn about you – sorry if that stings, but it's true. Not you, not anyone – even Hildy's no more than wallpaper in a room he's set to leave. But we do have something going, honey love, and it's worth fighting for. And you ain't a real fighter if you ain't willing to be ruthless to win.

'So what's keeping you? I won't give you a name at the Embassy: mine will be enough. All we have against us is time, and he, believe me, is the most ruthless fighter in the business. Those rumours . . . I still can't spell them out, and it wouldn't help if I did. If you won't come when I call you, I guess threats won't make you. But believe me, that fighter is not on our side, and he shortens by the minute.'

She pursed her lips into a kiss. 'Even in this. Take my love, honey, and bring it back to me. Soon.'

DD intercepted Michael on his way out, displaying a two-day stubble of beard. He claimed his hand shook too badly even for a protector razor, and flatly refused to use the cordless electric Michael had bought for him. It didn't give a clean shave, he said, caressing his stubble. He asked what they were having for supper, and Michael told him Mrs Featherstone from Lookout Street would be bringing something down. DD exploded.

'Mrs fucking Featherstone! That means either hotpot with gristle, or fish pie with skin and bones. I can't stand the woman, and I certainly can't stand the sweet-charity smile that comes with the delivery. The birds can have it, whatever it is. I'll manage with bread and cheese.'

'I'll get something from Brighton Marks & Spencer, if I have time.'

'I'm not blaming you,' DD said fretfully, 'but I get fed up

with all this. I ran across Beau Chambers in the High Street yesterday. Four-course meals in that residential place he's in, and a decent drop of wine with it, he says. He's put on half a stone. He said they might have a vacancy coming up.'

Over the next few days, Michael played Lucy's disc several times, and thought about it in between. The frank assurance of her demand exhilarated him; he was delighted when his own half-framed arguments and excuses collapsed before her cogency and his need. Occasionally he turned on the television. Newscasts were preoccupied with debates in the House of Commons in which some backbenchers bleated ineffectually about loss of sovereignty, while government and opposition front benches united in a show of uneasy reassurance. It was pathetic in its pointlessness.

There was nothing left to win here, he told himself, everything to lose. Graveny, as they were discreetly admitted through a green baize door, was equally dismissive of immediate prospects.

'The trouble is, we like our fetters. Nice solid clank when you wave your arms. And those ankle-chains keep you shuffling on at a steady pace. Who wants to break into a run, anyway?'

The restaurant was anonymous, though the PC-printed menu called it Luke's. It fell into a recognizable category, between official de luxe establishments and the increasing number catering for the increasingly penurious, where for lamb you could confidently read goat. Places like Luke's were ex-directory, word-of-mouth, and cash-only. But lamb was positively lamb, and in this case, as Graveny had promised, lusciously Icelandic. They also served cloud-berries, from the same forbidden island, as a pudding. The wine was French though, a vintage Nuits St Georges, and very good.

Afterwards they had coffee and brandy in an atmosphere wickedly tinged with cigar smoke. It was, all in all, a pleasant oasis in a rapidly spreading desert. There was no reason to presume such oases would not survive, Michael thought, and tried to convince himself it mattered.

They emerged into the cloudy chill of a dingy street, to the cries of rival newsboys. One had a stack of *Standards*, the other of the *London Evening Post*, Euro-funded to compete with its politically less reliable rival. Both boys were shrieking 'Sensation!' but while the *Standard* headline simply read GOVERNMENT FALLS, the *Post*'s, in heavier type, cried TREACHERY!

Graveny bought a *Standard*, and they scanned it together. An early morning meeting of the cabinet had ended in revolt, and the resignation of the Prime Minister. The new government, under the interim control of Joseph Wills-Parson, Minister for Defence, had issued an emergency order withdrawing the United Kingdom from the European Union. All powers and authority that had been conveyed to Europe, from the Single European Act onwards, were consequently rescinded, and re-invested in Parliament, the sole source and repository of British sovereignty.

'Well, I'm buggered!' Graveny marvelled, 'Unbelievable! Somebody's done something.'

Michael pointed to a smaller story in the bottom right-hand corner. It was an account of new ministerial appointments. The list included Helen Rackham, as Home Secretary.

'Haven't they just?'

Ten

It was dark by the time Michael got to Sheaf. There had been chaos at Charing Cross and he had waited two hours for a train. Rumours were rife: in the milling crowd he heard that Irish troops had occupied Anglesey, that there had been a threat to bomb London, that a special train had taken the royal family to the comparative safety of Scotland. That everything emanating from the bland television screen above the station buffet oozed reassurance did nothing to reduce speculation.

There were several unscheduled stops on the way down, one lasting over half an hour, and carriage and corridor were so crowded that it was better to endure the discomfort of a distended bladder than to try to force a way to the lavatory. When they finally reached Ashford, there was an announcement that service would terminate there: trains to stations further south were cancelled until further notice. The link to Sheaf was still operating but almost as crowded as the main-line train had been; it appeared that some people were taking any route out rather than stay in what they saw as a possible target area.

The phone network was out of action, so there was no point attempting to get through to DD. Michael doubted that DD, isolated in his music, would worry about his absence, but he needed to be fed and no replacement for Mrs Featherstone had yet been found. It was a relief when the train pulled in at the station, an even greater relief to find the town relatively deserted and wrapped in its customary evening stillness.

He opened the front door to the further reassurance of a haunting little *air de ballet* by Gretry, which DD had lately become obsessed with. The worry about food, it emerged, had been unnecessary: DD had found cheese and ham in the fridge and somehow concocted his private version of a *croque monsieur*, and had brought up a bottle of claret from the cellar to wash it down. It stood, barely a quarter full, beside the debris in the kitchen. DD had heard the official news from London, but was not much interested. His principal topic was another encounter with his old pal from the nursing home, who had been offering the delights of bridge as a further inducement.

'But you don't play bridge,' Michael said.

'Used to, when I was in the Army. They're short of a fourth, he said, since that old cow Tillie Smythe popped her clogs. I'm off to bed.'

Michael made a sandwich with what was left of the cheese and ate it in front of the television set. The late-night News had finally found something of substance to report. The French guards at Folkestone had defied orders to stand down, and had taken over control of the Tunnel entrance. A protest had been lodged with Brussels, and steps were being taken to rectify the situation.

After a night of fitful sleep, he woke to a distant throb of engines in the southern sky. He went to the window, though without much expectation of seeing anything: lodged as it was halfway up Friars Hill, the house's view was impressive to the north but southwards was limited by the stand of leylandii blocking off the High Street, and by the monastery's pointed roof. Between those two impediments there was only a narrow gap of powder-blue sky, but by chance it was along that channel they emerged: heavy military planes.

The first line was followed by a second, and he heard but could not see others crossing the town. The English Channel lay only a couple of miles south, which meant they must be coming from France. It was a few minutes to the hour, and he switched on his bedside radio. Janice always left it tuned to her favourite station, and he was anticipating having to switch over from a blare of pop music, but a public service announcement was in progress: '. . . take no action and as far as possible remain indoors. Only officially badged vehicles are permitted on motorways, and cars using other roads must carry an authorization, obtainable from local police stations, which will not be issued except in cases establishing an urgent need to travel. We repeat: the government has declared a state of emergency. Stay tuned for further announcements.'

When the news came on, the main item was an overnight statement from Downing Street. In view of the continuing rejection by French troops of orders to evacuate their bridge-head at Folkestone, and the refusal by the European High Commission either to confirm or deny reports that additional troops had been sent through the Tunnel to reinforce this illegal occupation, the British representative at the United Nations had called for an emergency meeting of the Security Council. In addition, the Prime Minister had made a direct appeal to the President of the United States.

The announcer's voice gave way to that of Wills-Parson. He sounded tired.

'We have to assume that other members of the Federation with seats at the United Nations may attempt to block our assertion of national independence, on the grounds that the issue is an internal Federation concern. Meanwhile, this country is under threat of imminent invasion by Federal forces. For that reason, I have requested the President to give us all help possible in our struggle, including military help. Twice in the last century the Americans came to the aid of liberty in Europe. The threat today is at least as great as it was in 1917 and 1941.'

The sound of aircraft, fading away in the north, was suddenly lost in a wild jangle of bells from St Anselm's

Norman tower. Moments later, Michael found DD at the door in his pyjama tops – he refused to wear the trousers.
'So it's on then!'
'On?'
'The invasion. That was what they told us in the Battle of Britain, in 1940. Church bells would mean the Germans had landed. They didn't manage it then, but the buggers don't give up, do they?'

The old man's mad certainty put Michael's own bewilderment in perspective. He said: 'It's not the same, DD. There's nothing to get worried about.'

'They never give up,' DD repeated. 'My dad and I were both in the LDV, before they called it the Home Guard. Patrolled together outside the Post Office in Winchester, kid of sixteen and a bald old sod left over from the first war. God knows why the Post Office: nobody said. With one rifle between us – he let me have that, and the two rounds of ammo, and he carried a pike. Bloody Germans – never give up.'

He was beginning to shiver in the morning's chill. Michael took his arm. 'Let's get your dressing gown on, and I'll make us a mug of tea.'

Sheaf was well provided with bakers, tourists offering a year-round market for rolls and sandwiches and sticky cakes, and there were two in the High Street. At each of them, just before nine o'clock, a queue stretched more than twenty metres from the door. Michael thought the shop at the top of Eagle Street, more out of the way, might be a better prospect, but the queue there was almost as long. He joined it, anyway. A notice in the window read: TWO LOAVES MAX PER PERSON.

A woman ahead of him was explaining about the early morning carillon. Graham Welby, a sidesman at the church whose eccentricity was sometimes indistinguishable from nuttiness, had apparently taken it on himself to revive the ancient alarm signal, and the Rector had been forced to rise from his bed to put a stop to it. There was a pleasantly comic element to this: the Rector had not long since taken as a bride a comely young woman who had come to Sheaf as his curate, and popular report held that he had been in a swoon of sexual ecstasy ever since.

The atmosphere among the queuers was generally one more of curiosity than alarm. He heard some anti-Euro sentiments voiced, but they were matched by others suggesting Wills-Parson had put himself out on a limb which would not bear him for long. There seemed to be general agreement that the call for American intervention was as crackpot as Welby's little fling with the bells. But there was no great sense of indignation. There was some speculation as to where the aircraft had been heading, but the principal conclusion was that, whatever their destination, it was bound to be a long way from Sheaf.

Re-entering the house through the garden, Michael noted that the magnolia had shed most of its remaining yellow-stained blossoms, but the azaleas were still burning brightly and the roses were pregnant with bud, some already in flower. On his way to the kitchen to put away the loaves, his eye was caught, through the hall window, by another unexpected flash of colour. He set the bread down on the painted chest, and went to investigate.

The car parked beside his own soberly blue Rover was a Citroen, in the flaming pink metallic paint which, together with bright green hub-caps, had been a feature of last year's range re-launch. Additionally, it was bedizened with eye-wrenching panels of white, boldly lettered in pillar-box red. The most prominent, taking up almost the whole of the nearside front door panel, proclaimed SODALITAS CAROLINGIANA, which closer inspection revealed to be repeated on the offside. The bonnet carried a similarly blatant message: PRESIDENT – SHEAF CIRCLE. There were also a couple of large stickers: EUROPE IS THE

FUTURE and FORWARD WITH THE CAROLINGIANS!
Their badge, a ring of big blue stars firmly enclosing a
miniature Union flag, was featured at the top of both front
and rear windscreens.

Michael was still studying the display when Souter came
into the courtyard. His appearance had been transformed by
a royal blue jacket with the Carolingian badge on the breast
pocket, and a gold-braided peaked cap.

He looked purposefully at Michael. 'You're back. Good.
I wanted to have a word. I tried your bell, but there was
no reply.'

Michael nodded. 'I've been getting some bread in.'

Souter looked cross. 'There's been hoarding.'

'I wouldn't call two loaves a hoard.'

'Not by you, necessarily. Anyway, we're getting the situation under control. I need to talk to you about parking.'

Michael hesitated before responding. Those privileged
to enjoy parking space inside the citadel defended it with
paranoid intensity: favours granted on a temporary basis
were not always easy to retrieve. Apart from the garage
adjacent to his shoebox house on Sheaf Hill, Souter had
some parking near his office which needed to be juggled
between partners and special clients. Presumably whatever
game he was playing with his Carolingians required, or
made him think he required, a supplement to that. And
the Georgian House courtyard was certainly underused
these days.

He said, warily: 'We could let you use part of this. But
if we get an influx of family . . .'

Sooter produced a legal-length document from inside
his jacket. It looked like a product of his office printer,
though the heading was not the familiar Barnes, Dickson
& Turnbull, but Sodalitas Carolingiana.

'I'll leave this with you. Putting it briefly, this courtyard
has been requisitioned as a car park by the Carolingian
administration in Sheaf.'

'The what?'

Earnestly, Souter explained: 'This is an emergency matter, and the emergency probably won't last long. Meanwhile I'm unofficially authorizing you to keep your own car here, at least for the present. If you have any problem with junior officials, refer them to me. We're working out of the Town Hall, incidentally.'

Michael wondered if, in a variant of Welby's campanological fit, the man had gone mad: the uniform and the technicolour car, with its messages and stickers and badges, hinted at it.

'Junior officials . . . ? Did you say Carolingian administration in Sheaf?' Souter nodded agreement. 'What does that mean, precisely?'

Souter brought his hands together, not quite rubbing them but with a positive squeeze of pleasure. 'Exactly what it says. I gather you missed the announcement. The Sodalitas has taken over local administration not – just here, but throughout the country.'

Mad or not, caution seemed indicated. Michael asked mildly: 'On whose authority would that be? The government's?'

'If you're referring to that treacherous lunatic, Wills-Parson, certainly not. Our authority is directly from the Federal High Commission.' He advanced and put a hand on Michael's arm. 'The trouble with people like you, Michael, is that you go with the tide. I suppose you can put up some sort of case for that, a selfish one, as long as you can be sure you know the way the tide will run. All this Little England stuff that's made the headlines over the past year . . . serious people understood that even though it was ridiculous it had to be taken seriously, to make sure it stayed ridiculous. Now the tide's on the turn, but we needed to be ready in advance, ready to take advantage of it.

'Right now the main function of the Sodalitas is as an arm of the Federation, defending it against subversion. That's very important, but there's more to it than that, Michael, much more. Once we've put things to rights here, we shall move on to revolutionize Europe as a whole. We're not going with a tide – we're creating one.'

Gait, Michael reflected, watching Souter's departure up Friars Hill, was always a giveaway: he might parade like a peacock but he walked like a budgerigar. Back in the house, he switched on the television but left it while he saw to things, like plant watering, which Janice could never remember to do. Anna, at least, had missed all this. He wasn't sure whether the play in progress was tragedy or farce, but if it had happened six months ago she would have been frantic over the risk it entailed for Adam. For both of them it was peace now, all risks ended.

He got back to the book room to find a news broadcast on. The face of the announcer was unfamiliar, but he had a jacket like Souter's. He was reiterating Souter's statement, that civil and military authority throughout the United Kingdom had been assumed by the Federal High Commissioner in London, acting for the European High Commission. Order was being re-established, and for the time being would be locally administered by the appropriate branches of the Sodalitas Carolingiana. Parliament had been suspended, and the former Prime Minister, Joseph Wills-Parson, placed under arrest in protective custody.

That was that, then. He wondered what he could give DD for lunch.

In the afternoon, while DD napped, Michael sampled television and radio. Everything seemed back to normal. Television offered soccer, a quiz show, a true-life drama and a sitcom re-run, with news bulletins that were uninformative but unalarming. The same atmosphere prevailed on radio, though he did find one station jammed into unintelligibility. He tried calling Lucy but got no joy: the network must be down still.

The town, when he went up on a quick shopping trip, also seemed normal, and there were no queues at the bread shops. He saw blue-jacketed Carolingians, but even with Heckler-Kochs they did not present a particularly disturbing feature – more a tawdry spectacle laid on for tourists; like the Town Crier in his scarlet waistcoat, or the Morris dancers with their staves and furbelows. St Anselm's clock struck the hour, shortly followed by the distant chug of the Sheaf Flyer pulling out of the station. Sheaf was at peace.

He got back, though, to find DD up, and in some agitation. He was in the hall, talking to a lad in his teens, a Carolingian who seemed partly belligerent, partly overawed by the encounter.

DD said: 'It's some bloody nonsense about wanting me to report to some Commandant. That's the Germans again, isn't it?'

The boy looked at Michael with relief. 'Mr Frodsham, sir? It's you the Commandant wants.'

'The Commandant – that will be Mr Souter?' The boy nodded. 'Did he say what he wants me for?'

'No, sir. Just you're to report to him, at the Town Hall.'

'I see. Thanks for letting me know.'

'Now, sir. I'm to bring you, right away.'

The belligerence was verging on desperation; he seemed near weeping.

'Bloody Germans!' DD said. 'I'll come with you.'

'No. Go and listen to them instead: Bach, Buxtehude . . . It won't be anything important, car parking probably.'

'Something to do with that tart's wagon sitting outside our front door? I'll come with you. I want the nauseating thing gone.'

Michael succeeded in soothing him and sending him grumbling upstairs before accompanying the boy up the hill. He doubted his own interpretation of the summons, and wondered what actually lay behind it. The possibility that

Adam's BA connection might, under present circumstances, have come up for re-investigation was a mildly disturbing one. He told himself he had been personally cleared by Security, but security services, as he well knew, were many-headed beasts.

It might, on the other hand, be something as simple as Souter inventing a reason for getting him along just to observe him revelling in the joy of his office and his new peaked cap. His reception tended to support that. Souter wasn't wearing the cap, but it was carelessly conspicuous on the edge of the Mayor's desk, behind which he sat hunched in a Victorian swivel-chair. There was a map of England on the wall, studded cryptically with coloured pins, and an impressive-looking intercom system beside the desk. At a suitably respectful distance from the great man, a blue-jacketed male secretary sat in front of keyboard and plasma screen.

Souter was busy with a telephone call; he nodded acknowledgement of Michael's arrival and carried on. It seemed to be a jurisdictional problem: the village of Nutarge, ten miles away, came under Sheaf in Souter's view but had been claimed by Ashford. Since Ashford was a much more important centre, one would expect the Commandant there to carry more clout, and Michael could not help being impressed by the firm, indeed truculent manner in which Souter fought his corner. He ended his conversation abruptly with the comment that he had sent a detachment to set up a command post in the Nutarge Village Hall, and had reported to London to that effect. Turning to Michael, he said: 'Teething troubles. Like the phone network: they say it's coming back on soon, but soon may not be today, or even tomorrow. Meanwhile, it's back to the old land line. That's why I had you paged. You're wanted, from Germany. I can get you through from here.' He clicked fingers at the secretary. 'Get the Frohsteig number for Mr Frodsham.'

The call came through surprisingly quickly. Within minutes Michael was handed the telephone. It was Dieter at the other end.

'Michael? You are all right?'

Souter was studying a map, under a transparent plastic cover decorated with coloured lines and stars and arrows. Michael said: 'Yes. We're both fine. Things are pretty quiet down here.'

'Good.' Dieter hesitated. Without a screen one missed the subtleties of facial expression, but nuances of voice became more obvious. Not good news, Michael felt. 'Your father . . .'

'What about him – what's happened?'

'I am sure it will not be serious. A heart attack. He is being well cared for, I assure you.'

'Has he been hospitalized?'

'Indeed, yes. In Nuernberg we have the best cardiac unit in Germany.'

'When did he have it, the attack?'

'It was in the night. I have tried to make contact sooner, but the way things have been . . . But I have spoken with his physician in the last hour. His condition is stable.'

'Is he conscious?'

'No, but that is because they prescribe total sedation – on life support, you understand. But you will wish to come, of course.'

He felt a tightness in his own chest. 'If I possibly can.'

'I am sure it is possible. It is fortunate Sheaf is in the occupied territory. Yet not a good idea for DD, perhaps.'

'No. I think not.'

'I spoke with Commandant Souter, earlier. It is better I speak with him again. I believe he will help.'

Souter was in fact extremely helpful. Michael heard him tell Dieter that Mr Frodsham's journey would be given top priority, and every facility that might be required. When they had finished, he turned to Michael: 'How long will you need to pack?'

'Half an hour. But I'll have to make arrangements for my grandfather.'

'Leave that to me.'

'He'd been thinking of trying out Mrs Bennett's Sunnyhill; but I'm not sure whether they have a vacancy, or if they could take him at such short notice.'

'I said: leave it to me. I'll deal with Mrs Bennett.' He checked the time. 'A car will come round for you at seventeen thirty.'

Something had been nagging in his mind. 'Dieter – my uncle – said something about it being fortunate Sheaf was in occupied territory. His English isn't perfect, but it's pretty good. It seemed an odd way of putting things.'

The glow of command in Sooter's face took on a more characteristically peevish aspect. He said, after a pause: 'There's a bit of trouble still, in the north.'

'What sort of trouble?'

'Resistance. It's meaningless, pointless. And illegitimate, of course. Quite apart from sovereignty of all former national states being vested in the Federation, a bauble doesn't justify anything. The woman's mad.'

'Woman?'

'Rackham. She got away when Wills-Parson was pulled in, and took the Mace with her.'

Johann met him at Nuremberg station. Another cold snap had set in, and the scar on his right cheek was bright, raw looking. He pulled Michael into an embrace.

'How is he?' Michael asked.

'Fine.' Michael freed himself to look into his step-brother's eyes; they were direct as ever. 'No, really fine. As well as anyone can be who's had a massive heart attack. He's stable, and the prognosis is excellent.'

Heinrich had the stretch Mercedes immediately outside,

taking up two places in a crowded taxi rank. As they purred away, Johann said: 'You've made good time.'

'It went very smoothly. Dieter's is a name to conjure with.'

Johann laughed. 'He has his uses! You'll be getting accustomed to that train journey. Just as well you didn't try to make a plane. They say Heathrow's re-opening, but God knows when. How's DD?'

'Delighted with life. Dieter's man in Sheaf got him fixed up in a nursing home where he has pals. I said I had to go to London for a few days, but I don't think he was listening. I didn't say anything about Father.'

'I'm glad. Adam, Anna . . . now this. It's been a fairly bloody year.'

'Yes, it has. You say Heathrow's still closed? So things haven't settled down yet. Exactly what is happening? Someone on the train was talking about an American landing, but that's obviously just another idiot rumour.'

'I'm afraid not.'

'You're not saying they responded to Wills-Parson's appeal? But they couldn't – there wasn't time. He wasn't in office much more than twenty-four hours.'

'Basically, it's a cock-up. You know they've had that aircraft carrier, the *Richard Nixon*, sitting off the west coast of Ireland? Aronheimer used it to send in a detachment of marines. He said it was simply to protect United States citizens at the American University in Liverpool. There'd been fighting in that area and he wanted to evacuate them. But the British Liberation Army put out a claim that the operation was in support of their revolt against the Federation.

'It's difficult to work out just what happened. Federal airborne troops had been sent north to deal with the Liverpool situation. There's a story that the Americans picked up their people, and were then prevented from getting away by the BLA. Whether or not that's true, they somehow got into a scrap with our lot. There were casualties, on both sides.

As things stand, the Americans are surrounded, inside the University grounds. The situation's highly tricky, as you can imagine.'

'Yes, I can imagine.'

He thought of Lucy. This wasn't anything she could have been involved in, or even known about in advance; but the repercussions were bound to affect her, affect them both. If it led to war . . . But he couldn't believe that. The whole business was too absurd . . .

Johann's mind had been working along the same lines. He said: 'I wouldn't worry about it. No one is looking for trouble. We certainly don't want it, with the British situation still needing to be cleared up. And I'm sure the Americans will be aiming for a way out of a mess they never wanted to get into in the first place.'

The Mercedes entered the ornamental gates of the Ost-Bavarisches Hospital and passed three *Parken Strengst Verboten* signs before depositing them at the front door. As they got out, Michael wryly compared the building's magnificence with the hospitals he was used to in England. The contrast was further underlined as a soaring walkway took them through space to the coronary care unit. Even the nurses' uniforms were better, he thought, or at least more impressively starched.

The figure in the bed, connected to drip and monitoring equipment, was motionless. Someone rose from the chair beside the bed as they came in. His surprise at seeing her surprised him; of course she would be here, she was his father's child too, and a closer one. Hildy opened her arms.

'Mikey! It's so good to see you.'

She drove the Audi Sport very fast, but also very well. They took a route between low hills, green with early summer, through several small villages to a still smaller one. Pritzendorf consisted of a few shops on three sides of a square boasting a nineteenth-century fountain presided over by a Rubensesque nymph, and was surrounded by substantial country houses dotted among woods and meadows. A couple of hundred metres beyond the village, Hildy swung expertly into and up a precipitously steep drive leading to a hilltop where a towered villa perched.

This had been entirely her idea, and he had demurred when she first proposed it. He told her he had come to Nuremberg solely on account of their father, but she overrode him firmly.

'Me, also. But we have seen him, and know he is getting the best care. His heart mends, and will mend no better if we sit all day beside his bed. We can't even talk to him.'

'If I can do no good here, I probably should be getting back to DD.'

'DD is fine. Dieter keeps check on that. Johann has been told Papa may be well enough to be taken out of sedation in a couple of days. You cannot go back to England sooner.'

His real reluctance, he knew, was at a deeper level. He did not want to think about Stern, or about whatever clinical error might have been responsible for Anna's death. It would not bring her back. There might not, in any case, be anything to it beyond the wild guesses of an emotionally unbalanced young man. Hildy herself had suggested he had been obsessed with Stern: that he had contrived to worm his way into Stern's home bore that out.

But she had been determined to get him out to the house where Berthold Gegener still lived with Stern's widow and two daughters. A further objection, that the widow might be distressed by a visit so soon after her husband's suicide, was confidently dismissed.

'She was OK when I spoke with her. Of course, we will not discuss this other matter in front of her. I said I would come to offer condolence, and that pleased her. And there is no reason my brother should not come with me. I don't know if she suspects it was because of Anna he killed himself, but anyway it is not wrong that you show good will.'

Frau Stern was younger than he'd expected, at least fifteen years her husband's junior, and though her hair was dark brown rather than flaxen, she was rosy-cheeked and altogether Germanic in appearance. He liked the new slant that put on Stern's reason for returning from Israel. Relationships, even – especially – conventionally romantic ones, provided a sounder basis for action than Jungian illusions. The girls were healthy fruits of the genetic mix: Trudi, a lively six-year-old, was a slim Semitic maiden, Hannah a sober Anglo-Saxon toddler, very like her mother.

They were given cakes and lemonade. The cake was practically identical to the one Michael had eaten at the Brosser Clinic, presumably also made from the recipe handed down by Stern's grandmother. Frau Stern apologized for having no alcoholic drink to offer; it had been a principle of Julius to have none in the house. They assured her apology was unnecessary, and sincerely praised the home-made lemonade.

Berthold Gegener had joined them. Michael recognized him from the Christmas party: thin, white, awkwardly put together and prematurely balding. He had been working in his room, he said, but volunteered no details. He seemed ill at ease, but this was plainly not through any lack of closeness to his adopted family. Trudi chattered to him like an older brother, and while his responses were not voluble, there could be no doubt of his fondness for them all.

No mention was made of Anna, or the Clinic, and Michael wondered how Hildy was going to manage the more specific interview she had in mind. It would suit him personally if she were frustrated. But she managed it very well, choosing the right moment to offer Frau Stern help in clearing dishes, and wondering, when she received the expected refusal, if Berthold could show them the garden; of which she knew Dr Stern had been very proud.

The girls came with them. Hildy was exercising her wiles on Gegener, but he seemed unresponsive. Michael wondered if he now regretted the letter which, he must know, had brought them here. Once the immediate shock of Stern's death was over he might have perceived his reaction as excessive.

The house stood on a knoll, with terraces going down to a kitchen garden on their left, level lawn and swimming pool to the right. All was fastidiously neat and well maintained. Further off the ground rose again, part orchard, part paddock, to a higher hill topped with pines. They were more than a hundred metres from the house when Hildy said: 'My cigarettes – I am so careless.' She ruffled the hair of the older child. *'Trudi, willst du mir meine Zigaretten bringen, bitte? Sollst auf dem Tafel finden – in kleine schwarze Kiste.'*

The child said reprovingly: *'In der Haus' ist Rauchen ganz verboten.'*

'Aber hier sind wir nicht zu Hause.' She smiled at Trudi irresistibly. *'Du bist ein' Engel.'*

As Trudi ran towards the house, she said: 'Now you can tell us, Berthold.' When he did not reply, she added gently: 'We do not try to blame Dr Stern. Whatever it was, he has paid for it. He chose the payment when he killed himself.'

Gegener turned to look her in the face. His own was twisted in either pain or anger. 'He did not kill himself!'

It was warmer here than it had been in Nuremberg. Butterflies danced nearby, and Hannah went off in pursuit. Hildy said: 'Berthold, I understand your affection for him . . .'

He spoke again, stumbling over the words. 'I found the journal, in which he wrote daily. It was not in his computer, but I found the *Abdruckscheibe* – the copy disk. There was something wrong in the Total programme of your sister. Something very bad – he did not say what. *"Allzu schrecklich für schreiben,"* he said – too terrible to write.'

'He called me in England,' Michael said. 'He was distressed, but he said nothing like that.'

'*Allzu schrecklich für schreiben.* Or was it from fear he could not write it down? But I know he asked you to come to the Clinic. He wrote that also.'

Michael saw again the agonized face on the screen, but still he tried to rationalize it away. 'He was obviously terribly upset. Maybe unhinged – capable of anything. Even of killing himself to put an end to his misery.'

'With a lethal injection of morphine?'

'If that's what killed him.'

Gegener stared at Michael, with bitterness. 'It is what killed him. That is certain. I saw a copy of the autopsy report. A lethal injection into the main artery of his left wrist. That was surely a remarkable feat of dexterity – by a left-handed man.'

Sitting up in bed, John Frodsham looked pale but not especially unwell. He gestured towards the enormous basket of fruit dwarfing the bedside table.

'Help me out, Mike. Maria-Mercedes will do a check on how much I've eaten when she comes in this evening. She's committed to generosity, but despises waste. At least have a kumquat or two. I never could stand them.'

'How are you feeling today?'

'Fine. They're very pleased with me. I'm to stay in till the weekend while they do a few more tests, but after that I'm on indefinite parole. MM's taking on a new cook, for the special diet, and buying me an exercise machine to sit beside her own. His 'n' hers exercisers – how's that for togetherness?'

His father had never, thankfully, put on a show of uxoriousness, but neither had he ever criticized his second wife; the acerbic note was new. Michael had a sense of barriers lowered. His father went on: 'I'm glad you came, but we mustn't keep you over here. You ought to be back in England, especially the way things are. Did you hear about the Americans?' Michael shook his head. 'It was in

the latest news bulletin. They've agreed to the Federation's
conditions for evacuation of their troops and civilians. The
marines aren't required to surrender arms, but will accept
supervision by Federal troops – running a moral gauntlet,
you might say, and the television crews will make the most
of it. Aronheimer has also agreed to support the Federation's
resolution in the United Nations, reiterating the principle of
no interference in internal affairs and accepting the Federal
High Commission as the only legitimate government of the
United Kingdom. I would say that just about kisses goodbye
to his chances of re-election in November, wouldn't you?
Do you think it's likely to affect your Lucy much?'

'I don't know.'

'I liked her.'

'Yes.'

'I've been wondering –' he tapped his chest – 'about this.
Doesn't have to be stress-related, of course. Infarctions
happen. I thought I might have one that day at Twickenham,
when you creamed the French.'

'With the help of the rest of the England fifteen.'

'Yes. Yes indeed. Sheer joy, that particular stress. But
I've not been liking what's been happening lately. Worry
into guilt, and guilt back into more worry. It just goes on.'

'Why guilt?'

'That's a never-ending why, isn't it? And family and
country get mixed up. Family guilts are easier to label: I
left two of you behind. I'd rather have taken you with me,
but you were old enough to make a choice. Respecting that
didn't remove the guilt though – how could it? Like that
fiasco at Christmas: Granny T. dead, so I try to bring Sheaf
to Frohsteig.'

'It wasn't a fiasco.'

'It was for me. And then there's the other guilt. Country.
Did you ever come across that bit by E. M. Forster – that if
he had to choose between betraying a friend or his country,
he hoped he'd betray the country? Bad, and mad. Or stupid.

Because country isn't an abstract, it's a sum of things. Things, and people. Parents, children, the friends you had at school . . . Not just DD, Granny T., you, Anna – but the woman who kept the sweetshop when I was five, that wonderful crippled lady with a body twisted from birth, who smiled whenever I met her in the High Street . . . hundreds of people, thousands.'

He took a grape out of the basket and stared at it. 'When I was little we had a neighbour who had a greenhouse with a Cannon Hall vine. It must be forty years since I tasted one. There have been gains to go with the guilt – of course there have. Two children I loved and left, two more since then. I wouldn't have wanted a world they weren't part of. But I won't pretend I don't ache a bit. Do you know what bothers me most?'

Michael shook his head.

'Growing old in a country where I can't swear in my own language, and be properly understood.'

'You could come back. Johann and Hildy are a lot more grown up than we were. Anyway, I sometimes think Johann sounds more English than I do, and Hildy seems to be permanently in London nowadays.'

'No. I can't do that. Things go past. But you should go back. You can see I'm all right.'

'I will, eventually.'

'Go now. There's DD to consider.'

'He's fine.' Michael drew a deep breath, not knowing why. 'I still have something to do here.'

207

Eleven

'What do you think?' Dieter asked.

'It's impressive.'

'Perhaps architecturally a little too severe for a castle of dreams? Maybe something like Neuschwanstein would look better. But I fear it would be less good for working conditions. Dreams do not require things like heating or air conditioning, but those who make them do. We take such matters seriously.'

The headquarters of Frohsteig Wissenschaftliches Verkehrs was sited conveniently on the Frohsteig estate. A pine-crested ridge concealed it from the Schloss, but twenty minutes' brisk walking brought it into view, and on this fine May morning that was what Dieter had suggested. The Mercedes would have taken almost as long, by the narrow road that twisted and turned round the side of the hill.

It was Hildy who had proposed the expedition, but Dieter had been quick to welcome the idea. He said to Michael: 'You have never visited our working centre? Johann has never shown you?'

Michael shook his head. 'We walked to the top of the ridge once, and I saw it from a distance. There's never really been time on a short visit.'

'And on this visit you have longer. Good, if not for a happy reason. But you are reassured about your father?'

'I had a word with his consultant. He said things were looking well.'

'And you will not find a better cardiologist in the world

208

anywhere. You must excuse our German prides, Michael. We have come late to nationhood – we achieved it not long before nations, in Europe, ceased to matter. But as a race we are old. We boast, it is true, but we try our best to set correct standards for the boasting. Anyway, what is important is you are content he is in good hands.'

This valley was broader and flatter than the one from which they had come, and had been cleared of all but ornamental vegetation. The complex itself was oval in shape, about two kilometres in length and a third of that across, surrounded by a ring road which offered access at four equidistant points, and was itself accessed through an approach road on the far side. From where they stood, it was possible to walk directly into it, through flowering meadows. Dieter's young black Labrador, George, ran ahead of them, occasionally stopping to look back with twitching impatience.

The actual buildings were of various shapes and sizes, successfully avoiding any monotonous uniformity; even the formal gardens which separated them offered variety as well as neatness. The gardens included a multiplicity of streams and pools, plainly artificial but contriving to look individual, as did the occasional piazza and the bridges and footbridges crossing the streams. When Michael made an approving comment, Dieter nodded satisfaction. Mies van Gebhardt, the industrial architect responsible for overall layout, had, he told them, spent a year studying garden complexes in China before making his first sketch.

They reached the ring road and crossed it by an underpass, spotlessly clean and with discreet lighting to illuminate pale green ceramic tiles underfoot, and mosaics of Chinese landscapes on the walls. Their voices induced a faint, tranquil echo.

As they came up the exit ramp and found themselves only a few metres from the nearest building, Michael said: 'I'm a bit surprised by the lack of security. The hospitals I visit in England have three- or four-metre electrified fences.'

'But what do we have to fear,' Dieter asked, 'here in this quiet land?'

'Industrial espionage? I seem to have heard reports of foreign spy teams on the loose in Europe. And you do claim to have the most highly developed technology in Virtual.'

'In Virtual, certainly. In Total even more, I would say, since we have achieved the direct cortical input. But we trust our American friends, and our Japanese friends and our Israeli friends. I am joking, you understand. We have protection, more subtle than electric fences and also more effective. We use electronic surveillance. From the top of the ridge, and still now, we are watched; and not by human eyes that can be distracted or nod into sleep. Our invisible watchmen scan perimeter and interior without ceasing, and alert guards if they detect a movement not programmed as acceptable – they will not cry wolf for a rabbit, or a deer even.

'Aesthetically better, would you agree? Psychologically also. Our technicians are happier that no barriers exist. The only exception is in the clinical application area, and that is for protection of the patients.'

He pointed to their right, in explanation. They had come through to one of the transverse roads. Several hundred metres along in that direction, the way was blocked by a checkpoint, guarding a gap in a fence. Beyond the fence stood buildings resembling the wards in the Brosser Clinic.

'The vagrants?' Hildy asked.

'You know of them?' He seemed surprised.

'Johann said something. Not much. Why do they need to be protected?'

Michael echoed her: 'Vagrants?'

Dieter shrugged. '*Vagabunden*. It is a term that is used. Some may indeed be such, but being without home explains more. Living in the streets, in holes in the ground – like animals, except animals look after themselves better. Without home, without aim, without hope. Except the hope of drugs, which is no hope. Some of them can be persuaded to give up the destructive dreams from drugs in return for the therapeutic dreams of Total. But in early days of treatment sometimes they are confused, deranged. There were cases of patients waking and wandering, and doing damage – to valuable equipment and also to themselves. It is chiefly from themselves they are protected.'

George, who had run ahead again, came tail-wagging back to a brief whistle from Dieter. His lead was put on and secured to a ring by the door of one of the buildings. Michael wondered if that, and indeed the dog's presence here, was in fact a status symbol. There had been no sign of other animals; the Labrador might well be an exception underlining a hygienic rule.

This building, unlike others they had passed, was windowless, semi-circular in section, and some twenty metres wide by fifty long. The rooms on either side of a central corridor were of uniform configuration but varied in size; Michael noted that the ceilings were grooved at intervals, so that partitioning walls could be slotted in and out as required.

Dieter pushed a door that swung easily and silently inwards. 'Here our authenticators work. Authentication is the *Grund*, the founding stone, for Total. The grass under the dreamer's feet must look like grass, and feel like grass, and smell like grass – grass maybe with sun and wind on it after rain. The ring on a beloved's finger must be genuine, its stone showing the gleam of diamond, not paste. It is a great skill, in truth an art, requiring imagination but also dedication to the littlest details, to perfection.

'Such dedication demands something better than laboratory conditions in which to work – white walls, bright lights, white uniforms. Here the authenticators choose what lighting suits their mood: the mood they are creating. It is

211

for them to select and control. Temperature and humidity also.'

They were standing just inside a room whose walls glowed in varying intensities of rose. The air was cool and fresh and faintly flower-fragrant. A helmeted woman, wearing something like a sari, manipulated with flying fingers the controls of a multi-screen console which dwarfed her. She did not turn round. Hildy whispered: 'Might we distract her?'

'There is no risk of that.' Dieter did not lower his voice. 'Environmental conditions are of importance as a background, but when working an authenticator is beyond distraction. Her mind concerns itself only with the scenes before her, with the new world she creates from the innumerable images to which the console gives her access. She is a little god.'

When they came out, George barked in excitement and relief. Releasing him from the hitching ring, Dieter cut him short with '*Schweige!*' but appeared dissatisfied with the response. He wagged a threatening finger. 'To be hesitant to a command is to be disobedient. And disobedience in a dog requires severe penalty, death even. *Also, sterbe.*' The Labrador dropped to lie at his feet, eyes closed and motionless. 'That is better. So, *lebe wieder.*' He smiled at Michael, as George jumped up, panting and wagging. 'It is a game we play. Now I will take you to meet a major god – a goddess.'

The building at the heart of the complex was a Chinese-style pavilion, of dark wood faced with red panels decorated with golden dragons. These chased one another's tails and breathed fire, but the chasing was more that of kittens at play than predators, and the crimson fire did not look as if it would singe a leaf. The pavilion was abutted by a veranda set with low tables and stools, and bird and animal sculptures. The corner supports were of bamboo, but immensely thick. It could be a veneer, Michael thought, over a core of steel.

Presumably their approach had been monitored by the computers. As they reached the steps giving access to the veranda, a figure emerged from inside. Dieter held his arms out, and was greeted with an embrace.

'Gundula, always it is good to see you. Hildy, my niece, you have already met.'

It would be difficult to guess her age: perhaps forty, but with a few years leeway on either side. Her chestnut hair was either natural or dyed with great discretion, and fell thickly and simply. Like Maria-Mercedes, her features showed a classical beauty, but without the cold stillness. Her smile was very warm. She wore a golden brown dress, if not silk then something very like it; simple again, but in classic lines accentuating an attractive figure. She offered Hildy a hand.

'Once or twice, I think, at parties.'

'It is not easy to persuade Gundula to attend social occasions. She is not a butterfly like you, Hildy. And this is my English . . . *Neffe?* Michael Frods-Ham, a sportsman of distinction.'

'Nephew. Yes, I know.' Her soft hand pressed Michael's firmly, and lingered. 'The rugby player who defeated the French – at Twickenham, not Waterloo. A scrum-half, but taller than most.'

Her English was excellent and almost accentless. Dieter said: 'I am always amazed by the wideness of your knowledge, Gundula, yet still surprised it includes rugby. I have not heard of you as a watcher of sports.'

'Sport is a major field in Virtual.' She looked at Michael, smiling. 'And while for German clients rugby is less important than soccer or athletics or tennis – than basketball even – it comes into consideration. You are eternal in our archives.'

'And almost everything in the archives is also in Gundula's memory,' Dieter said. 'An astonishing comprehension. And astonishingly accessible. She retrieves better than any database.'

213

'It is nothing,' she said. 'A knack, unimportant. What has Dieter shown you, and what would you like to see?'

'He showed us one of your authenticators at work,' Michael said. 'Impressive, but it's well beyond my grasp.'

Gundula nodded. 'High skills to an outsider are much like magic. And not all forms of magic are interesting to view. The authenticator builds worlds, but building signifies nothing to a spectator. It is not like watching a potter at the wheel. And nothing, certainly, like seeing a rugby player score a try. Perhaps there is something else I can show you?'

'The vagabonds,' Hildy said. Gundula turned to her. 'Is it possible to visit the Total wards?'

'Yes, of course.'

There had been an edge to Hildy's voice. Michael registered her dislike of the other woman, without understanding why. He felt Gundula had registered it also, though she gave no sign.

'We can do that right away.' Gundula stooped to pat the Labrador, who licked her hand. 'But we will not take George with us, I think. Although he is the essence of amiability, there is sometimes confusion when a patient emerges from Total, and we will not risk increasing that. However harmless, dog is a threatening image.'

The guard at the entrance wore an unmilitary light-blue uniform and did not carry a Heckler-Koch, though a stun pistol was holstered on his belt. He waved them through with a smart salute. Inside, the nursing staff were dressed like nuns, and Michael asked if they were members of a religious order.

Gundula shook her head. 'Again, a question of atmosphere. Our psychologists advise that the nun's habit is reassuring to the disturbed.'

There were two wards. Conditions, though far less luxurious than in the Brosser Clinic, were very much better than Johann's description of the Warsaw set-up. There was ample room between beds, and each had a locker and chair beside it. The cocoons were standard, and the figures inside them slept as peacefully. Two cocoons were open, and empty. There were pictures on the walls, abstracts in unchallenging pastel shades of colour; and flowers.

At the far end, the ward gave access to a room where there were easy chairs, and windows looking out on wooded slopes. The two patients temporarily out of Total sat there, with glasses of orange juice in front of them. They wore yellow robes and thonged slippers; they looked dazed, but not unhappy. Hildy spoke to them in German, asking how they were, and they answered in slow voices, hesitant but untroubled. One of the nun-figures came with a pitcher to replenish the glasses, and they thanked her politely.

When they left, Dieter drew in a deep breath. 'They would be better with fresh air and sunshine, but that is not at the moment in their case practical. What they have is better than drugs, violence, sickness, degradation. That is what always must be remembered. And now I think we go back. George will be impatient.'

It was Hildy who insisted on tennis. They hadn't played together since she was a schoolgirl, when he had been obliged to work hard at letting her win a few consolation games, and she surprised him, not only with her skill, but also with the strength in her slender arms. Her serves were low and powerful, her returns stingingly accurate. Michael did win both sets, but they were close run. After showering they lay by the pool, the sun's rays softened but scarcely dimmed by the UV blocker net floating between its support poles, high against the blue.

She said: 'I do not like her.'

'I noticed that.' He paused. 'You didn't like Lucy either, did you?'

She twisted round to stare at him indignantly. 'You think I do not like her because of you? Because she held your hand

215

too long on greeting, and tenderly again on parting? What pompous arrogance!'

'She kissed Dieter, and I didn't think you cared a lot for that. She is a woman who likes men, and shows it. What we English call a womanly woman, which I suspect could be what ruffles you. Birds in their little nests may agree, but that doesn't apply to coquettes.'

'Would you call this male observation? How can men observe anything, when they are so blind? Not to women's bodies, of course – their eyes gorge there – but to everything else, except the smile of invitation. I cannot help despising them for that.'

'Any more than you can help exercising the smile?'

'Yes,' she said restlessly. 'I can despise myself also, doing something that is so easy. Playing a part for Virtual is better. They see your face, but you do not see theirs. But this is nothing to do with Gundula. I just do not like or trust her.'

'Yet Dieter plainly does. May that not be the trouble?'

She said, angrily: 'It has nothing to do with you or Dieter! I think she is bad, evil maybe. I did not like any of it. Those poor old men thanking the *ersatz-Nonne* for their fruit juice . . . and the others lying in their plastic cabinets . . . There is a big difference between Virtual and Total, I think.'

'For whatever reason, you're being emotional about it. I don't know a hospital ward in England as well organized as the one we saw. Or as restful. Perhaps we've both been over-emotional. Berthold could have got it wrong.'

'Wrong that Stern found something – and that he was killed because of it, not a suicide?'

'You have to admit Berthold is a very odd character.'

'If he is odd, what is Gundula? But she flatters you.'

'I'd have thought Berthold's worshipful attitude at the Christmas party was pretty flattering, too.'

They went on wrangling, on Michael's part not unenjoyably. Gegener's tense white face and tortuous suspicions seemed a long way off. The sun was warm, the scene relaxing, his half-sister a pretty, lively young woman who no longer represented a threat. Lucy was his security, assured though remote. According to the bulletins, the American evacuation had been completed without incident and things were quiet in Britain. On a day like this, he could not believe that it would be too long before he saw her again.

The buzz of Hildy's phone interrupted them. Past the curve of her shoulder he saw Gegener's face, too small to reveal expression. But the voice, in rapid German, sounded strained.

It was not a long conversation. When it ended, Hildy said: 'He is at the Clinic. He wants to see us again.'

'When?'

'As soon as possible. Tomorrow morning.'

'At the Clinic?'

'Not at the Clinic. At Pritzendorf. He is driving back there tonight.'

Maria-Mercedes had a dinner party that evening, with Dieter presiding in place of her stricken husband. Guests were the von Grenzendorfs and two other couples who, though not specified as listed in the Almanac, looked as though they might be. The wild boar, presented whole on an enormous platter decorated with hunters in horned helmets, was devoured with relish, washed down with burgundy from silver goblets. Michael allowed his to be replenished more than he would normally have thought sensible, as a distraction from the conversation. It was conducted, for his benefit, entirely in English, and was banal in the extreme.

The port that appeared when the ladies retired was presumably for his benefit also, and the conversation relaxed to the extent of the gentlemen exercising their English in dirty and unfunny jokes. It was almost a relief when Friedrich von Grenzendorf switched into the familiar vilification of *Ausländer*. Foreigners, he translated helpfully: foreign vermin. But also dangerous, continually more bold. It was past time the situation was taken in hand, and Western Europe made safe for its ancient peoples.

Michael was alone in the breakfast room the following morning when a call came through from Johann – Dieter had left, Hildy was probably in her bath, and nothing was permitted to disturb Maria-Mercedes before ten thirty.

'How is Papa?' Johann asked.

'Coming on well. How's Tokyo?'

'As ever, boring. But I only have one more company dinner to endure. I'll be with you tomorrow, I hope. How did last evening go?'

'It was interesting.'

Johann laughed. 'Lied gallantly, like a true Englishman. Give everyone my love.'

Hildy came down dewy-fresh, and drove with her usual verve. He could have done with her taking it more easily, especially on the tight bends as the road wound up through the hills. He was glad to recognize a roadside shrine not far from Pritzendorf, then nauseated by her slamming on brakes as she came out of a curve. They were confronted by a road block.

The German was too fast for him to attempt to follow, but he gathered that the police *Unteroffizier* was prohibiting their onward progress, and Hildy was rejecting the prohibition. He heard her mention Frau Stern, and saw colour leave her face at the sergeant's response. She brought in Dieter's name then; emphatically, and with effect. The sergeant saluted and waved them on. As she weaved the car between the barriers, Michael asked: 'What's wrong?'

'A fire, he said. At the Stern house.'

The village was deserted as they drove through in silence. The explanation for that appeared when they came in sight of where the house had stood. The road was lined with figures, staring up at a heap of rubble from which a few rags of smoke still rose.

Hildy stopped short of the row of police cars, and they got out. Michael felt a different nausea, along with disbelief and something like dread. Hildy's voice, questioning the officer in charge, was weirdly distant.

'Well?' he asked.

Her face was tight. 'They are dead.'

He thought of cakes and lemonade, slim lively Trudi, younger, more sober Hannah. Healthy fruits of a genetic mix . . . beautiful laughing children . . .

'Are they sure?' He looked at the charred ruins, at no point more than a metre above ground level. 'They might have gone away – been staying somewhere else.'

She said in a bleak voice: 'They took four bodies out, he said. A man, a woman, two . . .'

He put an arm round her, trying to remember what it had been like all those years ago when she too had been a child, in a world that could offer no worse horror than the death of a puppy.

'Did he say how it happened?'

'*Ausländer*. Another house was burned some months ago, on the other side of the village, but the people there escaped. A heavy truck was heard going through, in the night. They used flame-throwers.'

The news had reached Frohsteig by the time they got back. Dieter was at the house, in the library. He poured brandy into Waterford glasses.

'You will need a drink. *Ist unmöglich*. How could anyone do such a thing? Those children . . . I have not been one of those who hated *Ausländer*. They are human beings, as we all are. But how could they do such a thing?'

For Michael, Dieter's words released doubts which had been suppressed under shock and horror. It wasn't *Ausländer* who had driven Stern to suicide – or murdered him, according to

Gegener. *Ausländer* weren't responsible for whatever had killed Anna. He wanted to say that, but saw Hildy look at him in appeal. She had asked him not to involve Dieter, and clearly still did not want to.

It was overwhelmingly important to think clearly and stay cool. He reminded himself that the human mind was desperately egocentric. As a boy he had believed in reincarnation simply because of a recurrent thought that there had once been a time when Sunday came before Saturday. The rationalization was that he must have been a Jew in a previous life, and could recall *Sabat* coming before the secular holiday. But there had been another, equally convincing, false memory: of a rugby international match being played, in his very early childhood, on the Flats at Sheaf. In the sophistication of teens, he had recognized the impossibility of the second proposition, and worked it out as resulting from confusion, in a childish mind, between a game shown on television and a local one witnessed on the same day, or near it. He had not been tempted by reincarnation theories since then.

The fact that man was a linking animal should not blind one to the possibilities and power of chance. Lucy was an example. Their first meeting had been at a party given by a London friend with vague US Embassy connections. Michael had quite liked her, but made no attempt to get a phone number, or angle for a date. It was some days later, dropping into an exhibition in Piccadilly featuring some of Anna's paintings, that he saw again the strikingly beautiful black girl in the next room, and went to her – propelled by a sense of destiny.

In love with her he had been tempted again, this time by the notion of a second encounter ordained by fate. The presence of both of them, in that place and at that time, had seemed a benevolent miracle: she had been on the point of leaving and he had come from a meeting which ended half an hour earlier than usual. But grasping the gifts of chance was not the same as assuming they were intentional. Whether or not there was an infinity of possible universes, the possibilities of the universe we actually knew were infinite; and indifferent.

That also meant that conspiracy theories were to be mistrusted, precisely because they harmonized with the mind's egocentric bias. Anna's death might, or might not, be linked with Stern's; or, more remotely, with Gegener's. To tie those events into an intrigue involving the German state police and the Bavarian fire services was as irrational as his boyish belief in reincarnation.

He felt slightly soothed by the brandy. He simply said: 'No, I don't know how anyone could have done it.'

Lunch was subdued. Even Maria-Mercedes seemed shocked out of her calm. '*Fürchterlich . . . unglaublich*,' she murmured, shaking the bell of her matutinally refurbished coiffure. Afterwards they went different ways, in Michael's case to his room. He felt tired, and lay on the bed, trying to make sense out of confusion.

The line of suspicion which had started with Stern had led to Gegener, and had ended with him. Despite Hildy's reluctance, there could be no way forward now except by involving Dieter. Yet there was nothing positive to show him, nothing even to pass on except the suspicions of a man Dieter had already dismissed as unbalanced, and those of his fanatical disciple.

The console beside his bed buzzed softly. This was part of the technological luxury of life at the Schloss, a system providing television, and internal as well as external phonecalls. A green light on the panel winked under 5. Hildy: he pressed for receive, and she came in view.

'Can you come to my room? Now?'

Her door opened to a push. She looked at him from a chair behind her desk. The expression in her face was not one of

221

welcome, but a look of cold fear. Her left hand was clenched in her lap. Her right held a letter, a couple of pages in crabbed German script.

'It came in this morning's mail,' she said. 'I have not looked at it till now.'

It was another minor luxury that Moritz took in the household mail, sorted it, and had it despatched to the appropriate room, where it was left in a mahogany rack inside the door. Mail usually arrived about nine, and was delivered before ten. They had been on their way to Pritzendorf soon after nine.

'From Berthold.'

'Go on.'

'He found something else. He found what Stern had found – that which was too terrible to write down. He has not written it, either. He wanted to see us, talk about it. But he thought he might be under suspicion, like Stern. That was why he told us to come to Pritzendorf, not the Clinic. And in case something happened to him, he sent a copy of what he had found.' She opened her left hand. 'This is it.'

He recognized a Virtual disk, a small square of metal and plastic holding thousands of gigabytes of electronic memory: enough to fuel the creation of a new universe. With a sick conviction of knowing the answer, Michael asked her: 'Does he say what it is?'

'He says: a part of Anna's Total program.'

'What part? What's in it?'

Hildy shook her head. 'He says only – horrible.' On her desk lay glove and helmet. 'I thought I should esp it, but I could not. I am a coward, Mikey.'

He did not know how he could face it either, but knew he must. He put out his hand for the equipment, and the disk.

At first there was an unsettling sense of duality: he was at the same time experiencing, and a spectator to, the experience of another. He understood it was an artificial world, and knew it was Anna's, created to nourish her imaginings and longings. There was colour and sound and tactility. He – or she or they – walked through a landscape very like Flintly Woods, a few miles north of Sheaf. The season was spring, early April perhaps. Daffodils fluttered in a gentle breeze, and the ground was patched thickly white with anemones. Birds sang: he recognized blackbird and thrush, a dove, the harsh chatter of a magpie softened by distance and the beauty of the day. Everything breathed regeneration, and an imminent renewal of summer.

Gradually his identity faded into hers: this was Anna's world, and it was she who was walking along the bridle path, with tall trees close on either side and branches budding green against a bright blue foil of sky. He shared warmth and light and sensation with her, and also somehow anticipation of what lay no more than a few metres away, where the bridle path and a broader avenue joined.

And he felt with her the shock of joy as anticipation became reality. She came from the cover of trees into a long march, empty except for one thing, one person. Adam stood there, regarding her gravely for a moment, then running to her – crossing the aching distance on a child's stumbling feet. Her arms opened, and the boy came into them. In a world already bursting with loveliness, the feel of his flesh against hers, the unforgettable smell of his body, was an all-surpassing ecstasy.

After ecstasy there was ordinary happiness. They walked down the march together, soft grass underfoot, the breeze mild on their faces. It was good to have the small hand clasping hers, but good also to see him dart away to investigate a rabbit hole or dabble his fingers in an unexpected stream, knowing the physical separation would so soon be ended by his return. He chattered to her – of a party he'd been to, his new school, the dog he might have for his birthday – and she answered, not knowing what she said, nor caring.

They reached a pond, where a kingfisher flashed and flew

away. He cried: 'Mummy, look!' – not at the vanishing brilliance of emerald and tangerine, but towards the ropes of frogspawn he had glimpsed in the clear water of the pool. He knelt to peer more closely.

Then nightmare tore the universe apart.

Wrenching loss was at the heart of it, but everything had gone – sunlit sky, trees, grass – replaced first by bitter-tasting blackness, then unspeakable horror. There was slime on her skin, mixed with burning acid and crawling filth. Eyes and ears were assaulted, battered, by sounds and images out of Hell. A chilling, pitiless voice condemned her, not to death but to an eternity of pain and degradation; and the condemnation became real in whips and burning pincers that tore and gouged her flesh. She knew with a dreadful certainty this would go on forever, and knew there was no way of escaping it – no hope of oblivion. The voice issued from a face against which she could not shut her eyes: hateful and hating, rotten-fanged, stinking close. She was utterly at its mercy, and knew that in this world mercy did not exist.

All the while, more intense even than the fear and pain and despair, was the greatest torture: where was Adam? Was this agony, this undying death, happening to him too?

It was unbearable. Selfishly, ruthlessly, finally Michael fought for his identity. Even when he regained it, he felt helpless, incapable of moving a finger. He fought again, for his life this time, and found and pressed the switch.

It was an evening ritual that Moritz served drinks in the Pink Room at six o'clock, and equally established that after one vodka with low-calorie tonic, crushed ice and lemon zest, Maria-Mercedes retired for her pre-prandial bath, and change of gown and make-up. From their chairs in front of the great fireplace, crimson with the flames of massed azaleas, Dieter, Hildy and Michael watched as she ascended the staircase, until it turned and took her out of sight.

Dropping the mask of brightness, Hildy said: 'Dieter, we must tell you . . .'

She broke off. He gazed at her benevolently, champagne cocktail in hand. 'Tell me what?'

For a moment, she turned to Michael in appeal. He had no answer to it. It had been her decision to do the talking but even if she wanted to change her mind he did not feel he could help her. He was back inside Anna's dream, knowing again the fear and disgust and despair.

Hildy drew breath, and talked. She told the story brokenly, but in full. As though through the wrong end of a telescope, Michael saw Dieter, listening impassively. At the end she said: 'Michael esp'd it – went into the dream. I couldn't. He told me about it, as much as he could tell. It wasn't the same as being in it – how could it be? – but I saw his face. Dieter, it was Gundula, I know it was. She is in charge of everything, you said so. But why, why? Even for such evil, there must be a reason.'

Dieter set down his glass on the table by his chair. He said: 'For evil, perhaps you can seek a reason. But there is no evil in this.'

She stared at him. 'You knew . . .'

'A reason for evil,' Dieter said, 'but not always for error. Mistakes happen, sometimes very bad mistakes. They cannot always be reversed. All that is possible is to try making right what remains.'

Her eyes had not left his face. She said: 'Anna . . . it was the bad dream that killed her. It was so terrible, and so strong, that Michael found it almost impossible to switch it off, even from Virtual. In Total, there is no switching off, no way out. Instead, her heart stopped.'

'When Anna came to us,' Dieter said, 'her condition was very bad. Suicide was possible – probable even. She was given best care, by Stern himself. Dreams were planned for her – dreams that centred on Adam. The initial programming, as always, was here in the complex. Then the program is sent to the Clinic for adjustments. At the last, it returns here. For perfecting, you understand.

'For authentication one needs talent that is close to genius, for dream-making much more – true genius. And with genius are always problems. The gods fight in vain against stupidity, but stupidity can be seen at least, and understood. This is not so with genius. We gave Anna's programming to our best man. There had been problems with him too, but his work, at its best, was the finest. And the problems were thought not to lie outside the normal parameters. One does not lightly hand such a one over to the psychotherapists, who adjust the emotion and maybe kill the creative part. Gundula judged him reliable, and I accepted her judgement. We were wrong. When the programme came back, for finishing, he overwrote the end with this new one.'

His eyes went to Michael: a reasonable look, man to man, expecting understanding. 'When Anna died, Gundula did her duty. She checked, with thoroughness, and discovered the program disk. Then she called in the psychotherapists. They examined the programmer. The problems had been greater than she knew, or could have guessed. He is diagnosed psychotic, now strictly confined. They do not think he will recover. It is probable he suffers great mental torment, which cannot be helped or ended without also ending his life. And of course the law forbids that.'

'And Stern?' Hildy asked.

'He had first queried the cause of Anna's death. Through him, Gundula obtained the program disk. She explained to him fully: the mistake, the results of the clinical examination of the programmer, the steps taken to be sure it will not happen again. He was a man of guilts – he could not see things rationally. He called you, Michael, and that would not have been the end of it. He was Director of the Clinic and felt responsibility. I think perhaps he would have killed himself, anyway.'

'But Gundula arranged it for him,' Michael said. 'Even though, as you say, the law forbids it.'

Dieter shrugged. 'All laws are in hierarchy. What the lower forbids, the higher may require.'

'And the higher is – saving Gundula's skin, and yours?'

'No. The higher law in this case is the security of the state – beside which the life of an individual is unimportant.' There was a silence, as Michael looked at him. 'There was connection with a project which must not be put at risk.'

He had been rattled after all, despite his apparent composure, to let that last bit slip out. Another connection suddenly dropped into place, like a jigsaw piece one had been looking at but not properly seeing.

'Your vagabonds,' Michael said, 'the ones without homes, without friends . . . do they sometimes die of heart failure in the middle of their Total dreams?'

'Oh, no. That is not possible!' Hildy exclaimed. 'It could not be . . .'

Deliberately, Dieter picked up his glass and drank. 'You have suspicions. It is better if they are not roused, or are dismissed. But if not, next best is to explain. But the explanation must stay within this room.'

'You and I, all of us, make plans against the future – for ourselves, as individuals. The state is bigger, and less selfish. Since many years the economics of the world have got worse, and get worse still. Masses of people – tens of millions, hundreds – are unemployed, unemployable. It is a situation from which only disaster can come, for everyone.

'The state has asked our help. With Total we can make things easier, putting men into dreams where they make few demands on the economy. Yet they cannot remain in Total always. They must come back to the real world, which is more grey than the bright world of dreams. That is where our latest research may help. It is possible that in the dreams there can be also persuasion – patterns of contentment may be created which continue after the dream is taken away.'

'By which you mean brainwashing,' Michael said. 'Much more sophisticated than the old combination of drugs and sensory deprivation and suggestion. With permanent serfdom as its end product, a *Lumpenproletariat* of happy slaves. And a little research on the side into ways of killing them by nightmares in their sleep, just in case it doesn't work?'

For the first time, Dieter looked disturbed. 'I told you, that was one man, a madman. Whatever he did was not authorized. How could you think it possible I would authorize such a thing? You have known me a long time, Michael. Do you think me vicious?'

'Vicious? Anna died, in a manner horrible beyond belief, and your whole concern was to cover it up. You had Stern killed because he refused to go along with that. Then Gegener. But not just Gegener – an innocent woman, two children, burned to death . . .'

'It should not have happened – Stern's widow and children. We had information they will go to visit her sister the day before, that they are not at the house that night. We did not know the sister cancelled this visit.'

'So that was just another mistake,' Michael said. 'An error that cannot be reversed, so you make good what remains. Do I think you vicious? It doesn't matter what I think, does it? What matters is your utter blindness – to what you've done, what you're still doing. For the glory of the state?'

Dieter rose from his chair. 'Argument is for individuals. There comes a point at which it is useless, dangerous. Whether or not the state has glory, it is above such trivialities. It enforces duty, and its own preservation. This includes the preservation of its secrets. Now let us look at things reasonably. We are not only friends, but of one family.' He stood before Hildy. 'This goes no further. I have your word?'

Michael looked past him at her. 'Anna, dying in torment. Stern, killed for his Jewish conscience. Berthold, burned to death because he was going to tell us what he'd found. Elizabeth Stern . . . Trudi . . . Hannah . . .'

Dieter reached down, and took Hildy's hands. She looked very small against his bulk. But there was more to it than that, Michael suddenly saw. In his look there was unassailable confidence – the confidence of one who knows his power is beyond question, the power of the seducer over the seduced.

'I have your word, Hildy.'

It was not a question. She nodded, without speaking. Dieter let go her hands and turned to Michael. 'I do not need to ask you, do I?'

Twelve

He woke to unobtrusive birdsong. The initial confusion over where he was turned to helpless anger as he remembered. Underlying the birdsong he could hear the hum of an air-conditioning unit. He was on a futon in a room about four metres square, with a white sanitary unit – WC, wash-basin, shower – neatly taking up one corner. Other furniture consisted of a small table and two chairs, one upright at the table, the other a lounge chair. Surfaces were rounded and padded, and he guessed they were bolted to the floor.

The floor itself was dark blue, the windowless walls and ceiling azure. A television screen was sealed into one wall, with controls recessed in the desk. Above the screen, plexiglass protected a camera lens which covered the room on wide-angle, but was switchable to close-up. The room, Dieter had assured him, was sound-proofed as well as air-conditioned; the door had no handle on this side.

So what about the birdsong?

Of course. Dieter had also explained the room's normal function: for the safe securing of disturbed patients. Birdsong was probably deemed therapeutic as a background, like the two-tone colour scheme. Blue for serenity.

He threw back the flimsy cover and got up. He had slept naked, but the light robe he had been given when his clothes were taken was lying across the easy chair. He put it on, tying the belt, and slipped on the sandals that had also been provided. The desk control panel featured buttons additional to those for television and phone. A setting marked 'Auto' toggled with 'Off': the birdsong ceased when he pressed it. There was also a Call button, and he pressed that.

From the wall-speaker, a male voice asked in clear English: 'May I help you? Do you wish something?'

'Breakfast?' Michael asked.

'Of course. What do you choose?'

'What do you offer?'

'Anything the kitchen can provide. Most things, that is. English breakfast, if you wish. Bacon, eggs, sausages—'

'Coffee and a croissant will do.'

He clicked off and paced the room, recalling the previous evening. Although the confrontation must have taken Dieter by surprise – the failure to monitor Hildy's mail had presumably been another unfortunate error, like the killing of Frau Stern and her children – emergency precautions had been in place. It would not have occurred to Michael to expect Moritz to arrive, armed, to a bell cord summons. The security guards had been there soon afterwards.

Otherwise Dieter's reactions had been in character and, after the revelation of the nature of the Total research programme, predictable. Hildy's had been less so. Michael's appeal to her had fallen not so much on stony ground as into an echoless abyss. He had looked at her as he was taken away by the guards, huddled small in her chair, refusing to return the glance. Whatever its roots, Dieter's dominance over her was of long standing, and absolute.

Breakfast arrived within ten minutes: the door opened without warning and one of the pseudo-nuns set a tray on the table, making no reply when he thanked her. There was a cafetiere of strong coffee, jugs of cream and hot milk, two croissants on a plate under a heat-retaining cover, a pot of butter and a small bowl of Cooper's Oxford marmalade. He was hungrier than he had thought, and left only crumbs. He had just refilled his cup when Gundula came in, similarly unheralded.

Her dress this morning was pale grey, but with flame-red revers at the neck and a broad belt in matching material. Like yesterday's, it clung to her pleasantly. The smile was as pleasant too.

'Michael. I hope you slept well.'

'Reasonably, all things considered. I can't offer you coffee. They only brought me one cup, and anyway I've finished the pot.'

She shook her head. 'I am just looking in to see you are OK.'

'You can see that from outside, of course, can't you?' He nodded towards the lens. 'But thanks for the call. I suppose you wouldn't care to fill me in on what happens next?'

'Dieter will have to explain that. I have executive function only.'

'And when may I expect to see Dieter?'

She shrugged, a pretty gesture. 'He is very busy, as you know. He will come to talk to you as soon as possible. Meanwhile, he is anxious you are well cared for. If there is anything you wish – books, magazines maybe . . .'

'If I'm to be here long, I imagine books will be useful. I'll make a list, shall I? Meanwhile, magazines in English would be welcome. Anything you have.'

'That will be arranged.'

Her nod carried a hint of mission completed. He had a sudden reluctance, fear almost, of being left alone. He asked: 'Do you have time to talk?'

She smiled warily. 'On what subject?'

She had already ruled out discussion of Dieter's plans for him. The question of the morality of mental experimentation on people without consent was unlikely to produce any more positive response. He said: 'Whatever you like. Anything.'

The smile became easier. 'That may be nice. But I too am busy now. Later, we will talk.'

Reading matter arrived within the half-hour – a couple of

general leisure magazines, an arts journal dealing principally with television, *Sport UK*, and *Spot-On*, a weekly news review. He glanced through that first. It included an account of the American withdrawal from Liverpool, emphasizing that it was not only a surrender, but a mortal blow to the anti-Euro forces in Britain. A boxed editorial crowed in bold face that this was the moment of truth. There had always been, at the heart of the reactionary movement, the ludicrous dream of reverse colonization: of American forces crossing the Atlantic to detach the British Isles from Europe and turn them into a fifty-first state. Sadly for them, but coming as long overdue relief to the British people as a whole, that dream was now finally exposed as a treacherous sham. America had been taught a lesson; and Europe and Britain – Britain within Europe as history and logic demanded – could get on with their lives in peace and security.

Time passed. Michael skimmed through the remaining magazines, tried to follow German television for a while, then went back to the magazines and read them more thoroughly. *Sport UK* had a piece on rugby: the expected arrival on the international scene of Germany, with a side to be managed and coached by Michael Frodsham of Wasps and England, was yet another sign of the healthy spread of British influence in European sport.

He was given a generous choice of menu for lunch, and it was served with the half bottle of red wine he'd asked for. Later there was tea – a choice of Assam or Earl Grey, and the tray included a slice of English fruit-cake. His father always insisted on fruit-cake for tea at Schloss Frohsteig; he wondered if he had been told anything but guessed not. Dieter would think it wrong to risk unnecessary distress to someone recovering from a heart attack. Michael recalled his plaintive response, the previous evening: 'Do you think me vicious?'

Later still, there was dinner, and another half bottle of wine. The nurse collected the tray afterwards, uncommunicative as ever. He suspected that was it for the day, brushed

his teeth, showered, and made himself ready for bed. The
TV clock told him it was a little past nine.

The call buzz made him wonder if in-house comforts
extended to cocoa and biscuits, but it wasn't the guard's
face that came on screen. 'Mike? OK for me to come in?'
Johann said.

He nodded. 'Nice of you to ask.'

Johann hugged him on entering; the pressure of another
body was a comfort. When they separated, Johann sat on
the edge of the table, looking at him.

'I got back less than an hour ago. The usual flight delay.
How are you?'

'Fine. Well looked after. A little curious as to what
comes next.'

'Dieter's filled me in on things – from his point of view,
it goes without saying. I'll run it through, so we know
where we stand.' He did that quickly and comprehensively.
'Anything important I've left out?'

'Not from Dieter's point of view. No, I wouldn't say
he omitted anything. Taking his word for good intentions,
and giving him the benefit of all doubts, it's just a simple
story of large-scale experimentation on human beings, with
the unfortunate side effect of Anna dying under mental
torture, and a cover-up featuring two planned plus three
unintentional deaths. Nothing important missing.'

'Tell me one thing.' Johann's voice was earnest. 'Do you
think I had any idea what was going on?'

'Which part of what was going on would that be?'

'Any of it.'

'No,' Michael said, 'I don't think you did. But you
do now. The question is – what do you propose to do
about it?'

'I've told Dieter it's got to stop.'

'Again, which part? The murdering, or the murderous
project?'

'Both.'

'And what did Dieter say to that?'

'The project's already being wound down. As he said, it was government-funded and government-controlled. And Top Secret, which was why I wasn't told. I've never been in on the research side, in any case. Computer Science wasn't a priority during my time at Eton.'

'Do you believe it – about being wound down?'

'I may not know anything about computer research, but I know a bit about committees. They're usually technically incompetent, but not keen to acknowledge it. In this case they took bad advice, and then pushed on with it because that's what committees do. But they can be shaken out of pushing on. It seems the report on Anna's death came as a nasty shock.'

'Well, it was, wasn't it? A very nasty shock. Literally.'

'Yes.' Johann was silent. 'I suppose I've been trying to avoid thinking about it. But the programmer was mad.'

'Even if you can be certain of distinguishing mad from bad, there are degrees of insanity. Which category would you say authorizing mind control came into? And committees – we're talking about people – can recover from shocks.'

'That's something I am in a position to do something about. Now I've been put in the picture, I'm not going to be put out again.'

He sounded as if he meant it. He was young, of course. Michael said: 'What about me, then? Can I go home?'

The hesitation was sufficient answer.

Johann said: 'Dieter says this won't be for long – a few days maybe. He said if he let you go now, he couldn't be sure you wouldn't blow the whistle right away, which could be disastrous. It's a delicate situation. He said you refused to give an undertaking not to.'

'I saw no point in lying. And I wouldn't have expected Dieter to believe me if I had.'

'Does that mean you don't trust us . . . me neither?'

'Trust is multi-factorial. Good will's one thing; good judgement's another.'

'I'm sorry you feel like that, Mike.' Johann gave a small downward jerk with his head. 'But you'll be out of here in a few days.'

'I don't think so.'

'I guarantee it.'

'You more or less guaranteed Anna too, didn't you? All right, wince; but I don't think the comparison's unfair. Neither Hildy nor Dieter have been to see me today, and I can understand the reason in both cases. Hildy simply feels bad about what she's done – or not done. Dieter doesn't want to look at what he's going to do – doesn't want to look into the eyes of a man he's condemned to death. It's almost endearing he should be so squeamish. He had Stern killed, and then Gegener, without a moment's hesitation. You may think he'll make an exception for me, because I'm family. You underrate him.'

Johann rubbed the scar on his cheek. 'You're wrong. I absolutely know you're wrong.' They looked at one another across the room. 'I'll come back in the morning.'

Michael felt surprisingly calm after Johann had gone, but not sleepy. He was lying on the futon, re-reading *Sport UK*, when the door opened to admit Gundula. She wore a loose robe of cinnamon-coloured silk. If there was anything underneath, it had to be extremely flimsy: the Emperor's new clothes, he guessed.

He said: 'I suppose people not knocking is one of the minor drawbacks to imprisonment. Trivial; like a hang-nail.'

She smiled it down. 'What are you reading, Michael? About one of your own exploits, perhaps?'

He shook his head. 'The rugby season's over, like some other things.'

'You said you would like to talk. I am not busy any more.'

He stood up. 'What do you think might be a good topic? Obviously not why I'm here, or what comes next. As you said, you only have executive function.'

'There are plenty of things we can talk about. Nice things, happy things.'

She made no move towards him, but every line of her body demanded the move from him. Her confidence, and his instinctive response to it, shocked him. Stimuli were stimuli, appetite a ravenous moron. Part of his mind was aware of lust almost as an abstraction, but another part screamed for surrender – of thought, will, everything, including loyalty.

He glanced up at the camera in the wall. 'A recorded discussion?'

She shook her head. 'It is disabled. The guard will not disturb us. I told him it may be some time before I need him again.'

The sense of inevitability, of sliding towards mindless satisfaction and release, was almost overwhelming. This was not the way it had been with Hildy. The further random thought, shattering the mood, was not of Lucy, but Dieter. Did he know about this? Had he even planned it, giving an instruction to his faithful aide? For some obscure manoeuvring purpose, perhaps, or out of his own twisted notion of benevolence? The condemned man enjoyed a hearty orgasm . . .

His trusted aide, his female doppelgänger. Whether on Dieter's instruction or not, she would bed him tonight and have him killed tomorrow with the same efficient smile. Lucy, my darling, he thought – I'm not going to see you again, and I don't suppose you'd reproach me too much if you knew, but I'm not going to betray you during the last bit of everything, for the momentary pleasure of fucking a heartless bitch like this.

'I'm tired,' he said. 'You can call the guard now.'

'Are you sure?'

She still did not move. Her lust, he guessed, was as strong

as his own had been, but she had it under control. Control was her métier. He speculated on the other satisfaction available, of putting his hands round her neck and squeezing the life from her beautiful body. The guard was not on watch, and even if she'd lied about that or the guard had disobeyed orders, he was confident he could strangle her before help arrived.

He shook his head. 'I'm sure.'

Michael was not much surprised when Johann failed to keep his promise of returning the next morning. He had made more of an effort than Hildy, but pressures were pressures, and Dieter was expert at exerting them. He followed the routines available – ablutions, breakfast, desultory scanning of television, lunch. When the tray was removed, the books he'd ordered the previous day were delivered.

He'd made a quick selection from the teletext list of books in English: a couple of thrillers, a biography (*Churchill, First European Federalist*), *Anna Karenina* in a new translation he'd seen praised, and *Northanger Abbey*. Time, he suspected, might be short: too short for *Anna Karenina* or *Churchill, First European Federalist*, or indeed, as far as the thrillers were concerned, for embarking on the solution of any puzzle whose resolution might survive his own. He settled instead for the chatter of Catherine Morland and Isabella Thorpe, and their shared ecstasies at the horrors of gothic imagination. He was reflecting on the calamity of rain threatening the prospect of another visit to the Pump Room, when Johann arrived.

'Good to see you, Jo',' he said.

His half-brother looked ill at ease, which was scarcely surprising. It was something that, unlike Hildy, he had not backed away from a guilt-inducing encounter. In a voice conspicuously lacking its usual lightness, Johann said abruptly: 'I'm quite sure you're wrong – about Dieter.'

There would be no point in arguing. Michael felt he could afford to make things easy for him. 'That's OK.'

'But it is my view, against yours, and if you were right . . .' Michael did not respond. 'Dieter's taking the early afternoon flight to an appointment in Berlin. Gundula was more tricky, but I've organized an emergency in our plant on the other side of the city. She's gone there to sort things out. It'll take her several hours, and meanwhile I'm in charge here.

'I've got people I can trust, who can get you to England. To Sheaf, if you want, but I'd recommend further north. The whole of the Southeast is under Carolingian control. If you really are at risk, you'd still be at risk there.'

'Further north? Then what happened at Liverpool didn't put an end to resistance?'

'No. The reverse, in fact. For some reason it made the other tribes on the islands rally in support of the English. Even the Irish. The present holding line runs from Cardiff to the Wash.'

'Someone once described that as a line north of which Hell begins. Maybe they got it wrong. You can really help me get to Sheaf? What about the risk to you?'

'If Sheaf's what you want. Don't worry about me. I can deal with Dieter.'

'I hope you can. I'm grabbing the lifeline, anyway.' He looked at Johann, and smiled. 'Thanks for everything. You may be right about Dieter's plans for me, but if you're wrong I owe you a life.'

Michael was dropped at the point he'd specified, near the bottom of Sheaf Hill. Hans, his driver and companion over the previous forty-eight hours, wished him luck with what sounded like sincerity. He was a dour Schwabian, plainly unhappy outside German-speaking territory, but they had got on well despite linguistic limitations. It had all gone very smoothly in fact. Controls were markedly in evidence, on the English side of the Tunnel especially, but Johann's *laissez-passer* went unchallenged.

He walked under a half moon down the narrow tree-hemmed stretch of Deadman's Lane, named for the bodies laid out there after one of the more severe French onslaughts of the fourteenth century. It offered an inconspicuous entry to the town, though he doubted if the Carolingians would be very active on night patrols anyway. Sheaf was a long way behind the lines.

Friars Hill indeed was empty apart from Ginger, a grossly overweight tomcat without a permanent home but on the hand-out list of most of the town's restaurants. He arched his back to be stroked, producing his incongruously plaintive miaow. The streetlamp on the hill lit up the side door, but the house was dark. Michael let himself in, and made his way through to the kitchen before switching a light on. It was suddenly of vital importance that the whisky bottle should be in its usual place, in the cupboard to the right of the Aga.

He turned, glass in hand, at the sound of footsteps. It could only be DD, but it didn't sound like him. Nor was it. He stared at her as she stood in the doorway, in wonder and amazement.

'They say you ought never to try pulling the same trick twice,' Lucy said. 'But I couldn't talk you into coming my way, and it didn't seem to leave much of an alternative.'

Thirteen

S heaf Harbour lies two miles from the town, connected
with it by the river Trug, whose broad channel meanders
between mudbanks across the Marsh. Towering steeply
above the river at low tide, at high tide the banks are
reduced to exiguous ramparts across which, in summer,
sheep stare at people in passing craft, virtually eye to eye.
It offers a prettily pastoral scene in the green heat of a sultry
afternoon. In the black chill of a winter's night, there was
nothing to see but the bobbing lights of other fishing boats,
ahead and astern.

Huddled inside his waterproof, Michael counted them
again, compulsively. Eleven: the full complement – for the
moment at any rate, the *Sheaf Princess'* dicky engine was
holding out. On two previous mornings, winds close to gale
force had prevented sailing. The south-easter against which
they were beating was still stiff, and the sea beyond the
harbour would be rough, but he had taken the decision to
go ahead. Two days confined below deck, with the constant
danger of a snap inspection by Federal troops, was more than
long enough. Apart from questions of morale, the forecast
had another low coming in from the Atlantic. This was a
poor weather window, but the only one they had.

Lucy squeezed his hand, and he ventured a quick embrace.
They had agreed, when she talked him into letting her come
along, to put physical contact into suspension, but the night
was very dark. He thought, as he had done many times
during the past days, that he ought to have been firmer

about insisting she stay behind. But she had turned his main argument on its head: since there were half a dozen other women on the expedition, their known relationship would have made rejecting her the wrong kind of discrimination.

He was in any case accustomed by now to her having the last word on major decisions. Her position, as she'd made clear the night he'd found her again in Georgian House, was simple. She was her mother's daughter; and having chosen her man would allow no obstacle to keep her from him. Which meant, since he would not cross the Atlantic to her, she had to come to him. Having done so, she was going to keep him in sight – something she had steadfastly achieved during the months of nomadic life in unoccupied Britain and through several guerrilla sorties to the south.

His secondary argument, relating to her special vulnerability through being conspicuous – a woman, American, and black – had received equally short shrift. If things went wrong, and they were captured, she wasn't likely to be treated worse than anyone else but probably a good deal better. The greatest hazard was likely to be over-exposure to camera lighting when they produced her as a television trophy. They would have a fine time with that, especially if they traced her connection with the once and yet again President of the United States of America.

That had been one of the happier surprises of the year. In the aftermath of the Liverpool fiasco, Aronheimer's hopes of re-election had plunged close to vanishing point. Even after he weathered a powerful challenge from inside his own party at the primaries, his presidential rival's rampant isolationism had seemed to echo irresistibly the mood of the nation. The British had gone into this European union of their own free will: if they found the fire too hot, that was no good reason for American fingers to get burnt plucking out their chestnuts. Opinion polls put Aronheimer more than twenty points behind, and there were forecasts of a clean sweep of the states.

Over the late summer months he had gradually pulled back, but had still gone into the election as the conspicuous underdog. His unexpected victory had been due principally, Lucy judged, to the continuing inability of the Federation to make an end of the British insurrection, and to one monumental miscalculation in particular. An attempt at a double coup, in Belfast and Dublin, resulted in two disastrous failures, and an unusual demonstration of Irish unity against a more distant enemy than the one they had so long cherished. The day before polling in the United States, television screens showed a march of triumph down O'Connell Street, with the Union flag waving alongside the Irish tricolour.

Apart from diminishing hope of a quick solution to the off-shore problem, Europe had had its internal troubles. The Prague revolt was quickly suppressed, but was followed by a state of simmering tension in Warsaw, in which the Russians were taking an increasingly overt interest. And as far as Germany itself was concerned, apart from the usual neo-Nazi riots directed at foreign workers, there had been more general disturbances in a number of cities.

One such was reported from Nuremberg, following the mysterious death of the boss of the Virtual empire, Dieter von Frohsteig. There were rumours of suicide, of assassination, of a heart attack in the course of a sexual orgy. This last, Michael felt, was highly unlikely, but he was fascinated by the subsequent news that the company had been taken over by von Frohsteig's nephew, Johann Frodsham. It would be interesting, some day, to find out exactly what had happened, and whether Gundula had survived the upheaval (he guessed she would); but that wasn't an urgent consideration. Other matters were more pressing. He had heard nothing of his father, but felt he would have his agreement on that point.

There was still a Federal High Commissioner in London, and what passed for a parliament. The original rump of less than a hundred members dwindled continuously, as more and more found their way to the new parliament in Edinburgh. On a briefing visit to the Commander in Chief, Resistance, Harry Porter, Michael had attended a session and listened to the Prime Minister addressing the House. He had sent in a note afterwards, not really expecting a reply, but she had summoned him that evening to her quarters in the Castle.

Helen Rackham had not changed much, but he had not expected she would have. As always, her manner alternated almost flirtatious amiability with casual brusqueness, and she did not offer him a drink. The only difference he noted was that her Australian accent had broadened, possibly to distance her from the Thatcherite image with which she had not infrequently been associated. The questions she put to him were brief but searching, and he soon worked out that she knew about Lucy, and that her principal objective was to probe the possibility of using her in some kind of diplomatic exercise. When he firmly declined on Lucy's behalf, she shrugged and let it drop.

He asked her if she had heard anything of Peter Graveny, and she looked surprised.

'He's dead. I thought you knew. In Liverpool.'

Liverpool had been the scene of the heaviest fighting, and had recently been re-taken for the third time. Having grown accustomed to news of sudden death, the pang and automatic disbelief surprised him. 'On his home territory, at least,' he commented. 'There are worse ways to go.'

Helen Rackham laughed. 'Certainly on his home territory, and I guess also the way he'd have chosen. He had a heart attack in a pub in Lime Street.'

'You're a cold bitch, Helen.'

It was the first time he had addressed her by name. Neither that nor the remark seemed to bother her. 'I know,' she acknowledged, 'but sometimes that's what's needed. Tell your Lucy to contact me if she changes her mind.'

Items of Sheaf news had been gleaned from local resistance members during their enforced sojourn at Fisherman's
Quay. Souter, he was told, had commandeered Bull House,
a notable National Trust mansion close by the church, where
he lived in style and with a show of authority. An oversized
Carolingian shield had been nailed to the fumed-oak front
door, and the Carolingian and Federal banners flew side by
side above the Jacobean roof. Michael's informant on this
point, a middle-aged man called Kim whose complexion
suggested an ancestry more Mediterranean than English,
though his accent was pure Sussex, added that Souter had
also acquired a chateau in the Dordogne, to which his new
Rolls and a special Tunnel dispensation conveyed him most
weekends.

'Not that it doos 'im much good,' Kim said. ''Is wife
always goes with 'im. As I reckon she will too when we
kick the boogers out, and 'e makes a run for it.'

Other sources reassured him about DD, who seemed to
be well, and well content, in Mrs Bennett's Sunnyhill. Less
welcome but not unexpected news was that Georgian House
had been taken over as yet another Carolingian administration centre. One needed to be philosophical about that,
Michael thought. The house had survived many changes of
occupation and fortune since its foundation stone was laid
early in the reign of Elizabeth I. It would survive this too,
whether or not he did.

Outside the harbour the waters were as unpleasant as
the skipper had warned. The boat rolled and wallowed
as they headed east, battered by a beam sea. Up to this
point the little fleet would have appeared perfectly normal
for the time and place, but to continue in line rather
than dispersing to various fishing grounds was likely to
arouse suspicion. They had to rely on doused lights and
the cover of darkness. As the boat rolled more heavily
and his stomach heaved, Michael hoped his youthful sailing days would continue to stand him in good stead. He

turned to the skipper, Dan Hayes. 'How long would you say?'

'With this sea an hour, maybe hour and a quarter.'

'And that will coincide with first light?'

'Near enough. We've lost the *Princess*.'

'How do you know?' Without lights the other boats were invisible. 'I can't see a thing.'

'She packed in, coming out of the harbour. I didn't think that engine was going to do.'

Only ten boats then, and a dozen fewer in the landing party. His stomach heaved again, as horizontal rain slashed like pellets of cold steel across the deck. The rational assessment he had been suppressing – that the scheme was totally hare-brained, more dependent on several kinds of luck than any kind of judgement – took over briefly before he hammered it down again. Rationality, at this stage of the game, was a dog to kennel.

He became aware of an alteration in course, with wind and waves now hitting them from the stern. 'Is this it?' he asked Hayes.

'By my reckoning.'

With navigation purely by compass and hard-earned experience of this stretch of coast, that was something else to take on trust. He asked: 'And the tide's right to bring us close in?'

'You'll get your knees wet. Your bollocks too, most likely. But close enough.'

He checked his Heckler-Koch inside its waterproof cover, and felt the adrenalin starting to pump. Peering towards the still invisible beach, he thought it was a bit like running on to the pitch at Twickenham. He could see surrounding faces more clearly. Lucy, incredibly, was smiling. He wanted to tell her he loved her, but knew it wouldn't do.

Less than an hour later, with daylight as full as could be expected on a dull December morning, Michael watched as the explosives team completed its work in the front carriage of the train standing at the southern departure platform. They came out with thumbs up, and shortly after that Steve, who had driven a Channel link train before the occupation, finished his work in the cab and jumped off as the wheels began to turn. Gathering speed, the train rolled towards the distant Tunnel mouth, and was swallowed up by the tiny far-off rectangle.

It had gone better than he could possibly have hoped. The first two guards had been surprised and killed silently – he would not forget the yawn on a sleepy face just before his hand fastened on the gaping mouth and the knife slid home. A third was shot down before he could bring his Heckler-Koch to the ready. By that time they were inside the station, and the remainder of the guard, stumbling out bare-legged in their shirts from the guardroom on the platform, had not offered serious opposition. They themselves had suffered a man hit in the hand, a woman with a leg wound, neither life-threatening.

As he had urged Porter, in obtaining his sanction for this second assault on the Tunnel, the smaller the engagement, the greater the advantage of surprise. But there was more to it than that. In the eyes of Europeans, and even of some natives, the Tunnel had put an end to Britain's geographical isolation, and to the basic concept of insularity. The land link, as far as they were concerned, was in place, now and forever. Having Folkestone meant maintaining a foothold which was an extension of continental Europe; through it troops and supplies could flow, unchallenged and unrestricted – and with them, control. The occupied South and Midlands had essentially represented a defence in depth of that vital bastion. Holding on to it, one could forget about the troublesome nuisance of the sea.

But the sea, with its perils and possibilities, remained deep-rooted in the hearts of the islanders, and in their thinking. Thousands of years of watching and learning, of calculating maritime risks and stratagems, were not to be uprooted by a sudden storm of technology. If it had been us holding Calais instead, Michael thought, I don't think we'd have fallen for this.

The *crump* was faint in the distance, but its insignificance was belied by the eruption, seconds later, at the mouth of the Tunnel. A swelling cloud of grey-brown dust burst out and debris whirled through the air. Someone cheered, and others joined in raggedly, conscious of achievement but still unsure just what had been achieved.

As to that, Michael felt reasonably confident. Almost certainly the Tunnel would not have been breached by the sea: defence against explosion had been a major consideration in its planning. But it must have suffered sufficient damage to produce a total blockage – now, and at a conservative estimate, for weeks, perhaps months ahead. There would be time enough for Porter's counter-offensive to sweep the occupying Euro troops, discouraged and no longer reinforced, into surrender or the Channel.

What followed would lie, as all events ultimately lay, with the goddess Fortuna. But she was, he hoped, a deity who would take some account of effort. It was highly unlikely that Aronheimer would authorize another landing of US troops, but with Britain firmly back in British hands it would be surprising if he failed to give diplomatic recognition to an independent United Kingdom.

International affairs could anyway be left to themselves; personal survival mattered now. Steve had been checking the train on the opposite platform. After a final burst of fire at the guardhouse, to keep the disarmed Euro troops quiet, they climbed aboard and it headed north. Lucy hung on to Michael's arm, and he hugged her. The small battle was over, and warriors could take their ease.

They were several miles north by the time the helicopter gunships came in view, heading towards Folkestone from their Heathrow base.

'Just as well you decided against a beach pick-up,' Lucy said. 'We'd have been a sitting-duck target.'

Michael nodded: another risk had been that the gunships might strafe the train, but they stayed on course. The Euro troops would be expecting to deal with the train at Ashford, where a barrier would be going up, if not already in place.

Lucy said: 'I didn't fancy another sea trip right now, anyway. Nausea should serve a better cause.'

'Such as?'

The train was slowing to a halt. All round them, wooded and meadowed, soggy with rain, occupied only by gazing sheep, lay the Kent countryside, a landscape in which to disperse and be lost. She touched him lightly.

'Pregnancy was what I had in mind.'